MASKED
DANCERS

MYSTERY NOVELS BY JEAN HAGER

Featuring Chief Mitchell Bushyhead

MASKED DANCERS
THE FIRE CARRIER
GHOSTLAND
NIGHT WALKER
THE GRANDFATHER MEDICINE

Featuring Molly Bearpaw

THE SPIRIT CALLER
SEVEN BLACK STONES
THE REDBIRD'S CRY
RAVENMOCKER

JEAN HAGER

MASKED DANCERS

THE MYSTERIOUS PRESS

Published by Warner Books

A Time Warner Company

Mysterious Press books are published by Warner Books, Inc.,
1271 Avenue of the Americas, New York, NY 10020.

Visit our Web site at http://warnerbooks.com

 A Time Warner Company

The Mysterious Press name and logo are registered trademarks of Warner Books, Inc.

Printed in the United States of America

First printing: May 1998

10 9 8 7 6 5 4 3 2 1

Library of Congress Cataloging-in-Publication Data

Hager, Jean.
    Masked dancers / Jean Hager.
        p. cm.
    ISBN 0-89296-641-6
    I. Title.
PS3558.A3232M37   1998
813'.54—dc21   97-34560
                                                        CIP

MASKED DANCERS

1

The sky was an ominous pewter color by the time Police Chief Mitch Bushyhead reached the station. He found Helen Hendricks, the dispatcher, looking anxiously out the window. "Morning, Chief."

Mitch went to stand beside her. "Looks like we could have a toad-strangler," he said.

Studying the sky, Helen nodded. "We're about due for one of our March storms."

A jagged lightning spear split the sky, followed by a crack of thunder as loud as a cannon blast. Helen jumped back. "My God, that must've hit something."

"A tree, maybe," Mitch said, noticing that the two oak trees on the corner next to the drugstore appeared unharmed. In fact, he couldn't see any evidence of a lightning strike from where he stood. He stepped closer to the window to peer at the dark clouds piling up overhead. Raindrops splattered the sidewalk and began to gather momentum. On the corner, the oak trees creaked and swayed in the wind.

All at once, the sky opened up and the rain poured down in sheets, pounding the walk and pelting the windowpane. Mitch could no longer see anything but rain beyond the window.

Glad to be indoors, he went over to the coffeepot and poured himself a cup. Helen threw another worried glance at the window and returned to her desk.

Just then Shelly Pitcher, Buckskin P.D.'s only female officer, rushed in, holding an open newspaper over her head. In the few feet from where she'd parked the patrol car to the station house, the newspaper had been soaked through and water dripped off the collapsed edges.

Shelly tossed the paper into the wastebasket. "Sorry I'm late. I had to call somebody to jump-start my car." She looked down at her khaki uniform and groaned. "I'm soaked."

"Don't you have a raincoat?" Helen asked.

"I didn't think I'd need it when I left the house." Shivering, she pulled a comb from her uniform pocket and ran it through her damp, sandy hair. "Is Duck here?"

"He went out on patrol a little while ago," Helen told her. She cocked her head, listening to the rain hammering the roof. It sounded like drumsticks rat-tat-tatting furiously on a snare drum. "He's probably waiting out the rain somewhere."

"The Three Squares would be my guess," Shelly observed. Duck's wife, Geraldine, was a waitress at the Three Squares Café on Highway 10.

"Oh, Chief," Helen said. "Before you got here, we had a call from Dr. Vann at the Cherokee clinic. They had another anonymous call yesterday."

That made the third such call in the last month. So far no one at the clinic had been able to identify the caller's voice. According to Rhea Vann, it sounded like a man. The caller lowered his voice to a guttural level to camouflage it and spoke barely above a whisper. "Dr. Vann meant to call us yesterday," Helen went on, "but she had an emergency and spent most of the day at the hospital, didn't remember to call until this morning."

"So far all the guy has done is make annoying phone calls," Mitch said. "I'm beginning to think he's all talk."

"What'd he say?" Shelly asked.

"The usual," Helen said. "Ranted about the clinic being operated with honest taxpayers' money which they weren't entitled to. Said the Cherokees called themselves a nation, and he wasn't a citizen of it, so they had no right to *his* tax money. He said people were sick of paying for the Indians' free ride."

"Same as before," Shelly observed.

"Only this time, he said the clinic should be blown to smithereens. He didn't say it *would* be, just that it should."

"Sounds like a bomb threat," Mitch said, alarmed. "He's never been that specific before."

"The call came from the same phone number as the last one," Helen said. Rhea Vann had had caller I.D. installed on the clinic phone after the first anonymous call. They'd traced the second call to the pay phone in the basement of city hall. "The doctor claims she knows who's making the calls and asked what we were going to do about it."

Mitch and Rhea had discussed her suspicions the last time they'd had dinner together, the third time they'd gone out in the last couple of months. He liked her a lot, and she seemed to like him—at least, she'd accepted his dinner invitations—

but she kept him at arm's length. The last time he'd taken her home, he'd asked if he could come in. She'd put him off. He'd been a little offended, wondering if she'd just been going out with him because she felt sorry for the poor, lonesome widower.

He'd considered calling her several times after that, but each time he'd suppressed the impulse. They hadn't spoken in more than two weeks now.

"She thinks it's Dane Kennedy," Mitch said.

"Frankly, he's the first person who comes to my mind too," Shelly admitted.

Mitch nodded. "I phoned Kennedy after the first call, hinted broadly that we thought he was making threatening calls to the clinic. He got mad—of course, he stays mad most of the time—and flatly denied making the calls. Until we can prove otherwise, there's not much we can do."

Dane Kennedy lived on a farm near Buckskin. Every summer ten or twelve men wearing camouflage and carrying guns showed up at the Kennedy farm for a week-long survival camp Kennedy ran. Since they had to go through Buckskin to get to Kennedy's place, Mitch knew when they arrived and when they left. He'd stopped a few of them for exceeding the town's speed limit and taken the opportunity to examine their guns to see if they were loaded. They hadn't been, and the men always claimed they'd brought the rifles for hunting and the handguns for a little harmless target practice.

Other than the yearly trek through town, they stayed out at the farm and did their thing, which, Mitch figured, mostly involved fueling each other's anti-government suspicions. Nevertheless, with the fiascos at Ruby Ridge and Waco, followed by the Oklahoma City bombing, Mitch was antsy while

Kennedy's survival camp was in session. It was always a load of worry off his mind when the campers left the area.

Kennedy alone seemed little more than an irritant, but if he was making bomb threats, he'd become a serious problem.

"As soon as the rain lets up," Shelly said, "I could go out to the clinic and take the employees' statements."

"Do that, Shelly," Mitch said. "We'll need a history on file if we I.D. this guy or, God forbid, if he ever decides to do more than talk."

"At least," Shelly said, "they'll know we're taking their complaints seriously. They're all women out there. Just the doctor and two employees, and those calls are scaring them." She glanced over at Mitch. "I like Rhea Vann. She's a real classy lady."

Mitch mumbled an acquiescence, ignoring the questions in Shelly's eyes. His love life—or lack thereof—was nobody else's business.

The rainstorm lasted about thirty minutes, then stopped as suddenly as it had started. Duck arrived and Shelly left for the clinic. Mitch worked in his office for a while, until Helen buzzed him.

"Phone call for you," she said.

Mitch picked up. "Hello."

"Mitch, this is Betty Roberts, Temple's mother." Temple Roberts was Mitch's daughter Emily's best friend. Emily and another friend, Carrie Lou Dunning, had slept over at the Robertses' house last night. Today was Friday, but school was out for a teacher's meeting.

"Yes, Betty. How are you?"

"Right now I'm a little worried about the girls."

"Aren't they at your house?"

"They got up early and left on their bikes. Then that storm came up, and they still aren't back."

"They probably stopped somewhere to get out of the rain."

"Maybe. But I drove around town and I didn't see their bikes anywhere. Before they left the house, I heard them saying they might ride out to the lake. If they got caught in that storm out in the countryside . . ."

Mitch felt a clutch of panic. "When did they leave your house?"

"About twenty minutes before the rain started."

Enough time to have been closer to the lake than to town, and far from any shelter that Mitch could think of. "I'll go out that way and look for them," he said. "You stay by the phone in case they call."

2

Before leaving town, Mitch drove by his house on Pawnee Street. Emily's '85 Mustang was there, but her bike was gone. He left a note for Emily to call the station if she got home before he saw her. Mitch was driving his Toyota Landcruiser and Helen would immediately relay the message to him on his cellular phone.

Still hoping they'd never left town, Mitch drove around, trying to spot the bikes that Betty Roberts had missed. He saw a lightning-struck maple tree split in two in a yard near the business district, the strike they'd heard at the station. But he didn't see the bikes.

He headed toward the lake, all the time thinking that surely the girls would have noticed the threatening clouds and not gone so far.

But who knew what kids would do? When he recalled some of the dumb, reckless stunts he'd pulled as a teenager, his worry intensified.

Then he remembered Eagle's Nest Lodge, a vacation resort with two golf courses, a swimming pool, boat rentals, and walking trails, which overlooked Lake Tenkiller, and he felt a little calmer. Maybe the girls had taken refuge there.

He reached for his cell phone and dialed the station. "Any messages?" he asked when Helen answered.

Helen's voice came through crackling static. "No messages. And I haven't heard from Emily. I told you I'd call if I did."

"Thanks," Mitch said, and hung up. To himself, he muttered, "Don't borrow trouble."

But he kept picturing what could have happened to three sixteen-year-old girls. A lightning strike that hit a bike—or a girl. One or all of them hit by a car, the driver unable to see them in the pouring rain until it was too late. Or they could have accepted a ride with somebody who only seemed harmless.

Halfway to the lake, he had worked himself into a state of anxiety so intense he felt nauseous. Emily had always been such a joy to him, and since his wife's death, he'd probably come to depend on her company around the house too much. Even as his throat tightened and his gut twisted, he was aware that he was probably overreacting right now. He worried about Emily far more than he had when Ellen was alive. An irony, since he used to tell Ellen that *she* worried too much. His wife's death at thirty-five had changed a lot of things. For one, it forced him to face the brevity of life and the swiftness with which his daughter's childhood was passing. He couldn't imagine an existence without Emily.

Stop it, he told himself, his apprehensive gaze sweeping the shoulders of the road, first one side and then the other. Don't torture yourself. She's all right. She has to be. He didn't convince himself.

Then he saw the tracks. He whipped the Landcruiser onto the shoulder and jumped out. Narrow tire tracks—bicycle tracks—crisscrossed each other in the mud alongside the road and led into the trees. He ran into the woods.

A few yards off the road, Mitch saw the back end of a bike sticking out of a thicket of brush. He pulled it out. It was Temple Roberts's red mountain bike. He pushed back more of the brush with his arm, revealing the other two bikes.

They must have hidden the bikes and gone on foot to find shelter. But the lodge was still two miles distant. Where the hell would they find shelter around there? And why hadn't they retrieved their bikes when the rain stopped? Mitch struggled to control his rising panic as he headed into the woods, slapping at branches and yelling, "Emily! Emily!"

It was like a nightmare. The air was still, sodden with rain, the woods oppressive. He didn't know how long he stumbled around among the trees. Once he got his foot tangled in some brush, tripped, and sprawled on his face. Within a short time, he was splattered with mud and felt scratches stinging on his face. And he was hoarse from shouting his daughter's name.

Mitch was not ordinarily a praying man, but for the last few minutes he'd been praying for all he was worth. "Oh, God, don't let them be hurt. Don't let them be dead." He would have tried to make a deal with God, but he couldn't think of anything he could offer that God might want in exchange for his daughter's safety.

Finally, he stopped to rest next to an old elm tree, supporting himself with a hand spread on the trunk. Blood oozed from a scratch on the back of his hand. He pulled a handkerchief from his uniform pocket and blotted the blood, then pressed the handkerchief against a couple of places on his face that smarted. The *splat-splat* of water dripping off the trees and the sound of his own labored breathing surrounded him. For a moment, he felt disoriented. He wasn't sure exactly where he was and could picture himself wandering in the woods endlessly.

He bowed his head and closed his eyes. "Let them be all right," he whispered over and over. When he opened his eyes, he noticed a pile of feathers near the tree where he'd stopped. Bending down for a better look, he saw it was a dead bald eagle with a bloody wound in its breast. An arrow, probably used to kill the bird, lay nearby.

Damned poacher. Bald eagles were protected by the Endangered Species Act. He heard a noise and lifted his head. Something was crashing through the underbrush some distance away. He grabbed the eagle's legs, lifted it, picked up the arrow by its steel tip, stuck it in his hip pocket, and reeled toward the sound.

Minutes later, he stopped beside a copse of cedar trees to catch his breath. He knew exactly where he was now, and the crashing sound was coming closer.

Mitch had opened his mouth to call Emily's name again when the three girls stumbled out of the trees in front of him. They looked like refugees from a bombing raid.

"Daddy!" Emily staggered forward and stumbled into his arms. She was trembling uncontrollably and gasping for air. "We were lost—how did you know to look for us?"

Mitch dropped the eagle carcass and hugged her tightly. "Temple's mother got worried when you didn't turn up after the storm." He didn't mention how terrified he himself had been.

Carrie Lou and Temple stopped behind Emily, their shoulders hunched as they sucked in great gulps of air. "There's—" Carrie Lou gasped, but she couldn't finish, hadn't recovered enough breath yet to talk.

Carrie Lou's short brown hair was plastered to her head, and her glasses were so streaked with mud Mitch could barely see her eyes. Between the smudges of mud on her face, freckles stood out against her pale skin. Temple's wet hair had turned from red to a rusty brown and her thin cotton shirt clung like a second skin. Tears trickled down her face, unheeded.

Emily's trembling arms gripped Mitch's waist convulsively and her breath caught in a sob. "Oh, Daddy, he's dead," she mumbled against his chest.

Carrie Lou glanced over her shoulder and she and Temple edged closer to Mitch and Emily, as if for protection.

"What did you say, honey?" Mitch asked.

Emily started to cry.

"There's a dead man back there," Carrie Lou managed in a shaky voice, and shot another anxious glance over her shoulder.

Temple merely nodded, as if words were beyond her, and kept on crying silently.

"We went in there to get out of the rain," Carrie Lou said, "and found him. His head's all bloody."

Mitch stared into the trees. "Where?"

Emily lifted her tear- and dirt-streaked face. "The outlaw cave, Daddy."

Mitch had forgotten about the cave, only a few hundred yards from where they stood. He and Emily had discovered it on a walk through the woods two years ago. According to legend, the cave had been a hideout for outlaws in Indian Territory days.

It was dark in the cave. Could one of them have imagined they saw a dead body, then scared the others into believing it?

Temple finally spoke for the first time. "It was awful. I threw up."

All three girls were close to being in shock, Mitch realized. "The first thing we have to do is get you home," he said. "Do you think you can make it to my car? It's not far."

They nodded. Mitch picked up the eagle and, with his other arm around Emily, Carrie Lou and Temple on their heels, they wobbled slowly toward the car.

After a few moments, Emily stopped trembling. She looked up at him. "What are you going to do with that dead bird?"

"It's a bald eagle," Mitch told her. "Protected species. I need to turn it over to a game warden."

They finally reached the Toyota. All three girls fell into the back seat and Mitch loaded their bikes into the rear. He found a stick and raked off some of the mud on his boots before he slid into the driver's seat. He hadn't had the heart to tell the girls to take off their shoes before they got in.

As they approached town, Mitch said, "The man in the cave—did you recognize him?"

All three girls agreed that they'd never seen him before in their lives.

"He was wearing some kind of uniform," Emily added.

"A police uniform?" Mitch asked.

"Kind of like that," Temple put in, "but not exactly."

"We didn't stay long enough to get a very good look," Carrie Lou added.

Mitch said no more about the dead man. He clung to a fragment of hope that, with the storm howling outside and the darkness inside the cave, they'd imagined the whole thing.

"It must've been dark in that cave," he said.

"I had my flashlight. I lost it in the woods coming back," Carrie Lou said, effectively extinguishing Mitch's theory that the body was nothing but a figment of somebody's overblown imagination.

As soon as he got the girls home and settled, he'd pick up Duck and go back to the cave. He wished the city council hadn't annexed all that land around the lake for the tax base when people started building houses out there. If there really was a body in the cave—and he no longer had much doubt—it was in his bailiwick.

After delivering Carrie Lou and Temple and their bikes to the Robertses' house, Mitch drove home. While Emily took a warm bath, Mitch grabbed a quick shower and donned a fresh uniform.

Emily was in the kitchen heating water for hot tea when he came downstairs. She wore an old terry-cloth robe and fuzzy house slippers. She'd washed her long hair and brushed it straight back from her face to dry.

"You okay?" he asked, leaning in the doorway.

She managed a smile. "Now I am." She took a deep breath. "Oh, Daddy, I'm so glad you found us. We were so scared, and I guess we sort of panicked. I don't know when we'd have found our way out of the woods."

He went over to her and hugged her. At times like this, she still seemed like a little girl to him. "If you think you'll be okay here alone, I need to get back to work."

The kettle started whistling. She turned back around and set it off the burner. She looked at the cup containing the tea bag, which she'd set on the cabinet. "Maybe," she said, "I'll go back to Temple's house."

"I'd like that better than you staying here by yourself. Get dressed, and I'll take you over there."

"I can drive my car."

He hesitated. "Are you sure?"

She nodded. "Yes. I just don't want to be alone for awhile, that's all."

It was only a few blocks to the Robertses' house. Mitch stifled his overanxious fatherly impulse to refuse to let her drive. But as he left, he couldn't help saying, "Be careful, honey."

He made sure the front door locked behind him.

3

"He hasn't been here long," Officer Harold "Duck" Duck-worth said, leaning over the body to snap a picture, while Mitch provided illumination with his flashlight. "Doesn't even smell yet." Duck looked to one side. "Or if he does, the stink of that puke's covering it up."

"Temple Roberts upchucked when they found the body," Mitch said, trying not to breathe too deeply. He touched his shirt pocket, where he carried his cellular phone. He'd already called for an ambulance and placed a second call to Ken Pohl, the medical examiner in Tahlequah, to alert him that the body was coming.

"It must've happened early this morning, before the rain started. His uniform's dry," Mitch said, thanking God that the killer had left before the girls reached the cave.

"You ever seen him before?" Duck asked as he positioned himself for another picture.

"Don't think so."

The man's eyes were open, empty. He had a round face and, though he looked young, his hair was already thinning and receding from his forehead. His left cheek appeared to be crushed, and there was blood all over that side of his face and crusted in his hair around a dent above his left ear.

Sewn to the man's front pocket was an Oklahoma Department of Wildlife badge. Remembering the dead eagle that was still in the Landcruiser, wrapped in a plastic bag, Mitch wondered if it was connected to the warden's presence in the area that morning. "They hired a couple of new game wardens for our part of the state recently. Must be one of them."

When Duck finished taking pictures, Mitch said, "Roll him over on his side for a minute."

Duck grabbed one shoulder and pulled the body on its left side, revealing more bloody, matted hair in two places on the back of the head. "Gawd Almighty, look at that," he said. "The guy really took a beating. Wonder what they hit him with?" They had not found the murder weapon in the cave.

"A pipe, maybe," Mitch said. "Or a log." He fished a wallet from the man's back pocket and flipped it open. The bill compartment held two twenties and a five. "Well, he wasn't killed for his money." The driver's license identified the man as Arnett Walsh. According to the birth date, he was thirty-three years old. The address on the license was in Yukon, Oklahoma, a suburb of Oklahoma City. If Walsh was one of the new wardens, he hadn't even been in the area long enough to update the information on his license.

Mitch tucked the wallet into his shirt pocket with the cell phone. "I'll contact the Wildlife Department and find out where he lives, see if they know the next of kin." Reaching in

Walsh's side pocket, he fished out a ring of keys. "Here's a GM key. His vehicle has to be around here somewhere."

Duck eased the body down on its back, the way they'd found it. Mitch took out a small tablet and sketched the scene. Before leaving the cave, they took another look around and found nothing else but moss and rocks.

As they left, Mitch took his first deep breath since entering the cave, inhaling the clean scent of wet earth and trees. They walked back to where they'd left Mitch's Landcruiser. Mitch had scraped out the worst of the mud left by the girls' mud-caked shoes in the floorboard behind the front seat. Now he and Duck pulled off their muddy boots, set them on the newspapers Mitch had spread on the floorboard, and put their shoes back on.

Then they got in and waited for the ambulance, which arrived within minutes.

After directing the ambulance attendants to the cave, Mitch and Duck followed the road as it circled the woods, looking for Arnett Walsh's vehicle. "There's a graveled road leading into the trees around the next curve," Mitch said. "It's a little closer to the cave than where we went in."

Sure enough, a Chevrolet pickup with the Oklahoma Department of Wildlife insignia on both doors was parked where the road dead-ended. They got out, and using the keys he'd found in Walsh's pocket, Mitch unlocked the driver's-side door. While Duck walked around the pickup, Mitch searched the glove compartment and the compartment between the seats for anything that might be a clue to Walsh's murder. If Walsh saw something suspicious before leaving the truck, he might have jotted down a name, a license tag number—or, at least a description. That would be a bit of luck.

But it wasn't going to be that easy.

He got out. "Nothing in here. Find anything out there?" he asked Duck, who had been walking slowly over the area around the truck, scanning the ground.

"A bunch of tire tracks."

"A lot of hunters park here," Mitch said.

"Teenagers come here too, to make out," Duck added. "If the murderer parked here, he must have left before it rained, because none of these tracks are very clear." He held out his hand. "Found these in the grass."

Mitch looked at a couple of cash register receipts from a local convenience store, one for soft drinks, another for beer. Both were faded and mud-smeared. They'd been there for a while. He tossed them back into the brush.

The third item Duck had found was more interesting—a picture of a woman's head, in a plastic holder about an inch in diameter. She was young, probably in her early thirties, with medium brown hair. It was hard to tell what color the eyes were in such a small snapshot. She wasn't smiling. Her expression was solemn, as though she hadn't been thinking happy thoughts when the picture was taken. Or maybe she just didn't like being photographed.

The holder, which had a plastic eye on top so that it could be strung on a cord or chain, was scratched, and the picture looked faded, even though it had been protected by the holder. Hard to tell how long it had lain there, but Mitch didn't think the plastic was weathered enough to have been exposed to the elements for a very long time. If it had been there a good while, it had been sheltered by weeds or a rock.

"I don't recognize her. Do you?" Mitch asked.

"No."

"She looks sad. Not a ghost of a smile."

"Maybe she's got bad teeth."

Leave it to Mr. Sensitivity to come up with that explanation, Mitch thought. Duck had been gripping the holder by the little plastic eye. Mitch pulled a plastic bag from his pocket and held it open so Duck could drop it in, then he tucked it in his shirt pocket. "You drive Walsh's truck back to the station," he said, tossing Duck the keys. "I'll let the wildlife guys know where they can pick it up."

Less than two hours later, Mitch was at the Wildlife Department office in Tahlequah, the county seat. He handed over the dead eagle, stiff now inside its plastic covering, to Dick Nash, the warden who was manning the desk. Nash, a square-built man with thick, graying hair so straight and coarse it looked like brush bristles, gazed curiously at the scratches on Mitch's face.

"Looks like you been in a cat fight," Nash said.

Mitch touched the Band-Aid on one cheek. "I was in the woods, looking for my daughter and a couple of her friends. They got caught in that rainstorm this morning."

"They okay?"

"Yeah, they're fine."

Nash stashed the carcass in the back room. They'd collect the feathers before disposing of it.

"Damn," he said as he returned to Mitch, "that's the third eagle killed over in your part of the county in the last few weeks. The other two were pretty well plucked, though. If the same person killed this one, wonder why he didn't take the feathers?"

Good question, Mitch thought. Maybe the eagle killer was interrupted—by Walsh?—before he had a chance to strip the bird.

Nash sat down at his desk. "Arnett Walsh—he's one of the new hires—was assigned to investigate."

"Does Walsh live in Buckskin?" Mitch asked.

"Yes. He and his wife just moved there a few weeks back."

Mitch tossed Walsh's wallet on the desk. Nash opened it and looked at the license, then he glanced at Mitch with a frown. "Where'd you find this?"

Mitch put Walsh's car keys on the desk too and told Nash the whole story.

As he listened, Nash slumped down in the chair behind his desk and held his head in his hands until Mitch finished. Then he said, "Oh, shit. He hasn't been married very long. They're expecting their first baby in a couple months." He sat with his head bowed for a long moment. When he looked at Mitch, his eyes were red-rimmed. "You say you found the eagle not far from the cave?"

"A few hundred yards," Mitch said. "I've got the arrow we think killed the eagle in the evidence locker back home. One of my officers dusted it. Found a good thumbprint. The way it was placed indicates the shooter was right-handed. Could be a connection between the eagle and Walsh's murder."

"You really think so?"

"It's just one among several notions at this point. Do you have Walsh's address?"

Nash pulled a folder out of his desk drawer, flipped through it, found the sheet he wanted, and passed it to Mitch with a hand that was none too steady.

"Could I use your phone?"

Still looking a little dazed, Nash got up and let Mitch have his chair. Mitch dialed the Buckskin police station and told Shelly to see if she could find Walsh's wife at home and give her the news before one of her neighbors did.

When he hung up, Nash asked, "You really think some Indian murdered Walsh because he caught him killing an eagle?"

Mitch relinquished the desk chair to Nash and pulled another chair up to the other side of the desk. "Why do you assume it's Indians who've been killing the eagles?"

Nash spread his hands on the desk and slowly lowered himself into his chair again. "Who else would take the feathers?"

"I don't know. Maybe somebody who makes those cheap souvenirs they sell at flea markets. Doesn't have to be an Indian."

"I'd agree, except for the rumors we've been hearing. The Cherokees have been holding Eagle Dances out in the country west of Buckskin. I've never seen an Eagle Dance, but I've been told the dancers wear a lot of feathers. The first eagle carcass turned up around the time the dances started. From what you've told me, the carcass you brought in was found in the same general area as the other two." He raked his bristly hair back with both hands. "No offense meant. This is all hearsay, you understand." He eyed Mitch measuringly. "You been to any of the dances?"

Mitch shook his head. He was half-Cherokee, but everything he knew about the Cherokee culture he'd learned in the last few years on what you might call a need-to-know basis, as he dealt with traditional Cherokees involved in police cases. He'd attended one stomp dance in his life, with Rhea and her grandfather. He knew nothing about the Eagle Dance and had not heard the rumors of dances being held west of Buckskin. But then, there were several stomp grounds in the area, and the Cherokees didn't necessarily advertise their dances.

"Can you be more specific about where the Eagle Dances are performed?"

"One of the wardens was told they take place on land owned by a Cherokee named Brasfield, Vian Brasfield."

Mitch took a second to digest that. Vian Brasfield was the principal of the high school and highly spoken of by those who knew him better than Mitch did. Mitch's conversations with Brasfield consisted of greetings exchanged at high school ball games. Judging from his appearance, Brasfield was less than a quarter-blood. Which didn't prove the rumors false. There were tribal members with only a small fraction of Cherokee blood who were more "Indian" than some full-bloods. Mitch had lost count of the pale-skinned out-of-towners he'd run across in Buckskin trying to trace their Cherokee roots so they could get their Certificate of Degree of Indian Blood. That little card they could carry in their wallet seemed to be a badge of distinction. These days it was evidently trendy in some circles to be Indian.

In other circles—militia enclaves like the Kennedy compound outside Buckskin, for example—anybody who wasn't white and male was a second-class citizen. Fourteenth Amendment Citizens, they called them. According to some convoluted logic, the U.S. Constitution and original Bill of Rights, which were meant only for whites, were the only legitimate laws. Minorities were granted citizenship rights later, which made them some kind of an underclass.

"I'm puzzled about something," Mitch said. "Why would

Cherokees risk killing eagles for their feathers?" The penalty for killing an animal or bird protected by the government's Endangered Species Act ranged from a stiff fine and a warning to ten years in prison. "I thought Indians could get eagle feathers legally, from the Wildlife Department."

"Not all Indians," said Nash. "Using feathers in ceremonies must be a tribal tradition. As it happens, Cherokees qualify. But the applicant has to file a request along with papers signed by the principal chief and a tribal religious leader confirming that the feathers are to be used for religious purposes."

"You're saying that Brasfield, or whoever's behind the Eagle Dances, doesn't want to go through the rigamarole?"

Nash shrugged. "Could be. I've been told the Eagle Dances weren't done much—at least in your area—until recently. Somebody would have to initiate the feather request process. It can take up to a year to be approved. Besides, Mitch, you and I both know it wouldn't be the first time an Indian's taken an eagle illegally."

Mitch conceded the point. "Aside from the long approval process," he mused, "I imagine some Indians resent the mere idea of having to apply for the feathers."

"You got that right. They used eagle feathers for generations before they were protected by law. They feel the government has no right to interfere with their ceremonies, especially when they're held on Indian land."

Defining what is legally "Indian land" could get complicated too. Brasfield could feel, as many Cherokees did, that any land owned by a tribal member was Indian land, even if the courts did not always agree. In fact, the state had won lawsuits against several smoke shop owners who weren't paying taxes on tobacco sold on land owned by an Indian because that particular land didn't fit the legal description of "Indian land."

Nash's next words seemed to confirm what Mitch was thinking. "I checked, Mitch, and there have been no new requests for eagle feathers from Cherokee County in almost two years."

"Were the other eagles killed by arrows, too?" Mitch asked.

"We didn't find any arrows, but the wounds were consistent with that kind of injury."

Mitch wondered if Vian Brasfield was a bow hunter. Remembering that the teachers were having meetings at the high school today, he decided to visit Brasfield after lunch.

"How recently did you talk to Walsh?"

"Yesterday."

"Did he mention he was investigating the eagle killings?"

"Just in passing. Said he planned to patrol the area where the carcasses were found on a regular basis, hoping he might catch somebody in the act." He shifted uncomfortably. "Crazy as it sounds, I'm beginning to wonder if that's what happened." He shook his head. "But what kind of insane SOB would kill a man over a bird?"

"Hard to imagine," Mitch said. "People kill for the most petty reasons. But it could turn out there's no connection at all." He had a hard time believing anyone would commit murder to keep from being charged under the Endangered Species Act. On the other hand, it nagged at him that he'd found the eagle carcass so close to the cave where a game warden's body lay. "Well," Mitch added, rising from his chair, "I guess I better get back to Buckskin before the outlaws take over the town."

"Could you give me a call after Mrs. Walsh has been noti-fied of Arnett's death?" Nash asked. "This is gonna be real hard for her to handle. I want to pay a visit. I'll take my wife, maybe take a potted plant or something, see if there's any-thing we can do to help. Then I can stop by the station and drive Walsh's pickup back."

"Sure thing."

As Mitch reached the door, Nash said in a strained voice, "Mitch?"

He turned around.

Nash's hands were clenched into fists on his desk, and his eyes were bleak. "It's not right. There's gonna be this little baby who'll never know his father."

"Yeah," Mitch agreed, thinking of his own father, whom he'd lost at an early age, and the hole left behind that could never be filled. But at least Mitch had those first eight years and some good memories.

"Catch the bastard who did this," Nash said, his voice rough with anger and grief.

4

The sun burned away the remaining clouds as Mitch drove back to Buckskin. The sky was so brilliant it hurt the eyes. Spring green sparkled on the trees and the new grass in the fields alongside the highway. On several stretches of road, wildflowers cast a blue mist beside the fencerows, and in the hills pink blooms, like puffs of cotton candy, decorated the redbud trees. Mitch loved Oklahoma's brief spring.

Back in Buckskin, he had a grilled chicken breast and baked potato at the Three Square Café on Highway 10, the main route through town. One of the town's two stoplights was at the intersection of the highway and Buckskin's main street, Sequoyah, named for the man who'd invented the Cherokee syllabary. The second light was at the other end of Sequoyah, where a left turn on Division Street would take you to the high school.

When Mitch returned to the station, Shelly and Duck

were working at their desks. Helen was eating yogurt from a paper cup at the dispatcher's desk. The jail's current total prison population, eighty-year-old Gus Ahrgrin, in jail-issue orange coveralls, was flicking a lamb's-wool duster over the furniture. To save money, Mitch had assigned Gus the cleaning duties, giving the janitor a month off. The station had to be staffed all night with a prisoner in residence, which required additional overtime pay. Virgil Rabbit usually volunteered for the job; with six kids he could always use the extra money. And saving one month's janitor's wages would partially compensate for the added overtime.

Gus didn't seem to mind cleaning. It gave him something to do while he put in his time for accumulated unpaid traffic tickets. Gus's eyesight wasn't good and his reflexes were shot, so after repeated car wrecks, the municipal judge suspended his driver's license. Gus still had an old car that ran some of the time and, once in a while, his foot itched to tread on the accelerator. As a result of his little joyrides, he'd acquired more than three hundred dollars worth of traffic tickets, most for driving with a suspended license, so the judge ordered him to pay or spend thirty days in jail. Gus said he didn't have the three hundred and chose the jail time.

Gus dawdled over the janitorial chores to make them last as long as possible. He liked being out of his cell and loved talking to Helen and the officers and eavesdropping on their conversations. Furthermore, Gus probably ate better in jail than he did at home, where he fixed his own meals. Here, carry-out restaurant meals were brought to him. Mitch figured he would have to kick Gus out on the street when his thirty days were served.

"How's Emily, Chief?" Helen asked as Mitch stood watching Gus work.

"She's fine."

"I'm so sorry those girls had to be the ones who"—she glanced at Gus—"well, you know."

"Found a dead man, did she, Chief?" inquired Gus with a snaggletoothed grin, his rheumy eyes glistening with a need for all the gory details. "Poor little thing."

Mitch gazed at him for a moment, wondering who'd told him. Probably, he decided, Gus had been eavesdropping on the officers again. "She decided to go over to Temple Roberts's house for the rest of the day. At least she's not sitting home brooding over it."

"Heard it was a game warden," Gus put in. "Young fella."

Mitch lifted an eyebrow. "Where'd you hear that?"

"Couldn't help overhearing the officers talking," Gus said baldly, confirming Mitch's suspicion. He ran his duster over the table where the coffeepot sat. "O' course, as an employee here, I would never repeat any police business I happen to hear."

In a cocked hat, Mitch thought. "You're no employee, Gus," Mitch reminded him. "You're just a prisoner doing your time."

"Right, Chief," Gus agreed. "I'm paying my debt to society. Getting plumb rehabilitated." He cackled happily.

"Go and dust in the back," Mitch told him. Looking offended, the old man shuffled out of the common room. Mitch turned to Shelly, who was engrossed in paperwork.

"Did you get hold of Mrs. Walsh, Shelly?"

She looked up. "Duck and I went out to her house." She sucked in a breath. "It was pretty bad, Chief."

"She's pregnant," Duck put in. "Turned as gray as a corpse

when we told her what happened. A wonder she didn't drop that baby right then and there."

"We grabbed her and laid her down on the couch before she collapsed," Shelly said, and shook her head. "It's amazing what people will say when you hit them with something like that. Mrs. Walsh kept saying, 'But we haven't even been married two years,' as if that could make it not true. We got a neighbor to come and stay with her till one of her sisters could get there. The closest one is in Oklahoma City."

Duck rubbed his hands over his face. "I purely hate making that kind of call. But Shelly didn't wanta go by herself."

"I *said* I could handle it," Shelly protested. "Didn't I say that, Helen?"

"You did. I heard you."

"Yeah, but I could tell you needed moral support," Duck said. "You were just too stubborn to admit it. Females get all emotional at times like this."

Helen snorted.

"Oh, stuff it," Shelly said, disgusted. She got up and poured herself a cup of coffee.

"Were you able to question her at all?" Mitch asked.

"A little," Shelly said. She came back to her desk, perched on a corner, and began to swing one long leg. The police department's khaki uniform looked good on Shelly, who was tall and very slender, unlike her partner. Duck was only a couple of inches short of six feet, but slender was not a word that had ever been applied to him.

"After she'd cried herself out," Shelly went on, "I fixed her a cup of tea and sat with her." She glanced at her cohort, who was tugging on the too-tight collar of his shirt. If Duck gained another few pounds, he'd have to buy bigger uniforms.

But he was resisting going up another size. "My moral support collapsed and went outside to wait for me."

With an angry jerk, Duck loosened his top shirt button and took a deep breath. "I thought she'd talk more if I left you two alone," he said sulkily.

Mitch cut in. "Did her husband tell her where he was going when he left the house this morning?"

Shelly nodded. "Out to the lake to patrol the area where they've found dead eagles. The one you found isn't the first."

"So Warden Nash says."

"Walsh left the house about seven, told his wife he'd be patrolling around the lake all morning, hoping to run into whoever's been killing the eagles. He'd got wind that there's some kind of dance scheduled tonight where the Cherokees use eagle feathers."

"Did he have a suspect?"

"If he did, he didn't tell his wife."

Mitch watched her take a sip of coffee. "Did his wife know of anybody he'd had a falling out with recently?"

"Nope. According to her, he was the most easygoing guy in the world. Never had a problem with anyone. Wouldn't even argue with his wife. She said it drove her crazy when they were first married. She'd get worked up over something and want to have a good, air-clearing fuss. He'd just walk away from her."

"Everybody who believes that can stand on their head," Duck muttered. "Never saw a married couple that didn't yell at each other once in a while." He cut his eyes toward the dispatcher's desk. Helen was thrice-divorced and had sworn off ever getting married again. "Am I right, Helen?"

"I hate to say it," Helen said, "but all my husbands raised

their voices once in a while. I'm not saying I didn't give as good as I got, mind you."

"I'm merely reporting what the woman told me," Shelly said.

"Duck showed me that picture he found out at the lake," Helen said to Mitch. She was in her fifties and had lived in Buckskin all her life.

"You recognize the woman?" Mitch asked.

Helen had spun around in her chair, her brow creased. "I keep thinking there's something familiar about her, but I can't put my finger on it, Chief. Maybe it'll come to me."

"Whoever's here at four when Virgil and Roo come on duty," Mitch said, "needs to show it to them." Virgil Rabbit had lived in Buckskin all his life too. "If she's from around here, surely somebody will recognize her, though the picture probably has nothing to do with the murder of Arnett Walsh."

"Yeah," Duck agreed. "The place where we found the picture is used by hunters and hikers and teenagers—all kinds of people. Anybody could've dropped it."

"Shelly," Mitch asked, "did you go out to the clinic?"

"Sure did. I was writing that report when you came in. Didn't find out anything we didn't already know. All three calls came at about the same time. Ten o'clock on a weekday morning. Wonder if that means anything."

"Could be the caller's doing it on his coffee break or something," Duck suggested.

Shelly cocked her head. "Maybe, but if Dr. Vann's right and it's Dane Kennedy, he could make the calls any time of the day when he happens to be in town. He'd know calls from his home could be traced through the phone company's records."

"I meant to mention this earlier," Mitch said. "Duck, I want you and Shelly to check with the people at city hall and the other businesses close by. See if anybody saw Dane Kennedy hanging around there yesterday morning. I'm going to run out to the high school."

"School's out today," Duck said.

"I know that, but the teachers and administrators are supposed to be there. Dick Nash thinks the principal, Vian Brasfield, might have some information on the eagle killings."

"Say what?" Duck asked, surprised.

"I'll fill you in later," Mitch said, preparing to leave. "By the way, let's try to watch our tongues when Gus is around."

"Aw, he's harmless, Chief," Duck said.

"He may not mean any harm," Mitch said, "but you know when the weather's nice he spends a lot of time with that bunch of spitters and whittlers who hang out on those benches outside city hall. When he leaves us, he'll be the center of attention for months. You know Gus. He'll repeat what he heard here and add his own creative touches, just to make a better story."

Duck nodded, unworried about what Gus might tell his cronies down at city hall. To everybody but Mitch, their prisoner had become a sort of pet around there.

5

Mitch pushed through the high school's double glass entry doors into silence. The school smelled of floor wax and something else that might have been chalk dust, but the thundering herd was missing. As he walked down the tiled hallway, he heard muffled voices coming from one of the rooms.

He tapped on the door, then opened it and stepped inside. A fortyish woman in a red pantsuit was addressing about twenty teachers seated at student desks. Everybody gazed at Mitch curiously.

"May I help you?" asked the woman at the front. Her blond hair was caught on top of her head with an elastic band, the ends falling helter-skelter in straggly curls down the back of her head. She had a ruddy complexion, as if she had been running or was excited about something. It made her look lively, charged up.

"I'm looking for Vian Brasfield," Mitch said.

The woman glanced at her audience. "I'll be right back."

Mitch followed her from the room. She closed the door and turned to him, her hand extended. "I'm Virginia Craig, the guidance counselor."

"Mitch Bushyhead. Pleased to meet you."

"Are you Emily's father?"

He nodded.

"Emily's a sweet girl. You must be very proud of her."

"Guilty as charged."

She smiled, but her mind seemed to be elsewhere. Her blue eyes held a troubled look. "Mr. Brasfield isn't here," she said.

"Oh. Well, do you know where I could find him?"

She hesitated and the furrows in her brow deepened. "I'm sorry. I wish I could help you, but I don't know where he is."

"I'll try his house."

Mitch was already turning away when she said, "He isn't there, either. When he didn't show up here at school this morning, we delayed starting the first meeting to wait for him. After a half hour, one of the teachers called his home. His wife said he left very early, before seven. She thought he was going to have breakfast somewhere before coming to school."

"He hasn't been here at all?"

She tucked a dangling curl into the mass atop her head. "No, and to tell you the truth, I'm a little concerned. Hunter Kennedy, our vice-principal, called his home again when we took our lunch break about"—she glanced at her watch—"forty-five minutes ago. His wife still hadn't heard from him."

The vice-principal's name caught Mitch's attention. "Is Hunter Kennedy related to the Kennedy who lives on a farm west of town?"

She pursed her lips. "Dane Kennedy, you mean. He's Hunter's father, but"—she paused as though to select her words with care—"Hunter doesn't share Dane's political views. I think his father embarrasses him. I know I'd be embarrassed if he were my father." She glanced at Mitch with a rueful smile. "Hunter is a good man, relates well to the students. They all seem to like him, even those he has to discipline." She noticed Mitch's questioning look. "That's part of the vice-principal's job, you know—discipline."

Actually, Mitch hadn't ever thought about it. "I'd like to talk to Kennedy. And anybody else who might have an idea why Brasfield didn't come to work today."

She hesitated only briefly. "I'll get Hunter and Troy Reader. Troy's been here for a number of years."

She went back into the classroom. Moments later, a stockily built young man came out followed by another man with an angular face, who appeared to be in his forties. The older man had white-blond hair and a neatly trimmed mustache.

"Hi," the younger man said. "I'm Hunter Kennedy and this is Troy Reader. Virginia said you wanted to see us."

Mitch introduced himself, then said, "Mr. Kennedy, the counselor told me you talked to Vian Brasfield's wife less than an hour ago. I'd like to know what she said."

Kennedy exchanged a questioning look with Reader. "About Vian, you mean?" With one hand, he raked back a forelock of hair the color of heavily creamed coffee. "Nothing, really, except that he left home earlier than usual this morning. He said he was going to have breakfast and catch up on some work in his office before the teachers' meeting started."

"Does he usually eat breakfast in town?"

"Once or twice a week," Reader said. "Sometimes I join him so we can discuss things at school. I'm president of the Classroom Teachers' Association."

"But you didn't meet him today?"

"No."

Kennedy pointed down the hall. "Let's go around to the teachers' lounge and get a cup of coffee."

"Sounds good to me," Mitch said.

The lounge was a small, square room midway down a second hall. Kennedy and Reader took mugs bearing their names off hooks. Reader picked up an extra mug for Mitch and filled all three from the large pot that sat beside a microwave oven on a shelf attached to the wall. They sat at one of three square tables.

Kennedy looked at Mitch over the rim of his mug. He had smallish brown eyes set in a square face. "We're all puzzled about why Vian never arrived here today. I guess somebody got worried enough to call the police station."

Mitch ignored the implied question and asked one of his own. "Did anybody check the coffee shops?"

Kennedy said, "His wife told me that she did, after one of the teachers called her earlier. Vian usually goes to the Three Squares, but the owner said he hadn't been in this morning. Mrs. Brasfield called several other places that serve breakfast, where she thought he might have gone. Nobody had seen him."

"And that's all she said?"

He frowned. "I think so. Wait. When I said good-bye, she asked me if Virginia Craig was here. I said yes, did she want me to go get her. She said no and hung up."

Mitch mulled that over. "Did you think it odd that she'd ask for Ms. Craig, then hang up before talking to her?"

"No—well, I did wonder why she'd asked about her. I guess she just wanted to be sure she was here, for some reason."

Mitch fixed his eyes on the other man. "What do you think, Mr. Reader?"

He half smiled and said dryly, "I don't know why she asked about Virginia. I don't think Virginia and Vian's wife are particularly friendly."

"Ms. Craig said you've worked here a good while, Reader. Are you a friend of Brasfield's?" Mitch said.

He shrugged. "We're not all that close. Since I represent the classroom teachers, I probably talk to Vian more than anybody else. But we don't socialize much away from school."

"Did Brasfield ever say anything to you about hunting eagles with a bow?"

Reader looked blank. "No. He mentioned hunting once or twice, but I assumed he used a gun. I don't even know if he owns a hunting bow."

Mitch let that drop. If Brasfield didn't turn up soon, he was going to have to talk to his wife, anyway. "Could Brasfield have been here earlier and left before the teachers arrived?"

The other two men thought about it. "Well," Reader said, "his office was locked when we all got here about nine-thirty. After a while, Virginia got the extra key we keep here at school and went in and looked around. As far as she could tell, he hadn't been here. Of course, we can't be absolutely sure."

"Strange," Mitch mused.

"It is," Kennedy agreed. "But his wife didn't seem concerned, just pissed because Vian didn't go where he told her he was going. To tell you the truth, I'm getting worried because it's so unlike him to miss a teachers' meeting. In fact, I even called the hospital after lunch. I thought maybe he'd had a wreck."

Odd that Mrs. Brasfield wasn't worried too. If her husband had gone eagle hunting this morning—and she'd known it—wouldn't it occur to her that he might not have come to work because he was being detained for illegal hunting? That ought to worry her, so *if* Brasfield was the eagle killer, it could be his wife knew nothing about it. "Does he make a habit of disappearing like this? In general, I mean. Not just missing a teachers' meeting?"

Reader glanced at Kennedy, who shrugged and said, "Maybe on the weekends. You'll have to ask his wife. I'm new at the high school this year. Been away from Buckskin for more than ten years, so I've only known Vian since September. All I can tell you is he's a good boss, fair in his dealings with the teachers. You can ask anyone."

"Like Hunter said, this thing today is out of character for Vian," Reader put in. "He rarely takes a day off unless he's too sick to get out of bed. He was scheduled to start off the meeting this morning. He wouldn't have forgotten about it. And I can't see him just deciding to do something else without telling somebody."

Mitch stared out the room's only window. Two young boys raced by on the school ground, trying to get their kites airborne. He sipped his coffee, detecting a touch of cinnamon. He turned back. "Either of you know anything about the Eagle Dances held on land owned by Brasfield?"

Reader gave a soft laugh. "Oh, yeah. If you're around Vian

at all, you'll hear about that. He lives two blocks from the school, but he has a few acres out west of town where they do the dances. He talks about it all the time. He's just an eighth Cherokee, but he's real proud of it. Says he's dedicated that land to the preservation of the Cherokee culture. He's invited all the teachers to come out to see the dances. I've gone twice. Virginia's been more than any of us, four or five times, I think . . . well, that's what I've heard." He paused as though to gather his thoughts, as though he wished he hadn't said that about the guidance counselor.

Then Kennedy said, "I went out there once. Took my wife and two boys." He stretched across to another table and opened the lid on a bakery box that still held a couple of pastries. As he did so, Mitch noticed his wristwatch, a fancy sports model with a red line bordering the face.

"That's a nice-looking watch, Kennedy."

Kennedy smiled. "My wife got it for me after I started running with Troy here."

"She had to order it out of Tulsa," Reader said, looking covetously at the watch. "It's got all the bells and whistles."

"Doesn't make me run any faster, though," Kennedy said with a sigh. "I still have to bust my butt keeping up with you, Troy."

"Laying off those doughnuts might help," Reader said, grinning.

Kennedy shrugged and offered the box to Mitch and Reader, who shook their heads. Kennedy took the doughnut with red and white sprinkles on it, leaving the long john with the caramel icing in the box, which he replaced on the next table.

"Kennedy, you were saying you went to the dances at Brasfield's place," Mitch prompted, wanting to keep the conversation going, to learn more about Vian Brasfield, whose disappearance had raised troublesome questions in his mind.

Kennedy took a bite of doughnut before answering. "Sometime last January, I think it was, during the time we had a break in the freezing weather. My boys are just three and four and I figured we wouldn't be able to watch the dances very long because they'd get bored. But they loved the drums and the dancers, especially when they wore those crazy-looking masks."

Mitch didn't notice masked dancers at the stomp dance he had attended. But whether the dancers out at Brasfield's were masked or not didn't seem relevant to his current inquiry. "All that noise could be irritating to the neighbors," Mitch observed, thinking of Dane Kennedy, whose farm was west of town too. Kennedy didn't have any use for Indians to start with.

"I guess." Kennedy tucked the last bite of doughnut into his mouth and washed it down with coffee. "From what Vian says, they go on until all hours." He got up to get a napkin and raked the sprinkles that had dropped from his doughnut off the table into his hand, then tossed them in the wastebasket.

Kennedy's casual tone and manner made Mitch think he hadn't made the connection between Brasfield's possibly irritated neighbors and his father. "Is Brasfield's place close to your father's farm?"

Reader looked sharply at Mitch as Kennedy turned from the wastebasket to sit back down, ducking his head, as though embarrassed by the mention of his father. "Vian's land borders the farm."

"Has your dad complained about the noise?"

"I don't see him much."

"Oh? I thought maybe that's why you came back to Buckskin, to be closer to your family."

"I see my sister more often than Dad. She and her husband and little girl live at the farm with him."

"You don't have much contact with your father, then?"

His cheeks turned pink. "Not a lot. At first I hoped he might have mellowed while I was away, but if anything he's worse than ever."

"I guess your sister doesn't mind it."

He looked dispirited. "Her husband lost his job last year, and they moved their trailer out to the farm. Maybe they'll leave when they get on their feet again, I don't know. I worry about what my niece is seeing and hearing more than anything."

"Have you discussed this with your sister?"

He shook his head. "Dee and I don't talk about Dad's politics much. She takes a too benign view of the whole thing, in my opinion. Says it's just a bunch of grown men playing war games and that growing up with Dad wasn't as bad as I remember. I don't know if she really believes that or if she's trying to convince herself."

"People don't always remember the same things from their childhoods."

He acknowledged this with a perplexed frown, as though it were one of life's profound paradoxes. "Actually, I guess it wasn't so bad, as long as our mother was there to keep Dad in check, but she left when I was twelve. After that, I just hunkered down and tried to escape Dad's notice as much as I could, till I was eighteen. He refused to pay for college, said the professors were all dupes of the Zionist bankers and One Worlders. It took me five and a half years, but I worked my way through Kansas State."

Reader had slumped down in his chair and was sipping his coffee in silence.

"Feeling as you do, I'm surprised you decided to come back to Buckskin," Mitch said to Kennedy.

For a moment he looked down at the table, his expression sad, as though talking about his childhood had dredged up too many painful memories. Then he looked up and smiled sheepishly. "Sometimes I wonder about that myself. The thing is, this is the only offer I had and I wanted to get into administration."

"God knows why," Reader snorted.

Kennedy gave him a surprised look. "The pay's better than classroom teaching, for one thing."

Reader smoothed his mustache and shook his head. "Too many headaches come with it."

"You have to deal with parental complaints," Kennedy agreed, "and kids who make trouble, but the raise in salary makes up for that. Which is why I grabbed this job. When you're as young as I am—I won't be thirty for four months yet—it's pretty tough to break in. Vian and I seemed to hit it off when I interviewed and I suspect he had to make a case for me to the school board. As I said, he's a good boss. He's sure been good to me. I wish I could've had that sort of relationship with my father."

It sounded as if Brasfield had become something of a father figure to Kennedy. "Too bad you and your dad don't get along better. Kids need grandparents."

Kennedy shook his head. "I don't take the boys out there

anymore. I don't want them hearing all that paranoid insanity I was raised with. Last time I saw Dad, he was all worked up about getting a notice that his property taxes on the farm are overdue."

Kennedy glanced at Reader, who suggested, "Tell him what your old man said about that."

"You won't believe this, Chief, but Dad's decided that, since he owns the land free and clear, he can declare it a sovereign nation and be exempt from taxes. Said if the Cherokees can do it, why can't he." He pushed back his forelock. "You can't reason with him, so I gave up trying. I decided I'd just go on with my life and have as little to do with him as possible. The problem is that everybody here knows he's my father."

"And we know you're not like him," Reader put in.

"People still give me a pretty wide berth till they get to know me." Kennedy lifted his shoulders, as though throwing off a weight. He gripped the edge of the table with both hands, preparing to push back his chair. "Listen, if that's all you want from us, we need to get back to the meeting."

"One more question, if you don't mind."

Kennedy sank back into his chair. "Sure."

Mitch had more than one question circling in his mind. Where was Brasfield? Had he been in the woods that morning? Had he seen Arnett Walsh? If so, and Walsh had tried to detain him, would he have resisted arrest? "Does Brasfield have a temper?"

Reader looked startled by the question. He set down his empty cup and considered his answer. "Everybody's got some temper, I guess. But I've never seen Vian really lose it. Oh, he'll reprimand a teacher when he thinks it's called for, but he's always extra considerate of them afterward. I think he really hates having to call anybody on the carpet."

"What's he like away from school?" Mitch asked.

"Pretty much the same way he is here, I guess," Reader replied.

"Is he a drinker?" Mitch had known the most mild-mannered men to become violent when they were drinking.

"He doesn't drink to excess, if that's what you mean," Reader said. "I've only seen him drunk once since I've known him. And that was at a conference in Oklahoma City. I guess since he was out of town he felt he could let his hair down a little. It was like he turned into somebody else—he got loud and maudlin. It was embarrassing."

"Maudlin? How do you mean?"

Reader exchanged a look with Hunter Kennedy, then said to Mitch, "This is confidential, right?"

Mitch nodded.

"After Vian had several drinks, he went on and on about how life is short and full of regrets. How he'd do a lot of things differently if he could live his life over. Said one thing he'd change was he'd marry another woman. Then he put his head down on the table and started bawling and begged to be forgiven."

"Forgiven?" Mitch asked. "For what?"

Reader looked at Kennedy, who said, "I think he wanted Troy to forgive him for hiring me as vice-principal instead of Troy."

Reader hesitated. "I don't know if that was it or not. I've told him I didn't want the job, and I didn't see any point in going over it again, especially when he was drunk. I went back to the hotel shortly after that."

"And left me to get Vian to his room," Kennedy said with a grimace. "Not an easy task. I practically had to carry him."

"The next day," Reader added, "Vian apologized to both of us."

It didn't sound as if Brasfield had a violent streak, sober *or* drunk. "Okay," Mitch said. "That about does it. Thanks for your time."

Kennedy preceded Reader out the door. Once Kennedy was gone, Reader stepped back inside. "We all make jackasses of ourselves once in a while, Chief. I wouldn't want Vian to know we told you about Oklahoma City."

"As I said," Mitch assured him, "I can't think of any reason to repeat what you told me to Brasfield."

As Mitch left the school, he decided, since Reader, Kennedy, and the guidance counselor were concerned about their boss's absence, he'd have a talk with Vian Brasfield's wife right away.

6

The Brasfield house was a handsome old two-story Victorian with green shutters and a wraparound porch across the front and one side. Gingerbread typical of early twentieth century Victorians trimmed the edge of the porch roof. Mitch's own house had the same trim around the front windows.

A plump woman with lots of dark, permed, gray-streaked hair came to the door, drying her hands on a tea towel. Mitch remembered seeing Mrs. Brasfield at ball games with her husband.

"Yes?" she said, speaking sharply, holding open the glass storm door and frowning as she said it, as though he'd interrupted her in the midst of doing something important.

Already Mitch was beginning to think that stopping at the Brasfield place was, if not a bad idea, at least premature. But he couldn't retreat now, so he gave her a big smile. "I'm the chief of police, Mitch Bushyhead. Just want to check on your husband, ma'am. He hasn't been at the high school all day, and the teachers are getting worried." Let her think he was there at the behest of the teachers.

She wore a pair of brown slacks that were too tight across her heavy thighs and a blue-and-white-checked shirt with the tail hanging down over her stomach and butt. "Oh, for heaven's sake. There was no need to call the police. I suppose this was Virginia Craig's idea. I would think Virginia had enough problems of her own without tending to other peoples'. Well, come on in if you want to."

Mitch wondered what problems she referred to as he stepped into a long living/dining room with a dining table and chairs of dark cherrywood. In the center of the table, English ivy trailed from a big brass pot across a crocheted tablecloth. A sofa covered in gray velvet and two flowered armchairs, with a dark butler's table between the sofa and chairs, occupied the other end of the room.

"Vian will put in an appearance eventually. Do you want me to have him call you when he comes in?"

"If you would. But as long as I'm here, could I ask a couple of questions?"

She balled the tea towel in both hands with exasperation. "If it's really necessary."

"I'd appreciate it, ma'am."

She sighed. "I was getting a roast ready for the oven. Wait here and I'll stick it in the refrigerator."

Mitch wandered around the living room, which smelled of lemon-scented furniture polish. Every surface gleamed like glass.

Mrs. Brasfield returned without the tea towel. She gestured toward an armchair. "Would you like to sit down?"

Her words were grudging, and Mitch declined. "Thanks, but this'll only take a minute. Have you heard from your husband since he left the house this morning?"

"No, but he rarely calls home during the day."

A big calico cat wandered into the living room from the kitchen, saw Mitch, and streaked out again.

Mrs. Brasfield stared at him, waiting. There was something not quite approving about the set of her jaw and the way her lips puckered, as though she were drinking something through a straw. Mitch had a feeling that the woman's outlook on life and other people was more often critical than not, and he began to understand Brasfield's drunken confession that he'd married the wrong woman.

"So you're not worried about your husband?" Mitch asked.

She settled on the arm of a chair. It might have been Mitch's imagination, but it certainly seemed that she found his concern for her husband nothing but a bother and an interruption of her work. "No, I'm not worried. He'll turn up around suppertime."

"You seem real sure of that. Does he often disappear without telling you where he's going?"

"All the time," she said in a voice tight with irritation. "When he's not at the high school, he's out digging into his Cherokee heritage. He's obsessed with it." She hopped off the chair with surprising agility, given her size. "Come back to his study and I'll show you."

She led the way through the kitchen and utility room to a small room at the back of the house. There was an oak desk, probably salvaged from a schoolroom, and bookshelves covering one wall. She walked over to the books and ran her hand across several spines. "All of these books are about the Cherokees."

"Every one of them?"

"Actually, some of them deal with other things and refer to the Cherokees only a few times. Vian will buy a book if the Cherokees are mentioned just once. He's spent a fortune on books. He's got five or six used book dealers searching for some that are out of print. And here." She walked to the desk and picked up a thick stack of xeroxed pages. "He copied these from material in the reference room at the university in Tahlequah." She slapped the stack angrily back on the desk. "We even had to spend our vacation last year at the Cherokee reservation in North Carolina. I thought we'd stay a day or two and go on somewhere else. But I couldn't tear Vian away. I ended up reading five novels in a motel room while he wandered all over the reservation, taping interviews with Indians. We came back with a trunkload of books. They're still in the box." She gestured toward a large cardboard carton in one corner. "No more room on the bookshelves."

"I see what you mean about him being obsessed," Mitch said.

She bobbed her head. "Sometimes I think Vian's gone totally crazy on the subject. When he first got into this, five or six years ago, I thought it was a passing fancy. Now he says he needs all this material"—she threw out both hands, taking in the room—"because he's going to write the definitive history of the Cherokees when he retires. If I had to guess, I'd say you could find Vian in Tahlequah right now, either at the university or out at the tribal offices. Or maybe at the University of Tulsa. They have a big Indian collection."

"According to the teachers, he was supposed to be at a teachers' meeting."

She shrugged that off as of no consequence. "He probably heard about a book or master's thesis somewhere dealing with some obscure tidbit about the Cherokees and he couldn't wait to get his hands on it." She poked a plump finger into the mass of hair and scratched. Then she turned and walked out of the office. Mitch followed her back to the living room.

Mitch wasn't sure what else to ask. "So, you're confident he'll be home this evening."

"Oh, yes. There's a dance scheduled tonight. He wouldn't miss that for the world. He'll probably come home just in time to eat dinner on the run. He didn't feel like eating dinner last night and he forgets to eat when he's doing research, so he should be ravenous this evening. At any rate, he'll be out at the dance ground, hopping around and hollering like an idiot."

Mitch couldn't help smiling at the description. "Is there a cabin on that land of your husband's west of town?" He was beginning to wonder if Brasfield was in hiding. If so, that seemed a likely place.

"No. Vian would like to build on the acreage, but I told him we'd have to keep this house too, because I wasn't moving. I don't want to be stuck out there by myself with that raving lunatic Dane Kennedy right next door."

"Where else might your husband go to get away?"

She gave him an odd look. "Away from what?"

"I wouldn't know. I'm just trying to get a line on where he might be."

"I already told you where he probably is. Tahlequah or Tulsa."

"Well, if I don't hear from him, I'll check in tomorrow, just to be sure he's okay. Sorry to have bothered you, Mrs. Brasfield."

"That's all right."

As he stepped out the door, Mitch thought of another question. "Does your husband own a bow and arrows, Mrs. Brasfield?"

"Why, yes." She held the storm door open as her sharp gray-green eyes studied him closely. "Why do you want to know?"

Mitch ignored the question. "Did he happen to have them with him when he left this morning?"

"He always has them. Keeps them in the truck, along with his booger dance costume and the other paraphernalia he uses in the dances. But you didn't answer my question. Why do you want to know?"

"Some dead bald eagles have been found near town, killed with an arrow."

She stiffened. "Isn't it illegal to hunt eagles?"

"Yes, ma'am."

"Are you accusing my husband of breaking the law?"

"No, ma'am. It's just that I was told there've been Eagle Dances out in the country, on that land your husband owns. They're getting the feathers somewhere." He gave her what he hoped was a disarming smile. "If your husband's gone crazy, as you say, on the Indian stuff, maybe he decided to take some eagles the way his Cherokee ancestors did."

Mitch could tell she hadn't thought of that before, but now that she had, she couldn't dismiss it completely. She went immediately on the defensive. "Let me tell you something, Chief Bushyhead," she snapped. "You better have some proof before you come around here saying they're getting eagle feathers from my husband. Half the Indians in the county have bows and arrows. Some of them even make their own."

"Yes, ma'am."

"Is that all?" she demanded.

"Yes, ma'am." Mitch barely got the words out before the storm door slammed in his face. Then the inner door banged shut so hard it rattled the walls. Mitch heard the bolt sliding into the locked position.

Charming woman, he told himself as he got back in the car. She'd found Mitch a bother even before he told her about the dead eagles, and after that, she'd taken a distinct dislike to him. Didn't seem overly fond of her husband, either. And Virginia Craig was definitely on her shit list.

Back at the station, Shelly and Duck gave him a rundown on their futile quest to find somebody who could swear to having seen Dane Kennedy in town yesterday. One man thought he saw Kennedy's pickup but couldn't be sure.

"Guess we could drive out to his farm and ask him," Shelly said.

"I don't think so," Duck protested. "That old man's deranged. He'd just as soon shoot us as look at us."

"We've got nothing substantial to question him about," Mitch said. "He'd probably stop us at the gate, and he'd be within his rights."

"Yeah, and he's flat-out touchy about his rights," Duck said.

Mitch went into his office and called to check on Emily, who asked if she could spend the night with the Robertses again.

"It's fine with me," Mitch said, "but aren't you afraid you'll wear out your welcome?"

"It was Mrs. Roberts's idea," Emily said.

"Okay, then, but I heard there's going to be some Indian dances tonight, thought I might run out there for a while." A couple of months ago, when Emily found out he'd gone to a stomp dance, she'd asked him to take her with him the next time.

"Oh, I want to go!" Emily exclaimed.

"I thought you might be doing something with Kevin Hartsbarger." Emily and Kevin had dated steadily last year, then split up. Now he was calling her again. Mitch worried when Emily went out with a different boy every few weeks, which had been more or less her pattern this school year, and he'd worried last year when she'd been seeing only Kevin. The fact was, he'd like it fine if she wouldn't date at all until she went to college. But he knew how unrealistic that was.

"I'm seeing Kevin tomorrow night," Emily said. "Can Temple and Carrie Lou come to the dances too?"

"Sure, the more the merrier," Mitch agreed. "I'll call later and let you know when I'll pick you up."

The dances didn't usually start until late, and sometimes they went on until dawn. But since tomorrow wasn't a school day, it wouldn't matter how late they stayed.

His hand rested on the phone after he'd hung up while he tried to make up his mind if he should call Rhea and ask her to go with them tonight. When they'd attended the stomp dance with her grandfather, she'd introduced him around and explained what was happening as the night went on. He'd even let her talk him into joining the dancers for a little while. To his surprise, he'd enjoyed it. Being with her and her grandfather, Crying Wolf, had given him a stamp of approval, and he'd felt welcome.

He'd be more comfortable showing up out at the Brasfield place if he was with Rhea, whose grandfather was one of the most respected medicine men in the county.

Which, of course, was why he was considering calling her, he told himself. But he knew he was looking for an excuse to call her. The dance just happened to be a credible one. He picked up the receiver and dialed the clinic. Rhea was with a patient, so he left word for her to call him back. Which she did ten minutes later.

She accepted Mitch's invitation without any detectable hesitation, Mitch wondered if that was because they'd have the girls with them.

"We'll have room for your grandfather too," Mitch said.

"He's nursing a bad cold. I told him to stay in bed for a couple of days. I wanted him to come stay with me till he's feeling better, but he wouldn't. He's a stubborn old coot. Doesn't mind me very well."

"You're not a doctor to him, you're just his granddaughter."

She laughed. "That's so true. I won't even tell him I'm going to the dances. He might want to come and I'd rather not argue with him."

"Any more anonymous calls since yesterday?"

"No. Shelly Pitcher came out and talked to my receptionist—she's the one who took the call."

"Shelly and Duck also went over to city hall, trying to find somebody who saw Dane Kennedy around there yesterday morning. No luck, but one man said he saw a pickup that looked like Kennedy's turning in at the Super Mart. Couldn't swear to it, though, and it's not illegal to buy groceries."

"The old man is seriously unbalanced, Mitch. He's like a ticking bomb. One of these days he's going to explode."

"I hope you're wrong. Even if you aren't, I can't do anything until he breaks the law."

"Until he kills somebody, you mean, or blows up a building."

"I know he thinks the government's oppressing him, Rhea, but his public protests have been fairly benign and certainly within the limits of the law."

She sighed. "I know."

"If you get another one of those calls, I'll have another talk with him. Not that I expect him to break down and confess."

"We're keeping the clinic doors locked and making people identify themselves before we let them in."

"Good. Whoever's making the calls is bound to slip up sooner or later, and we'll catch him. Now, about tonight, what time should I pick you up?"

"No point in getting out there before eleven," she said. "Why don't you come by about a quarter of."

"See you then."

He was smiling as he hung up, but the smile faded as he thought about yesterday's anonymous phone call to the clinic. Was Kennedy angry enough about the assessor's efforts to collect his property taxes to notch up his protests to the level of violence?

That had not been his pattern in the past. Once he and a few other like-minded "patriots" had picketed city hall when one of their friends was fined for driving with a suspended license. They'd carried signs that said YOU COULD BE NEXT and

STOP THE ABUSE OF OUR FREEDOM. Dane Kennedy had made a speech on the steps of city hall, the gist of which had been that the local police were tools of the traitors in the federal government and the elitists who own the Federal Reserve Bank. "If the police don't enforce treason, it won't be enforced!" Kennedy had raved.

Another time, after the local newspaper had carried a story about a couple of Buckskin men being sent to Turkey to patrol the no-fly zone, Kennedy and a couple other men had marched down the main street carrying signs that said, JOIN THE ARMY AND SERVE THE U.N.

Occasionally Kennedy wrote diatribes to the local newspaper. The letters, which were filled with warnings that the government was setting up concentration camps around the country and surveilling them from black helicopters in preparation for enslaving the populace, were printed in the letters-to-the editor section.

Other than such lawful protests, Kennedy kept to himself. Mitch fervently hoped it stayed that way.

7

"I like your daughter and her friends," Rhea said. "They seem like great kids."

They were seated on the second row of roughly constructed bleachers on one side of the dance arena. As Mitch had expected, he and the girls, accompanied by Rhea, had been warmly welcomed. When they walked in, people called the traditional greeting, *"O-si-yo!"* from all directions. Which delighted Emily and her friends no end. They'd immediately grabbed a soft drink from the hamper Rhea had brought and were wandering around the grounds, saying *"O-si-yo!"* to everyone they saw.

"They're the best," Mitch responded to Rhea's comment without a smidgen of shame. He unscrewed the cap from the big thermos he'd brought. "Want some hot spiced cider?"

"Sounds good."

The thermos cap held a nest of three plastic cups. He filled two of them and handed one to Rhea. When she'd

opened her hamper to get the girls drinks, he'd also seen sandwiches in plastic bags, apples, and grapes. Most people
brought food to the dances. Many of them would stay for
hours and eating was part of the affair.

At the stomp ground where Mitch had gone with Rhea
last winter, several people had even brought camp stoves to
cook on, but he'd seen none here. At one end of the camp-
ground, a couple of men had built a wood fire where people
could warm themselves, as the early March nights could still
get chilly. A few kids were taking advantage of the open fire
to roast wieners and marshmallows. Every once in a while one
of the men would lay another log on the fire.

At the dance ground Mitch had visited last winter, rough-
hewn log benches had been arranged around a fire in seven
sections, one for each of the ancient Cherokee clans. People
sat in their designated clan's section. But here there was only
one section of bleachers. Rhea said that Brasfield planned to
build benches for the seven clans as soon as he had the time
and money for the lumber.

Rhea laughed softly and pointed as Carrie Lou ran over to
the fire and snapped a picture. Carrie Lou was angling for the
position of editor of the school newspaper next year. On the
drive out, she'd told them she was going to write a story for
the school paper about the dances and had brought the
school's camera along to get some illustrations for her story.
"Carrie Lou is going to run out of film before the dancing
even starts," Rhea said.

"No, I saw several rolls in the camera bag she left in the
car," Mitch said.

Rhea glanced over at him. "What bad luck that they had
to be the ones to find that body." As soon as Rhea had got-

ten into the car that evening and greetings had been exchanged, Temple, fully recovered from her shock, had
launched into a blow-by-blow account of their morning's or-
deal, with Emily and Carrie Lou throwing in a few words now
and then for emphasis. Rhea had already heard about the warden's murder that afternoon at the clinic, but she hadn't been
privy to all the gory details.

"It's not something they'll forget for a long time," Mitch
agreed. "I'll be forever grateful that they didn't go in that cave
a couple of hours earlier."

"My God, you think the murderer was in the cave that
close to the time the girls arrived?"

"I don't have Doc Pohl's autopsy report yet, but I don't
think the body could've been there more than a few hours
when Duck and I saw it about ten-thirty. It was close to nine
when the rain started, and that's when the girls began looking
for shelter. None of them checked their watches, but Emily
thought it probably took fifteen or twenty minutes to find the
cave. According to Arnett Walsh's wife, he left the house
about seven. So we know the murder happened sometime between, say, seven-fifteen and nine-twenty, or thereabouts, when
the girls found the cave."

Rhea expelled a shivery breath. "They must've just missed
the killer."

Mitch nodded. Every time he thought of the close call the
girls had had, it made him feel sick.

"How big an area does one game warden patrol?" Rhea
asked.

Mitch shrugged. "Probably half a county, maybe more."

"You think somebody followed Walsh out of town to kill
him?"

The thought had occurred to Mitch. "I don't know, but I doubt it. It's possible he caught somebody out there in the woods engaged in illegal activity, and they attacked him." He shot her a sharp look. "It's just a theory. Keep it under your hat."

"Okay, but what makes you think that's what happened?"

"Walsh was in that area hoping to catch the person who's been killing eagles."

She lifted her chin, looking at Mitch with dark eyes. She leaned back against the edge of the bench behind them with a reflective expression. "Eagles? That wouldn't be why we're here tonight, would it?"

"Partly," he admitted.

"In other words, you know who's been killing eagles, and you think he'll be here?"

"It's not that simple. But the first eagle carcass was found, stripped of its feathers, about the time the Eagle Dances started out here. Vian Brasfield owns this land, and from what I hear, he's the one who started the Eagle Dances."

"Vian Brasfield!" She was shocked. "I know he takes part in the Eagle Dances, but Mitch, do you really think a man like that, a respected high school principal, is breaking the law to provide the dancers with feathers?"

"They're getting them from somewhere. I talked to a warden at the Wildlife Department earlier today, and there have been no requests for eagle feathers for ceremonial purposes from Cherokee County in the last two years."

"That doesn't prove anything. They could have gotten them outside the county. Or somebody here could have already had a supply."

"You're right. But I still need to talk to Brasfield. If he can convince me the feathers were acquired legally, then that'll be the end of it." He glanced over at her as she sat up straight and reached for the thermos to refill her cup. "One thing I didn't mention, though—and this is not for publication, either—I found a dead eagle not far from the cave where Walsh's body was."

She gave him a penetrating look as she screwed the cap back on the thermos and picked up her cup in both hands. "Hmmm." She blew on the cider. "Tell me, had the feathers been removed?"

"No. I figure the killer was interrupted before he had a chance to take the feathers."

She shook her head. "That's not how it works, Mitch—if it really was a Cherokee who killed that eagle to use the feathers for ceremonial purposes. The eagle killer fasts for a day or two before hunting the eagle. When he kills it, he says a prayer over it, but then he leaves it where it fell. Somebody else goes after the feathers and brings them back. That's the way it's done."

Mitch took this in. It was one more thing he hadn't known about the culture. Mrs. Brasfield had said that her husband hadn't eaten the previous evening, and even though he told her he was going to have breakfast in town that morning, he hadn't been seen at the café. If he was the eagle killer, he'd been fasting, and he'd lied to his wife because he knew she wouldn't understand, would probably scoff at him.

"I still can't believe Vian Brasfield is the eagle killer, Mitch," Rhea went on. "He seems like such a straight-up, law-abiding man."

"If not, maybe he knows who is."

She sipped her cider thoughtfully.

"I wonder where he is?" Mitch said, twisting to study the people sitting behind them, higher up on the bleachers. Two big lamps on tall poles stood at either end of the dance arena, throwing enough light for him to see the faces of those seated on the bleachers.

"I haven't seen him yet," Rhea said, "but he'll be here. He's probably getting ready for the first dance."

He turned back around and she smiled, tilting her head to one side. "I'm glad you asked me to come with you. I was beginning to wonder if you were ever going to call me again."

Mitch hesitated, then decided to be frank. "I almost didn't. I wasn't sure you wanted me to, after the last time we went out."

"The last time?" she asked blankly. Then it registered, and she set the cup she was holding on the bench beside her. "Don't tell me this is about my not inviting you in."

"Well, I did wonder about that. I mean, I thought we'd had a good time, but you kind of cut me off at the pass." She'd disappeared into her house so suddenly that Mitch hadn't even been able to kiss her good night, something he'd been thinking about all evening prior to delivering her to her door.

She frowned, studying him with what seemed a mixture of amusement and disbelief. "Your feelings were hurt because I'd had a long day and was tired?"

Put like that, it did sound childish.

"That's ridiculous. Come on, Mitch, we're not a couple of teenagers." And here he'd been thinking that, in those tight jeans and fringed jacket, with her long hair loose around her shoulders, she didn't look much older than Emily and her friends.

Her attitude was getting Mitch a little steamed, though. "We're not ready for the nursing home, either, Doctor."

She uttered an explosive little laugh. "You're actually angry. I can't believe it."

"Tell me something, Rhea. What am I to you, some kind of charity project?"

"What in the world are you talking about?"

"Did you agree to come tonight because you feel sorry for me?"

She laughed again. "Oh, of course. It's my mission in life to go out with men I feel sorry for."

He didn't find that funny. "Are there many of them?"

She gazed at him in bewildered silence. "Don't you cop an attitude with me, Mitch Bushyhead. Look," she said, twisting around till she was facing him squarely. Irritation flashed in her dark eyes. "You're the only man I've dated since I moved to Buckskin. And I would never have agreed to go out with you, tonight or any other time, unless I'd wanted to."

She reached over and laid her hand on his knee. "If I seem defensive at times, it's because—well, because I am, I guess. The few serious relationships I've had in the past have turned out badly. I don't want to rush into anything." She tucked a strand of long black hair behind her ear where a tiny gold stud sparkled. Her black brows rose questioningly. "Okay?"

He picked up the hand that rested on his knee, cupping it in his. "Sorry. I was being a jerk."

"Yeah, you were," she agreed, "and I'm glad we got that straightened out."

She pulled her hand from his as the three girls came clambering across the bleachers to sit down.

Emily scooted up next to Mitch, with Temple and then Carrie Lou on her other side. "This is so fun!" she exclaimed breathlessly.

"It's going to make a great story," Carrie Lou agreed.

Three men with drums had taken their places in the arena.

"I heard somebody say they're going to have the booger dance first," Temple said, craning to look around at Rhea. "Do you know what that is, Dr. Vann?"

"It's a humorous dance," Rhea said. "The dancers wear booger masks—that is, masks with exaggerated human, or sometimes animal, features—and they carry on like clowns. Real slapstick. You'll see. By the way, I thought you girls were going to call me Rhea."

"I forgot," Temple said.

Just then, Vian Brasfield's wife walked slowly along in front of the bleachers, looking up, scanning faces. When she saw Mitch, she frowned, then nodded curtly and sat down at the far end of the bleachers. Mitch looked around for Vian Brasfield, but didn't see him.

"Oh, look!" Emily cried. "Here come the dancers."

Around them, people hooted, laughed, and yelled taunts as a man came from behind the bleachers and entered the arena. He wore a dark red mask with heavy black eyebrows and black stains beneath the nose. "He's an Indian with war paint," Rhea said. The blue-and-white patchwork quilt covering his head and clutched under his chin fell to the ground, with only the toes of his boots showing. Leaning toward Mitch, she whispered, "I'm not sure, but I think that's Vian Brasfield."

Six other masked men trailed in behind the first man. "The second one's supposed to be a white man," Rhea said. The second man's mask was ghostly white, with eyebrows, mustache, and goatee applied in black paint. He wore ragged trousers and shirt with run-over shoes, whose holey soles he displayed for the audience to see. They shrieked and booed him.

Exaggerated audience reaction was evidently part of the fun. It made Mitch think of an old-fashioned melodrama where the audience hissed at the villain every time he came on stage. Emily and her friends were soon caught up in clapping and booing along with the rest. Everybody got into the spirit of the thing, except for Mrs. Brasfield. Every time Mitch looked her way, she was staring stonily ahead, her mouth set in a grim line.

All the dancers were dressed similarly, either in tattered garb or wrapped in a quilt or blanket. One of the red masks depicted an expression of fearful apprehension. A white mask had animal hair glued on it for head hair, eyebrows, and mustache. The only black mask—representing someone of African descent, Rhea told them—oddly had a pure white nose. One of the masks seemed to represent a bear. The noses on all of the masks were long, some of them curving down in an exaggerated hook.

Each masked dancer walked over to one of the drummers and whispered in his ear, after which the drummer yelled out a Cherokee word to the crowd, who laughed and clapped. "They're introducing themselves," Rhea said. "Each of the dancers has a fake name. They're usually pretty crude. For instance, the man in the black mask calls himself Black Buttocks."

The three girls shrieked happily at this bit of news.

After the dancers were introduced, the drummers began to play and chant as each masked dancer performed some sort of pantomime to the delight of the audience. Using a zoom lens, Carrie Lou snapped pictures while Rhea interpreted the pantomimes as they were acted out. The bear-masked dancer dramatized the tale of a man who was lost and found by a she-bear, lived with her, and had offspring. He hibernated with her and she fed him nuts whenever he was hungry. Then she was killed by hunters, who took the bear-man back to his home, where he slowly turned back into a man.

The other pantomimists were more clownish, dashing around, falling down, pretending to fight, often running toward the bleachers as though to grab the girls and women seated on the front row, whereupon the drummers would shout something in Cherokee and the women in the front row would scream.

"They're saying the boogers want girls," Rhea explained.

Occasionally a dancer tried to pull a woman to her feet to dance with her. The woman always refused.

Finally, the boogers grew quiet and sat on the ground and one of the drummers asked them a question, then spoke to the audience in Cherokee.

"He asked the boogers if they wanted to watch a dance," Rhea said. "They've chosen the Eagle Dance." The boogers got up and filed out and the audience began to stir. Mitch was watching Mrs. Brasfield, who stood and followed several other people from the bleachers around one end and out of sight.

Rhea said, "There's an intermission now. Anybody want a sandwich or some fruit?"

"I'm about out of film," Carrie Lou said. "I'm going to run to the car and put in a new roll before the next dance. Chief Bushyhead, could I have your car keys?"

Mitch handed them over, and she hurried down the bleach-ers and dashed out of sight while Rhea, Emily, and Temple ate. Mitch went looking for Brasfield.

Not spotting Brasfield among the people milling around behind the bleachers, Mitch walked beyond the pool of light toward the graveled parking area, hoping to run into Bras-field, who must have gone straight to his truck to change his costume for the next dance.

Mitch was walking along between rows of cars and pick-ups, looking in rear windows for Brasfield, when a female voice screamed, "Get away from me! No! Stop! Help! Help!" It seemed to come from the far end of the lot, where Mitch had parked the Toyota.

He ran toward the sound and deeper into the shadows. As he neared the Toyota, somebody barreled straight into him and grunted from the impact. Mitch grabbed her arms to steady her. She struggled to extricate herself. "Get away—"

"Carrie Lou?"

She stopped struggling. "Chief Bushyhead? Oh, thank goodness. You have to stop him! He stole the camera!"

Mitch peered around, but saw no moving shadow. Nor did he hear the sound of running feet. "Calm down, Carrie Lou. Who stole the camera?"

"I don't know. Just some man. He came up behind me as I was getting out of your car and grabbed it out of my hand. It was too dark to see. Besides, he was gone almost before I knew what happened." She flopped her hands in agitation. "You have to find him! That camera belongs to the school. It cost three hundred dollars. The journalism teacher is going to kill me!"

"Did you see which way he went?"

"It sounded like he ran that way." She pointed toward the fenced edge of the parking area, the boundary between Brasfield's land and Dane Kennedy's farm.

Mitch didn't want to leave her to find her way back to the bleachers alone, and he didn't want to wait before looking for the thief. "Come with me," he said.

They ran between cars until they reached the fence, then hurried along it toward the gate through which they'd entered the property. Near the gate, Mitch saw a movement beyond the fence.

He put a restraining hand on Carrie Lou's shoulder and whispered, "Wait here." Then he vaulted the fence and yelled, "Who's there?"

An elderly bearded man in overalls stepped forward without hesitation. It was Dane Kennedy. "You're trespassing," he barked.

"I'm looking for a thief who just stole a valuable camera."

"Well, I ain't no thief! I'm out here walking around because nobody can sleep or concentrate on anything with all that racket going on over there."

"Did you see anybody come this way carrying a camera?"

Kennedy hesitated. "I didn't see nobody carrying nothing. Now git off my property!"

Mitch had no evidence that Kennedy was the thief, so he couldn't make a search. He went back over the fence.

"You think that old man has the camera?" Carrie Lou asked.

Kennedy might be a little irrational, but Mitch had never heard of him stealing anything. "Not really," Mitch told her. "Looks like the thief's long gone."

"Mr. Blaylock will never let me be editor now," Carrie Lou groaned.

He took her arm, leading her back to the dance ground. "It wasn't your fault, Carrie Lou. I'm sure the school has insurance. They'll get another camera."

"You really think Mr. Blaylock will understand?"

"I'm sure of it."

She pushed her glasses up her nose. "At least I'd already put in a new roll of film. The roll with the booger dancers on it is in the camera bag in the Toyota. I can still do the story."

As they approached the bleachers, Mitch saw Mrs. Brasfield standing behind them, talking to a Cherokee woman. "I see somebody I need to talk to," he told Carrie Lou.

She nodded glumly and walked slowly around the end of the bleachers.

Mitch walked up to Mrs. Brasfield. "Evening, ma'am."

"Oh. Hello." She looked distracted.

"Is your husband around?"

"Yes. I tried to catch him before he got away, but I wasn't fast enough. He's probably gone to change his costume. The dancers always change back to street clothes after the booger dance. Then Vian will get what he needs for the Eagle Dance after intermission."

"He was one of the masked dancers?"

"Oh, yes," she said with a faint smirk. "He was the one with the red mask and blue-and-white quilt wrapped around him."

The same dancer Rhea had pointed out.

"I noticed he'd bought himself a new pair of boots today," Mrs. Brasfield went on, her voice tight with disapproval. "Then he came out here and scuffed them up stumbling around on the dance ground. Honestly, if he could make himself look more ridiculous, I don't know how."

"Well . . . it's all in fun."

She glanced at him sharply. "I don't mean to insult the Cherokees. I'm just upset with Vian right now."

"It seems that everybody knows who the dancers are, even though they use fake names," Mitch remarked.

"If they're regulars, they know. The dancers always wear the same costumes."

"I see."

She squinted toward the dim parking area. "When Vian didn't make it home for supper, I knew I'd find him here. I wouldn't have come otherwise. I've see it all before."

"Did he go to Tahlequah?"

Her face darkened with annoyance. "I haven't had a chance to talk to him yet. Believe me, he's going to get a piece of my mind for not letting me know he wouldn't be home for dinner. I fixed a big meal and had to throw most of it away. Vian doesn't like leftovers."

"You say he'll take part in the Eagle Dance?"

"He usually dances every dance. He'll be so tired when he gets home, he'll fall into bed and—" She halted to squint in the direction of the parked cars. "Now, where does he think he's going?" Mitch followed her gaze and saw a pickup creeping slowly across the graveled parking area.

"Who?"

"Do you see two people in that pickup?" she asked.

Mitch peered into the darkness. He couldn't see how many people were in the truck. "I can't tell."

"Oh, no, he doesn't!" she cried suddenly. "Excuse me." She stumped off, hurrying to intercept the pickup.

Was Brasfield leaving? But the dances had barely started. Mitch wondered if Brasfield had seen him and was leaving to avoid conversation with him. But if he hadn't been in touch with his wife, how could he know Mitch was looking for him?

Perhaps somebody at the high school had told him, somebody like Virginia Craig.

8

"The Eagle Dance was originally performed to prevent a diabolical person from using the eagle as a medium for working evil and causing sickness," Rhea said as an equal number of men and women dancers filed into the arena. Emily and Temple listened to Rhea, wide-eyed, and hung on to every word.

When Mitch had returned to his seat, Carrie Lou was still lamenting the loss of the camera, and the others were commiserating with her. But at last Carrie Lou seemed to have put the stolen camera out of her mind and was taking notes on a small tablet she'd brought with her.

Mitch was listening to Rhea at the same time that he studied the dancers, most of whom wore jeans and moccasins. Each of the seven male dancers carried a gourd rattle in his left hand and, in his right, a pole, about two feet long, with a ring lashed to one end. Attached to the ring were several eagle feathers, spread out like a fan. The women dancers carried only gourd rattles. One of them, whom Rhea identified as the lead female dancer, had tortoiseshell rattles strapped to her legs.

"This is traditionally a winter dance," Rhea was saying. "It's probably the last time it will be performed this year."

"Why is it performed only in the winter?" Carrie Lou asked.

Rhea smiled at her. "People believed if this dance was performed during the growing season, it would cause a frost that would kill the crops." She hesitated and a teasing glint came into her eyes. "And then, of course, there were the snakes."

"Snakes?" queried Temple, watching the dancers closely, as though she expected them to produce a sack full of writhing rattlers any minute.

"They thought that if the snakes heard the songs of the Eagle Dance," Rhea explained, "it would make them more poisonous than usual. Which is why the dance is only done in the wintertime when snakes are asleep and can't hear the songs."

"Oh," said Temple, visibly relaxing.

Emily leaned against Mitch. "Daddy, you look so serious. Are you thinking about how to catch the man who stole the camera?"

Mitch pulled his gaze from the dancers to meet his daughter's look. "That's not going to be easy, since Carrie Lou didn't see him. I'll alert the area pawnshops to keep an eye out for the camera. Thieves steal stuff like that to sell. Maybe we'll get lucky."

She returned her attention to Rhea. Mitch tried to take in Rhea's running commentary, but he had trouble concentrating on the dance. He was thinking about Vian Brasfield, who was not one of the eagle dancers. Mitch still had not caught so much as a glimpse of the man out of costume. And Mrs. Brasfield had not returned to the bleachers since the intermission.

Every time somebody sauntered from behind the bleachers to find a seat, Mitch turned to see if it was Brasfield, but it appeared he really had left the grounds.

The dance was a long one, consisting of several movements. First the men and women dancers lined up facing each other. They advanced, then retreated, in steps ranging from a dignified walk to the shuffling trot Mitch had learned at the stomp dance he'd attended earlier. Then the dancers circled the fire, shaking the gourd rattles, the men shaking the feather-poles, or wands, as Rhea called them. Occasionally they would crouch and jump, all the time moving around the fire, the men going clockwise and the women counterclockwise. When the song changed, the male dancers passed the feathers over their partners' heads, and the dancers re-formed in two lines, facing outward and then inward, always moving in time with the music. Finally, the women ran from the arena. When they returned seconds later, they carried baskets, which they set in the center of the arena. Then the dancers formed in a single line, feathers waving and gourds rattling.

"What are the baskets for?" Emily asked Rhea.

"They're symbolic of feeding the eagles to compensate them for their feathers."

As the dancers left the arena, Mitch looked at his watch. The dance had lasted for more than half an hour.

"Another intermission," Rhea announced.

The girls grabbed a handful of grapes or an apple and left

the bleachers to stretch their legs. "Want to talk a walk?" Mitch asked Rhea.

"Sure," she said, reaching for his hand. He pulled her to her feet and they walked around behind the bleachers. "Vian Brasfield wasn't dancing," Rhea remarked. "I thought I saw him in the booger dance. Wonder what became of him?"

"Maybe he's avoiding his wife," Mitch said. "I talked to her during the last intermission. He didn't come home for dinner. I think she came out here to lay into him."

"From what I've seen of his wife, she wouldn't hesitate to do that," she murmured. "Poor Vian." Then, "Carrie Lou was really upset about the camera."

"Yeah, but nobody can blame her for the loss. The school will buy another camera. I told her that."

"So did I," Rhea said, adding, "While you were gone during the last intermission, I talked to one of the men who was in the Eagle Dance tonight. I asked him where they got the feathers." She shivered, pulled her hand from Mitch's, and threaded it through the crook of his arm, tucking it into his jacket pocket.

"You cold?" he asked.

"A little."

"Come here." He wrapped his arm around her and pulled her close to his side. They walked along in companionable silence for a moment. "You were saying . . ." he prompted finally. "About the feathers."

"My friend said that Brasfield supplies the feathers; he doesn't know where Vian gets them. To tell you the truth, I'm not sure I believe him. I suspect he knows exactly where Vian gets them."

"You mean he knows Vian's killing eagles?"

She nodded reluctantly. "If he really was lying, then I think he knows who's killing the eagles, whether it's Vian or somebody else. I can't think why he'd lie to me otherwise."

Rhea shivered again and pressed closer to Mitch as she scanned the people behind the bleachers, who were standing around in clumps, talking. A woman near them waved and called Rhea's name. "Hi, Stella," Rhea called back. "Have you seen Vian?"

"Not since the booger dance," the woman replied.

Rhea looked up at Mitch. "Come to think of it, I haven't seen Vian's wife in a while, either."

"She didn't return to the bleachers after the first dance," Mitch said, peering through the darkness to where they'd parked the Landcruiser. He didn't really expect the thief to still be hanging around, but his feeling of unease which had started when he heard Carrie Lou's call for help had increased since the Eagle Dance ended. "Do you know what kind of vehicle Brasfield drives?"

"A dark blue pickup with an extended cab," she said. "A Ford, I think. Maybe a year or two old." The pickup that Mrs. Brasfield had gone to intercept could have been a dark blue Ford.

"Mrs. Brasfield has her own car, then?" There had been no car in the driveway when Mitch visited the Brasfield house earlier that day, but there could have been one in the garage. And she'd apparently driven herself to the dance ground.

"I've seen her driving a white sedan. Could be a Pontiac."

Mitch tugged on her hand. "Let's see if either vehicle is here." He headed for the parking lot.

She ran a few steps until she was walking beside him. "You don't think the thief is still around, do you?"

"No."

"Then what's wrong?"

"Nothing," he said. "At least nothing I can put my finger on. I'd just feel better if I could find Mrs. Brasfield and have a few words with Vian."

They walked in a big semicircle but didn't see a dark-colored Ford pickup with an extended cab, or a white Pontiac.

"Looks like they went home," Rhea said.

"Yeah," Mitch said, thinking that Mrs. Brasfield could have caught up with Vian and told him the police were looking for him. Either he'd been leaving already when his wife saw him, or he'd decided to leave when he learned Mitch wanted a word with him. And his wife had followed him home.

You don't run from the police unless you have something to hide. Brasfield's behavior was making him look guilty—of *something*. But was it the illegal hunting of eagles? Or an even more serious crime?

"Would you like to come in for a drink?" Rhea asked as Mitch pulled the Landcruiser into her driveway. They'd already dropped the three girls at the Robertses' house. Carrie Lou had decided to sleep over another night too.

Mitch hesitated, embarrassed because of their earlier discussion. "You sure?"

She smiled. "I wouldn't ask if I weren't."

"Okay," Mitch said. Well, he thought as he walked around the vehicle to open her door, she'd set the limits with the way she'd issued the invitation. He was being invited in only for a drink, but at least she was allowing him to come one step closer. Then he wondered again if she'd invited him in because he'd made an issue of her failure to do so last time. He decided to play it by ear, take his cues from her.

She didn't want to rush into anything, she'd said. Okay. He could live with that.

The Landcruiser sat higher than an ordinary car, and Rhea's legs weren't as long as his. She held on to his arm as she stepped down.

Rhea lived in a neat red-brick bungalow a couple of blocks off Sequoyah. There was a light burning over the front door and a lamp in the living room had been left on.

Inside, she tossed her fringed jacket in a chair, then retrieved the food hamper to take it to the kitchen. "I'm not much of a drinker," she said. "I've got half a bottle of wine in the fridge and, I think, a couple of Bud Lights."

"Beer's fine," Mitch said.

While she was in the kitchen, Mitch took off his jacket and wandered around the living room with his fingers tucked into his jeans pockets. Although the room was attractively furnished and decorated, it was not the least bit pretentious. It looked warm and welcoming.

Two couches, upholstered in mauve, gray, and white plaid, faced each other, separated by a large, low pickled-pine table. Other light-wood tables were placed around the room as well as chairs upholstered in shades of blue and mauve. Several framed prints hung on the walls. Mitch recognized the work of two Indian artists. He'd seen them the last time he was there, when he'd questioned a woman who was staying with Rhea. One print, however, he didn't remember seeing before. It was about as different from the others as it was possible for the work of one Indian artist to be from another. This one showed a desert scene in shades of blue, pink, and white. The only thing breaking the vast, flat lines of the landscape was the small figure of a woman with her back turned. Her black hair hung down in a single braid, and she wore a long dress with a shawl wrapped around her shoulders. A southwestern Indian, a Navajo perhaps. Which explained the vast difference in the prints. All the others were done by Cherokee artists and depicted woodland scenes.

Mitch walked closer to read the unknown artist's name. Deborah Hiatt.

"Do you like Hiatt?" Rhea asked, coming into the room. She set a glass of wine and a Bud Light on the low table between the couches.

Mitch joined her on a couch. "I don't think I've seen her work before, but I like it. I don't know a lot of Indian artists, although I recognize Jacob and Anderson."

"I picked up the Hiatt in Santa Fe in January when I managed to get away from the clinic for a few days." She handed him the beer, then sipped her wine and studied the print. "I'd love to have some originals one day. I saw some wonderful sculptures in New Mexico too. Indian and western. All very expensive. When you work for the Nation, you can't afford such luxuries."

"Have you ever thought about going into private practice?"

She shook her head. "Not for a while. It'd pay better, but I feel I'm making a difference where I am."

"Were you raised around here?" Mitch asked.

"On a farm about fifty miles from Buckskin," she said. "My parents sold it and moved to Oregon when I was in my last year of high school. We came back to visit Grandfather and various aunts, uncles, and cousins once or twice a year, but they stayed on the West Coast. They loved it out there. They were killed in a car wreck about four years ago."

"I'm sorry. Both my parents are gone too. Do you have any brothers or sisters?"

She shook her head. "You?"

"No." He went on to tell her about his mother, who'd raised him in Oklahoma City after his father died when Mitch was eight. "I lost her a few years back. She was one great lady."

The silence lengthened until it made Mitch feel uncomfortable. He swept another glance around the room. "I like the way you've decorated your house."

He had draped one arm along the back of the couch, and she moved closer so that she could rest her head on his shoulder. "What's your house like?"

He fingered a strand of her hair. "Totally different from yours. It's an old Victorian that my wife and I restored. Ellen—" He hesitated. "My wife liked lots of ruffles and throw pillows."

She turned her head to look up at him. "It's okay to mention her name."

He was silent for a long moment. "She's been gone two years now." His lips brushed her brow. "Sometimes it seems even longer. Sometimes it seems like I dreamed that whole part of my life."

"I know what you mean," she murmured. "Have you been involved with anyone since your wife died?"

He hesitated before he said, "Once. She was a teacher at the high school. It ended when she moved to California." He leaned forward to set the beer can on the table. She shifted to sit sideways, facing him.

"You don't hear from her?"

"Nope."

"Did you love her?"

He considered the question, determined to be perfectly honest with her. "Maybe. I thought I did for a while. I met her a few months after Ellen died. I was lonely, and she was new in town, divorced. I guess she was lonely too." He brushed a strand of hair out of her eyes, letting his hand linger on her hair. "Your turn. Have you ever been married?"

She reached for his hand, lacing her fingers through his. "No, but I was engaged once, when I was in college. He was a quarter-Sioux, from Wyoming."

"What happened?"

"Oh, we wanted different things. He didn't like the idea of my going to med school. He wanted to get married as soon as we graduated and move to Wyoming. He came from a big, close family—three sisters, two brothers. All but one of them lived within a hundred miles of Casper, where his parents lived. He wanted lots of kids and a wife who stayed at home with them. When I finally convinced him that I intended to finish medical school and take an internship in internal medicine, he gave up trying to talk me out of it. But by then I knew the futures we envisioned for ourselves were too different for us to ever make a go of marriage. Whatever we did, one of us was bound to be miserable."

"So you broke it off?"

She nodded. "He tried to change my mind, but once he got used to the idea, I think he was relieved."

"Is that the only close call you've had with the altar?"

With her free hand, she reached for her glass and gazed pensively into the ruby wine. She took a deep breath. "During my internship . . . there was a surgeon who was on staff at the hospital where I worked. We lived together for almost a year. We talked about getting married. Then one day I went home and he'd moved out. No warning. No note. Nothing. After that, at the hospital, he treated me the same way he treated the other interns. He was God and we were beneath his notice."

"The scum," Mitch muttered.

She looked up with a faint smile. "He's not the first surgeon I ever met with a God complex. It sort of goes with the territory."

He squeezed her hand. "I'm sorry. You loved him very much, didn't you?"

She took a drink of wine and set her glass on the table. "I'm not sure whether it was love or hero worship. I had deep feelings for him. But if we'd stayed together, I'd have ended up hating him. It would never have worked. He wanted a wife who would take care of his home and his children and not complain about the long hours he spent at the hospital. He wanted somebody who fit into his circle of friends, somebody who socialized with the wives of the other members of his country club, who would be a charming hostess at the intimate little dinners he liked to give. Eventually it would have meant my leaving medicine altogether. Can you see me in that role?"

"I can see you doing just about anything you set your head to do."

"That's just it. I realized, after I'd gotten over being dumped, that I didn't want a life like that. It was the same story as with my college sweetheart, although it took me long enough to see it. I'm a slow learner, I guess."

Mitch brushed his lips across the back of her hand.

Her dark eyes softened. "I seem to have chosen men who are bad for me, or maybe I was bad for them. Anyway, I've learned to be cautious. There are even times when I think I may never marry. Medicine is a demanding career. Long hours, calls in the middle of the night."

"Sounds a lot like police work."

She nodded. "It isn't always easy for a spouse to deal with, particularly when it's the wife who's out making the streets safe or sewing up knife wounds and the husband who's at home, waiting."

He grinned and cocked his head. "That's a sexist remark, Doctor. Have you been talking to my officer Shelly Pitcher?"

"Not about this," she said with a laugh, "but I'll bet she'd agree with me."

"I don't doubt it. And, for the record, it's not easy for the spouse when the cop or the doctor happens to be male, either." She nodded an acknowledgment, and Mitch went on, "I hope you're not advocating that all cops and doctors go to the other extreme and lead solitary lives."

She lifted her face to his and said softly, "No, I certainly wouldn't go that far."

He cupped her cheek with his hand. Her skin felt like silk beneath his palm. She sucked in a breath and ran the tip of her tongue over her full lips. Her eyes slowly closed as Mitch bent toward her.

The first kiss can be awkward and strange, but this one was sweet and searching, as they explored the taste and scent of each other. Mitch took his time, and she pressed closer to him, encouraging his arms to tighten around her. When, finally, he lifted his head to look down at her, her eyes were dazed and dreamy, and he knew that she was as reluctant as he to have the kiss end.

When he'd been in this house last December to talk to her houseguest, he'd gone into her bedroom to use the telephone. He could still visualize her big bed with the puffy white comforter as clearly as if he were looking at it, and right then, he wanted more than anything in the world to take her hand and lead her into the bedroom. There were a few fragile moments when she might even have gone willingly.

But he knew if he pushed too hard, he'd scare her away. He was beginning to think this woman could be a part of his future, and he didn't want to blow it.

She took a deep breath and shifted to put a few more inches between them. "You are one great kisser, Mitch Bushyhead."

He grinned. "It's a natural talent, darlin'."

"Modest, aren't you?" She hesitated. "Mitch, let's . . ." she said, and faltered.

". . . not rush into anything," he finished for her.

She nodded. "Please. Let's give ourselves some time to get to know each other. I don't want any more fractured relationships. Okay?"

"Okay," he said, and sounded almost as if he really *wanted* to get up off that couch and go home.

At the front door, he kissed her again. But this time he made it brief and got out of there.

9

Nicole Brasfield threw back the sheet and turned on the bed-side lamp. Sighing, she sat on the side of the bed and held her head in her hands. "You are mad," she whispered to herself, "or cursed."

The calico cat, curled at the foot of her bed, opened one eye to inspect her, then closed it and went back to sleep. Nicole envied the cat. This was going to be one of those nights when she wouldn't sleep until dawn. She lifted her head and picked up the framed photograph from beside the bed to look into the childish faces of her daughters. It had been taken when they were six and eight. Sometimes she could not find a trace of such sweetness and innocence in the self-contained, independent women they had become, and the craziest ideas jumbled around in her head. Looking at the photograph gave her reassurance that her memory wasn't completely gone.

After Vian had moved permanently into the bedroom down the hall, all those years ago, the girls used to snuggle in bed with her every night while she read to them. If she closed her eyes and concentrated, Nicole could still smell the soapy scent of them, fresh from their bath, and feel damp tendrils of their silky hair brush her chin.

"We can't go to sleep until you read us a story, Mommy," Kate would say, pressing her face against Nicole's arm.

Martha would add, "It's a tradition, and you can't break a tradition." Because Nicole had always called it their private tradition.

Nicole would have kept the tradition forever, but she knew that when the girls were older, they would no longer want it. She used to think how sad she would be when that day came. But the tradition hadn't ended because the girls outgrew it; Vian had put a stop to it before the girls reached that point.

They're too old to be getting in bed with their parents, Nicole. And she had known he really meant with her. He could barely stand to touch her anymore, and he didn't want the girls to, either.

But they're hardly more than babies.

Babies! They're both in school, in case you hadn't noticed. You're retarding the maturation process. You'll make them twisted.

That was all that was said, but she had known she had to stop the tradition. Because if she didn't, something terrible would happen.

After that, she tried sitting on each girl's bed, once she'd tucked them in, to read to them, but they had separate bedrooms and the one who had to be last was often asleep by the time she got to her. Or if not asleep, disgruntled because her mother had taken so long.

The tradition had died prematurely, like almost everything else in her life. The hugging and kissing had dwindled too, because Vian gave her such a mean look every time he caught her at it. To deaden the pain of loss, she had had to deaden all her feelings—to shut down. Until, finally, she had come to feel like a ghost, moving about her house, so insubstantial that surely light shone through her. There had been a time when she'd thought there was something inherently wrong with her, something in her genes that made her cold and undemonstrative on the one hand, and on the other, inappropriately emotional on rare occasions that always seemed to occur at the wrong time and place.

Frequently, Vian told her that she should be the most grateful woman in the world. She had everything a woman could ask for, didn't she? Two beautiful children. A home of her own and all day to take care of it. A husband who forgave her worst sins and went right on taking care of her.

That's how she'd thought of it then, how he had put it himself. Vian took care of her because she was obviously incapable of taking care of herself. Yes, he could be controlling and overprotective, but he only had her best interests at heart.

Then the girls grew up and went away and she rarely saw Vian except at the dinner table, where he preferred eating with a book open beside his plate. Somehow she had grown old before she realized that, like her, prisoners were protected and taken care of, while also being constantly monitored, their days rigidly scheduled for them. She was Vian's prisoner, and the cold hardness inside of her had become hate.

By the time she understood that, it was too late to start over.

Yet she had tried. She'd approached Vian with the idea of going back to school, earning a teaching certificate so that she could contribute to the family income.

He'd acted as if she'd suggested joining the circus as a trapeze artist or a lion tamer.

That's ridiculous. You're your own worst enemy, Nicole. Don't you know by now that you're not like other women? Left to your own devices, you'd destroy yourself and the rest of us with you.

No, Vian, she thought now, you managed that quite well all by yourself. She got up and put on her robe.

The cat watched with slitted eyes as she left the bedroom.

10

Saturday morning, Mitch had toast and coffee on his patio. It promised to be a perfect spring day. A morning person, he had never understood how people could lie in bed and miss the best part of the day.

Briefly, he imagined waking up with Rhea, warm and soft as satin beside him, then dragged his mind from fantasy to the odious task of cleaning house.

He spent a couple of hours making the house presentable enough for another week. He left a note for Emily, in case she got home before he did, and drove to the Brasfield house. He was still troubled by the obvious way Brasfield had avoided him last night. And he had nothing better to do, even if he was officially off duty and, therefore, not in uniform.

A white Pontiac was parked in the Brasfield driveway, but the pickup wasn't in sight. Possibly it was in the garage behind the house.

Several minutes passed after Mitch rang the bell before he heard footsteps approaching the door. He suspected he'd awakened the Brasfields and belatedly wished he'd waited until later in the day.

Mrs. Brasfield opened the door. She was dressed in the same slacks and shirt she'd had on when he was there yesterday. Her hair was neatly arranged. She even had on lipstick. He hadn't awakened her, after all.

She didn't look happy to see him, though.

"Sorry to bother you again, ma'am. But I need to talk to your husband."

She swept a glance over his jeans and denim shirt. "He's not here," she said with the barest civility.

"Is he at the high school?"

"No." Her lips clamped shut on the word.

This was like trying to get information from a post.

"Do you know where I might find him?"

"Norman."

"Norman? As in Norman, Oklahoma?"

She nodded. "He wanted to do some research in OU's Indian collection. Left before daybreak. Couldn't wait another day." She sounded very annoyed with her husband.

"Well, just tell him I came by. He can call the station and somebody will get word to me. If I don't hear from him, I might be back this evening."

She studied him with distaste. "Don't waste your time. He probably won't be back until late tomorrow night or Monday morning."

"Didn't you tell him I wanted to talk to him?"

"I told him."

"And?"

She shrugged. "He said he'd see you next week sometime."

"Did you happen to mention the dead eagles?"

She shook her head. "Why would I? My husband has nothing to do with that."

Mitch was pretty sure she wasn't convinced of what she said. She had the door half closed when he blurted, "Why did he leave the dance so early last night?"

"Upset stomach." The door closed and Mitch heard the sound of the bolt being thrown.

Upset stomach? Uh-huh, Mitch thought as he returned to the Landcruiser. Too sick to stay for the dances last night, but not sick enough to prevent his rising early that morning to drive two hundred miles to the University of Oklahoma campus in Norman. Mitch's suspicion that Brasfield was running from something—possibly Mitch—escalated. In his mind, Brasfield was fast becoming a serious suspect in the murder of Arnett Walsh. If Brasfield wasn't back in town by Monday morning, Mitch would put out an all-points on him.

Cherokee Officer Virgil Rabbit, Mitch's best friend, usually worked the four-to-midnight shift with Charles "Roo" Stephens, but he was filling in for Shelly today while she visited relatives in Broken Arrow, a suburb of Tulsa.

Mitch swung by the station and found Virgil and Duck in the common room. The dispatcher's desk was unoccupied. Helen Hendricks was their only full-time dispatcher. They had a couple of part-timers who sometimes worked weekends and evenings. Otherwise, one of the officers took the calls. When nobody was at the station, as was the case from midnight to eight A.M. when they had no prisoners in the cells, calls were automatically transferred to the officer-on-call.

"Virgil, you've been working sixteen-hour shifts. Isn't that enough for you?"

"After midnight, I sleep on that cot in the back most of the time, when Gus's snoring doesn't keep me awake. I'm just doing Shelly a favor today."

"So why aren't you men out fighting crime and corruption?" Mitch asked.

"Took care of that already," Virgil said.

"Yeah, had to escort the Kirkwood sisters out to their car," Duck added. "They saw a van drive by real slow this morning and decided it was a rapist who wanted to jump their bones."

The elderly, spinster Kirkwood sisters still lived in the house they grew up in on the edge of Buckskin, near the tribal boarding school. Since their retirements several years ago, they had too much time on their hands, so they imagined things. Especially Millicent, who was convinced the world, including Buckskin, was a dangerous place for two women alone. Every sound or strange car was somebody trying to break into their house or kidnap them for unsavory purposes. About once a week, they worked each other into a panic and called the station, demanding that an officer come and make sure their premises were secure.

Mitch poured himself a cup of coffee, his third cup that morning. He knew he was consuming too much caffeine. He had to cut back—but not right now. Maybe tomorrow. "What would we do without Polly and Millicent to keep us on our toes?"

Virgil leaned back in his chair with his feet on his desk. "You gotta love 'em," he observed.

Duck snorted. "Miss Polly's kind of a sweet old bird, but

that Millicent's hell on wheels. The old witch hasn't changed since she used to crack my knuckles with her ruler in the seventh grade." He studied the knuckles of his right hand with a frown. "That woman could hit hard. I got permanent calluses from it. If a teacher did that today, she'd get sued."

"Yeah, but Millicent sure didn't have any discipline problems, did she?" Virgil asked. "Fear is a great motivator."

"Well, I ain't afraid of her no more," Duck said. "Chief, we were at the Kirkwood house ten minutes after their call, and Millicent was fit to be tied because we weren't there sooner. I had to talk pretty stern to her."

Virgil guffawed and slapped his knee. "Stern, huh? Duck was trying to explain that we'd had to make a couple of other stops on the way, and she cut him off with one of her quotations. Something about his excuse for being tardy taking longer than what he was excusing."

Mitch chuckled. Millicent was never at a loss for a quotation, whatever the occasion. He grabbed a chair from Shelly's desk and pulled it over to sit between Duck and Virgil, placing his coffee cup on the corner of Duck's desk. "Thought we might toss around some thoughts on the Walsh investigation. If you can *call* something an investigation when there are no decent leads. Virgil, have you had a chance to read the case file?"

Virgil nodded. "Not much to go on, is there?"

"Not so's you'd notice. Duck, did you or Shelly get back to the wife?"

"I was there about eight-thirty this morning. Talked to Mrs. Walsh and her sister. Mrs. Walsh swore again that Arnett didn't have any enemies and the sister backed her up. Said even the people he fined for hunting or fishing without a license didn't hold it against him because he was so nice about the whole thing."

"That's what they say," Virgil put in, "but they weren't there, so how can they be so sure? I know I've made a few enemies issuing traffic tickets."

"Yeah, but nobody's out to kill you for it," Mitch said.

"Far as I know," Virgil mused. "But people get crazy enough these days to do most anything."

"Now you sound like Millicent Kirkwood," Duck told him.

Mitch looked at Virgil. "Did you see that picture we found near Walsh's truck?"

"Yeah, but I don't know who it is."

If neither Virgil nor Helen recognized the woman, it probably meant she didn't live in Buckskin. Mitch said, "I went out to Vian Brasfield's dance ground last night, hoping to talk to him. Sorry you and Trudy had to miss it."

"We probably wouldn't have gone, even if I hadn't had to work. Trudy's allergies are acting up. You get anything out of Brasfield about that dead eagle you found?"

Mitch shook his head. "Didn't even talk to him. He took part in the booger dance, then disappeared. His wife was there. She was ticked off because he hadn't come home for dinner, and when she saw his pickup leaving the dance ground, she took off after him. I went by their place before I came here this morning. Missed him again. Brasfield left early to go to Norman for the weekend."

"Almost sounds like he's avoiding you, Chief," Duck said.

"Yeah. I'm convinced Brasfield's the eagle killer the Wildlife Department is looking for, and he's afraid we're on to him. He could have another reason to make himself scarce too. Maybe when he killed that last eagle, he got caught."

Virgil gazed at him. "By Walsh?"

Mitch shrugged. "Walsh was out there looking for illegal hunters, and Brasfield's wife says he left early Friday morning and he never showed up at the café where he usually eats breakfast."

"If he was going to kill an eagle, he wouldn't eat," Virgil said.

Mitch nodded. "So he lied to his wife about having breakfast, went eagle hunting instead. That puts Walsh and Brasfield in those woods at the same time."

"Are you saying Brasfield killed an eagle, then killed Walsh to keep him quiet about it?" Virgil asked incredulously.

"It's crossed my mind."

"Aw, come on, Mitch. I know Vian. He wouldn't commit murder over a dead eagle. If he got caught, they'd probably just fine him and let him go. Vian ought to know that."

"The school board would take a dim view of it, though," Duck put in. "Might even fire him. But if Brasfield's as obsessed with his Cherokee heritage as his wife says, he might think he has a right to hunt as his ancestors did and that no game warden has a right to stop him. He could've seen Walsh as just another white man trying to control him. Happens all the time. Half the Indians I meet got a chip on their shoulder." He darted a look at Mitch, then Virgil. "Present company excluded, guys."

Virgil curled his upper lip. "Thanks a lot."

"Brasfield," Mitch inserted, "is the only suspect we have at the moment." Virgil was shaking his head. "Unless you know something I don't, Virgil."

Virgil, who liked Brasfield, looked as if he wished he could name another suspect or two. "For all we know, Walsh was killed by somebody he got tangled up with before he moved to Buckskin."

"At this point, we can't exclude anything," Mitch agreed. "Sometime today, maybe you can run down somebody he worked with in Yukon—that's where he lived before."

Virgil slid his feet off the desk and got up. "Okay. Right now I'm gonna go talk to a couple of the guys who take part in the dances out at Brasfield's. I oughta at least be able to find out for sure if Vian's the one who's been killing eagles."

Mitch and Duck watched Virgil leave, then Duck said, "Somebody who lives out on the lake road might have seen Brasfield's pickup parked on that road where we found Walsh's truck."

"Check it out," Mitch said.

Duck pushed himself out of his chair and headed for the door, trying to tuck his shirttail into the too-tight waistband of his trousers.

Five minutes later, Virginia Craig, the high school guidance counselor, phoned the station.

She identified herself and asked to speak to Mitch. "You got him," he said.

"Oh, good. I'd rather talk to you than anybody else. I mean, since you're the one who came to the high school."

"What's this about, Ms. Craig?"

"It's probably nothing. I just—well, I thought I'd better tell you since . . . Look, could we meet somewhere and talk face-to-face?"

Mitch thought a minute. "You know where the Three Squares Café is?"

"Doesn't everybody?"

"I'll meet you there."

"Fine. I'll be there in fifteen minutes."

Before leaving for the café, Mitch got his cell phone out of the car and took it back to Gus's cell. "In case of emergency, you can find me at the Three Squares Café," Mitch said.

Gus looked the phone over. "Never used one of those. How does it work?"

"Just punch 'Talk' and dial the number. When you're finished, punch 'Talk' again to hang up."

"Okay if I call one of my pals?"

"I guess so, as long as it's not long distance. I'll be back soon with your lunch."

Mitch left a note for Duck and Virgil and punched in the number of the car phone in Virgil's patrol car so any calls would be automatically transferred. Then he drove to the Three Squares. So much for his day off.

11

In jeans and denim jacket, her hair in a ponytail, Virginia Craig looked younger than she had at the high school. If you didn't notice the fine lines around her eyes and mouth.

"Now, what can I do for you?" Mitch asked as soon as the waitress, whose name was Sue, brought a Dr Pepper for Mitch and a diet Coke for the guidance counselor. Mitch had chosen the Three Squares only because he knew Geraldine Duckworth, Duck's nosy wife, didn't work on Saturdays. Geraldine would have turned the meeting into a romantic tête-à-tête and had it all over town.

The café was filling up with lunch customers and several people paused long enough to greet Mitch and Virginia Craig before finding a table. Then Mitch noticed that some of them kept casting curious glances toward the booth where they sat. No doubt there would be a few rumors even without Geraldine's help.

"I'm having second thoughts," Virginia was saying. "I don't really know why I'm here. I'm probably overreacting."

"To what, Ms. Craig?"

She picked up her glass, set it a few inches to the right, then traced the wet circle it left on the tabletop with a pink fingernail. She looked up and sighed. "Well, here goes. I've had three phone calls from Vian's home phone number in less than twelve hours. One at midnight last night—it woke me up—the other two this morning."

Mitch leaned toward her, his elbows on the table. "Vian Brasfield's been calling you from his house?"

"I don't know who it is. The caller didn't say anything last night, which made me think it wasn't Vian. He wouldn't hang up on me. I didn't answer the two calls this morning. I let the answering machine come on, but the caller just hung up again. I've got caller I.D. That's how I know where the calls are coming from." She hesitated, looking uncertain, then added, "I'm pretty sure none of the calls was made by Vian, or I'd have taken this morning's calls."

"Mrs. Brasfield?"

She lifted her shoulders. "Only two people live in that house."

"Let me see if I get this. You didn't answer the last two calls because you thought it was Brasfield's wife and you didn't want to talk to her."

She nodded, looking faintly embarrassed. "I can't imagine why she'd be calling me. She doesn't like me. We have nothing to say to each other. Of course, it doesn't have to be her. One of their kids could be home. They have a couple of daughters, but one of them lives in New Mexico, and the other in California."

"Why would their daughters be calling you?"

She looked away. "They'd have no reason. Actually, I've never even met them. It's just—well, I'm not *accusing* Vian's wife of harassing me or anything."

"It so happens I went by the Brasfield house earlier this morning. Mrs. Brasfield didn't mention that either of her daughters was home, and the only car in the driveway was hers."

She had reached for her Coke, but abruptly set it down at Mitch's words. "Did you talk to Vian?"

"He wasn't there. His wife said he'll be in Norman, doing research all weekend."

"If she knows where he is, then why would Nicole—"

It was the first time Mitch had heard Mrs. Brasfield's first name. Nicole? he thought. It didn't fit her at all; it was too exotic for the sturdy, opinionated housewife.

"You tell me."

Her gaze shifted from his and she slumped dispiritedly against the vinyl booth. "I don't know. Nicole is odd. I don't pretend to understand her."

"Are you married, Ms. Craig?"

She shot him a sharp glance. "Divorced."

"Then is it possible Mrs. Brasfield thinks her husband didn't go to Norman at all, that maybe he's with you?"

She fingered the collar of her denim jacket. "It's possible," she said finally. "It's more than possible. Nicole has a very suspicious nature." Then she straightened and leaned closer to Mitch. "Now that I know Vian's not home—well, she might think I'd go out of town with him." She spoke so low that he could barely hear her. "She could be checking to see if I'm at home this weekend." She drew in a sharp breath.

"Oh, dear. I've probably added to her suspicions by not answering the phone."

"It's none of my business, Ms. Craig, except that I need to talk to Brasfield in connection with a case I'm working. How . . . uh, close are you and Brasfield?"

Her eyes widened. "I'd expect that kind of question from Nicole, but not you," she said disgustedly. "I had to stop going to the Indian dances at Vian's place because every time I went, Nicole tried to stare a hole through me. She thinks I'm out to steal her husband."

"Wonder where she got that idea?"

She glared at him. "Vian and I are *friends*. That's all. Yes, he drops by my house occasionally, but just to talk."

Mitch nodded and waited.

"You don't have to believe me," she said defensively, "but it's true. Vian doesn't have anyone else to talk to. He gets so excited about his Cherokee research, and he shares things he learns. His wife certainly isn't interested. Honestly, sometimes I think Nicole doesn't care a fig for Vian's feelings. Anyway, Vian—he tells me his troubles, Chief Bushyhead."

"These troubles wouldn't include his marriage, would they?" A man who's bored with his wife, and a woman with a sympathetic ear. It wouldn't be the first time a sexual relationship grew out of such a situation. In Mitch's conversation with Hunter Kennedy and Troy Reader at the high school, he'd picked up nuances when Virginia Craig was mentioned. At the time, he hadn't been sure what the nuances meant. Now he thought the woman's co-workers, like Brasfield's wife, suspected her relationship with Brasfield was more than friendship.

His thoughts must have been written in his expression. "What?" she demanded. "Don't you think a man and a woman can be just friends?"

"Of course they can. At the moment, though, I'm only interested in what you can tell me about Brasfield."

She bowed her head for a moment. "All right," she said finally. "Vian and I are *not* having an affair, but"—she looked Mitch in the eye steadily, almost defiantly—"that's more to his credit than to mine." She took a long drink of Coke before continuing. "Vian and Nicole have been married for twenty-six years. I've known them almost that long. There was a time, seventeen or eighteen years ago, when something happened between them. I don't know what, but at that point he considered leaving her. He stayed because of his children. And he's still committed to keeping at least a semblance of a marriage."

"A semblance? What does that mean?"

She seemed to be turning something over in her mind. "Vian has told me things in confidence. Private things. I don't want to betray his trust."

"Ms. Craig, Vian Brasfield may be an important witness in a murder investigation."

She stared at him in shock. "*What?* What murder? When?"

"I'm not at liberty to say, but until I can locate Brasfield and talk to him, whatever you can tell me could be helpful."

"I can't see what his marriage has to do with being a murder witness." She paused, then expelled a breath and went on. "Vian told me that he and Nicole have separate bedrooms."

"Wouldn't be the first married couple. Maybe he snores. Maybe she does."

Her look was impatient. "You know what I'm trying to say."

"The Brasfields don't have sex?"

She shook her head. "Haven't for years."

Unlikely, Mitch thought. Sometimes men who were cheating on their wives—or thinking about it—said their sex life at home was nonexistent to disarm the other woman.

"Vian didn't go into the details," Virginia went on, "but I think Nicole may be frigid."

Maybe so, Mitch thought cynically, but it sounded to him like Brasfield could be working up to getting Virginia Craig in bed—if they hadn't been there already. Brasfield was sure playing on her sympathy. Maybe he was the kind of guy who wanted her to make the first move so he could blame her later if they got caught.

Mitch decided to switch directions, possibly catch her off guard. "Has Brasfield ever mentioned hunting eagles to you?"

She frowned. "No."

She appeared to be telling the truth, so Mitch tried another topic. "Hunter Kennedy and Troy Reader said that Brasfield rarely loses his temper. Is that true?"

She seemed bewildered by the quick changes of subject. "He told me that he was a real hothead when he was young. After it got him into a few unpleasant scrapes, he realized he had to learn to control himself, and he did. Vian is a very disciplined person."

"What about those unpleasant scrapes? Did he tell you about any of them?"

"No." She watched him thoughtfully, then glanced at her watch. "I have to go. I'm supposed to be at a friend's house in twenty minutes. Chief Bushyhead, I'm sorry I bothered you with this."

"No problem," he assured her.

"It was just that Vian never came to the high school Friday and I was worried about him. When I kept getting those calls . . ." All at once, her tone changed. "I've been watching too much TV, I guess. Right before I called the police station, I was struck by the crazy notion that Nicole wasn't home and Vian was injured or something and trying to get help. Now that I know he's fine, I feel pretty silly."

"It's all right," Mitch assured her. "It *could* have been something like that. Before you leave, do you have time for another question?"

"Sure."

"Troy Reader told me that he'd made it clear to Brasfield he didn't want the vice-principal job, so Brasfield then hired Hunter Kennedy instead. Is that what happened?"

She shook her head. "It surprised everybody when Vian didn't give the job to Troy."

"What was Reader's reaction at the time?"

"Oh, he was furious. It wouldn't have been so bad if Vian hadn't hinted that he was in line for the job. Troy confronted Vian in his office and they argued. Or at least Troy did. In fact, he yelled so loud half the school heard him. I don't think Vian intended to hurt Troy's feelings. Actually, I think he considered giving the job to Troy at first. But that was before he interviewed Hunter. Vian was impressed with Hunter. It turns out he was right too. Hunter is really good with the kids."

"Reader insisted he didn't want the job."

She smiled wryly. "That's just sour grapes. Troy wanted it,

all right." She glanced at her watch again. "Oops, I really do have to go."

He reached for their check. "I'll get your Coke."

"Thanks." She scooted out of the booth, pausing to look down at Mitch. "I wouldn't want Vian to know that we talked about his personal life."

"Don't worry about it," Mitch said. It seemed to satisfy her, and she departed hurriedly.

Mitch ordered a take-out pork chop plate lunch for Gus and finished his drink while he waited. It was almost noon, but he still felt full from the eggs and biscuits he'd had for breakfast. When a waitress brought Gus's lunch in a Styrofoam carrier, Mitch tossed a couple of ones on the table, paid the bill, and left. As he was unlocking his Landcruiser, a Chevrolet coupe pulled up beside him. Hunter Kennedy leaned across the seat from the driver's side and rolled down a window. "Chief Bushyhead, could I have a word with you?"

Mitch tossed the sack containing Gus's lunch onto the front seat and walked over to Kennedy's car. Two cute little boys peeked at him from their car seats in back. Blond hair, blue eyes, mischief written all over them. He recalled Kennedy saying his sons were a year apart, but they could've been identical twins.

"Hey, men," he greeted them, and stuck his hand in the window. "Give me five."

They slapped his hand and crowed with delight.

"Ryan and Rick, this is Chief Bushyhead." Mitch gave them a little salute and they saluted back.

"My wife and the boys have been gone a week visiting her folks, got home early this morning. I took charge of the boys so she could rest," Kennedy explained. "I'm no good in the kitchen, so we're having lunch out. I wanted to ask if you'd talked to Vian. He never showed up Friday at school."

"I haven't located him," Mitch said.

He frowned. "I wish I knew what was going on with him. Whatever kept him away from the teachers' meeting had to be something important. I was just wondering if somebody in the family was seriously ill. I thought you might know."

"I've talked to his wife, and she didn't mention any illness in the family," Mitch said.

"Oh, then, if you've talked to Mrs. Brasfield, he must be all right."

"As far as I know," Mitch said. "At any rate, he's all right enough to go out of town for the weekend."

"That's good." He got out, pocketed his keys, and opened the Chevy's back door. "Come on, boys. Let's go eat."

"If you see your father," Mitch said, "would you give him a message?"

He'd reached in to unbuckle a car seat, but at Mitch's words, he straightened up. "I don't know when I'll see him. I could call him if it's urgent."

"I wouldn't say it's urgent. You mentioned that you see your sister frequently. Next time you do, tell her to remind your father it's against the law to make threatening phone calls."

His face paled. "Sweet Lord, what's he done now?"

"The Cherokee clinic's been receiving calls. The caller doesn't identify himself, but he seems to share your father's political views."

He looked miserable. "Dad's as nutty as a peach-orchard boar these days. When I talked to him, right after I moved to Buckskin, he ranted on and on about Indians getting working folks' tax money, living off the dole, and keeping him up all night with some kind of barbaric ceremonies."

"Ceremonies? He must have meant the dances at Vian Brasfield's place."

"Probably. I don't pay attention to what Dad says when he gets started on his persecution theories. But that must be what he meant. Dad told me once that the Cherokees are teaching savage rites to little kids and ought to be stopped. He kept saying rites, so I didn't think dances. Dee told me that's one reason he's determined not to pay his property taxes, as a protest. Honestly, I sometimes think he's completely lost his mind. I hope he doesn't end up hurting somebody."

Mitch didn't like hearing his own thought issuing from Dane Kennedy's son. "Does your father have guns?" he asked, although he was pretty sure he knew the answer.

"God, yes. A regular arsenal. I don't guess there's anything you can do about that?"

"Not unless he breaks the law—and we can prove it. He's not engaged in trafficking in illegal firearms, is he?"

"I don't know." He sighed. "Look, I'm real sorry about those phone calls."

"It's not your problem. Just wanted to drop a word. If it is your father and he knows we suspect him, maybe he'll stop."

"I'll see that Dee gets the message."

"Good."

Mitch waved at the boys. " 'Bye, now. Have a large time, men."

They scrambled out of the car and looked Mitch up and down. "Are you a teacher, like my dad?" one asked.

"No, I'm a policeman."

"Where's your gun?"

"Left it at home," Mitch told him.

"Policemen are our friends," the other boy piped up. Sounded as if he were quoting from a book or perhaps his parents.

"That's right. You ever need any help, you look me up."

He nodded solemnly. Losing interest in Mitch, he turned to his father. "I'm hungry, Dad."

"Come on, then." Kennedy said good-bye to Mitch and led his sons into the café.

Mitch delivered Gus's lunch and retrieved his cell phone. Duck returned to the station, saying that he hadn't found anybody yet who'd seen Brasfield or Walsh on the lake road Friday morning, but he was going back for more canvassing later.

12

Emily came home at one-thirty. She hadn't eaten, so Mitch made sandwiches from leftover meat loaf. He loved thick slabs of cold meat loaf between slices of fresh whole wheat bread spread with lots of mayonnaise, liked it better that way than when it was still warm from the oven. He'd learned to make meat loaf after his wife's death, just so he could have the leftovers in sandwiches for a couple of days.

Droopy-eyed, Emily ate with her chin propped in one hand. "You don't look as if you got much sleep," Mitch observed.

"We talked till three A.M." She rolled her eyes. "You wouldn't believe how wired Temple and Carrie Lou were about the dances."

"What about you? You seemed to enjoy it too."

"Oh, I loved it! Anyway, we talked about that and the camera getting stolen for a while and then a lot of girl stuff."

"Boys and clothes, huh?"

Ellen used to have long, intimate talks with Emily about "girl stuff," but apparently Emily couldn't see her father taking Ellen's place in that regard. Occasionally, like now, he gave her an opening. She never took it.

Now she just grinned and said, "Yeah. Finally, Mr. Roberts yelled at us to shut up. Real loud too, so we knew he meant it."

"He waited till three A.M. to do that? The man is the soul of patience."

"Temple and her date are doubling with Kevin and me tonight, so she might come home with me and sleep over."

"You sure you want to stay up till all hours again?"

She waved a negligent hand. "I'll probably catch a nap this afternoon, after I wash my hair and do my nails. And I can always crash Sunday after church." Though Mitch didn't attend church services very often, Ellen and Emily had been regulars and Emily continued to attend Sunday School and church after her mother's death.

When Mitch peeked into her bedroom a couple of hours later, she was curled up in her bathrobe, her hair still wet, sound asleep. He closed the door softly and tiptoed toward the stairs. After leaving Emily a note on the message board in the kitchen, he went back to the station to see if Duck or Virgil had any new information that might be connected to the Walsh case. Even tenuously. He was getting nowhere fast on this one.

Duck wasn't there, and Virgil was on the phone. He hung up as Mitch entered, reached into a big bag of M&M's on his desk, and popped a few into his mouth. He pushed the bag toward Mitch. "Have some."

Mitch pulled out the chair from Duck's desk, sat down, and took a handful of candy, which he began to eat slowly, one M&M at a time.

"That was Stace Byrd on the phone," Virgil said. "He's one of the dancers at Brasfield's. I saw his brother earlier and asked him to have Stace call me. Nobody else would own up to knowing anything about the feathers used in the dances."

Mitch leaned back in the chair. "So what's Byrd have to say for himself?"

Virgil popped another M&M. "Wanted to know if I was asking about the feathers out of curiosity or in my capacity as an officer of the law."

"I see. And what did you say?"

"I told him I already knew Brasfield was supplying the eagle feathers for the dances. Said if he was killing eagles, it was the Wildlife Department's problem, not mine. I just needed to know if he was hunting in the woods near that out-law cave Friday morning, because if he was, he might have seen Arnett Walsh's murderer. Stace wanted to know why I didn't ask Brasfield, so I had to tell him we'd been unable to locate him." He tipped his head back and dropped another M&M into his mouth. He chewed and swallowed before con-tinuing. "Stace was real cautious, said he didn't have any first-hand knowledge but that he'd *heard* Vian had killed an eagle or two."

"Or three," Mitch mused.

"Yeah, and Stace allowed as how Vian *might* have gone hunting Friday morning."

"We'll have to go on that assumption till we know better," Mitch said. "I just wanted to hear that Brasfield has been killing eagles from somebody who knew. I think we can put it down as true that Brasfield was in those woods Friday morning and he killed that eagle I found."

"So," Virgil mused, "he killed it and left it for somebody else to pluck. Roughly about the time that Vian was doing that, somebody killed Arnett Walsh in the same area."

"I've given this a lot of thought," Mitch said, "and I came up with a couple of strong possibilities. Like I said earlier, Walsh could've caught Brasfield in the act, tried to arrest him, Brasfield panicked and killed him."

Virgil was shaking his head in disbelief. "Still can't swallow that. What's the other possibility?"

"Brasfield was hunting eagles. Walsh was hunting the eagle killer. Then a third party showed up and killed Walsh, not knowing there was anyone else in the woods to witness the crime. Brasfield saw what happened, dropped the eagle, and got the hell out of there."

Virgil pondered Mitch's words. "There's a big problem with that second one, Mitch."

"I know. If Vian witnessed a murder, why didn't he come straight to the police?"

"Exactly."

"I guess he could've been worried about being interrogated," Mitch said. "We'd want to know what *he* was doing out there. We might even think he was the killer and claiming to be a witness to throw us off."

"Okay, so maybe he decided to walk away and say nothing. Why did he disappear?"

"Could be like his wife said," Mitch replied, though he was beginning to doubt it. "He skipped the teachers' meeting to go somewhere and research the Cherokees. That's what he's doing this weekend."

"You really think a guy could witness a murder, then go merrily off to do some hobby?"

"You know Brasfield better than I do. What do you think?"

"I think he'd have come straight to the police, even though he might have to confess to illegal hunting. Unless . . ." He nodded vigorously as a new thought came to him. "Unless the killer saw Vian, recognized him, but Vian got away. He could be hiding out, afraid of being killed if he shows his face."

"So why doesn't he use the telephone and call us?"

"Maybe he's scared of the repercussions."

Mitch shook his head. "I like my first notion. Brasfield panicked, killed Walsh, then ran."

"I hate to say it, but it makes the most sense—or it would if it was anybody but Brasfield. By the way, I talked to one of Walsh's former co-workers in Yukon. The guy hadn't heard about the murder and was too shocked for a few minutes to be coherent. But when he got it together, he claimed Walsh was liked by everybody who knew him. Didn't have an enemy in the world, just like the wife said." He reached into the bag for more candy, frowned, changed his mind, and asked, "You want any more of these M&M's?"

Mitch shook his head, and Virgil rolled up the end of the bag and stuck it in his desk drawer. "If Duck doesn't find out I have 'em, I can make 'em last a week." He closed the drawer and turned to Mitch. "It's looking worse and worse for Vian, isn't it?"

"From where I'm sitting," Mitch agreed. "If he's not back Monday morning, we'll have to put his description on the wire."

At that moment, Duck strolled into the station. "You back, Chief? You need to get a life."

"Tell me about it," Mitch muttered as he got up to give Duck his chair. "You turn up anything?"

"Ooh, yeah. Woman named Thelma Fields lives on the lake road, spends a lot of time looking out her window. She had a pair of binoculars sitting on the windowsill. Claimed she likes to watch the birds." He flopped into his chair, sank down, and stretched his legs out. "But you want to know anything about her neighbors on either side, she can tell you. Couple who live on the north spend all their spare time working in their front yard. Thelma took 'em over some cookies right after they moved in, but they never even returned her plate. Thelma's still puffed about that. But at least the unfriendly couple don't make any noise. Now, the woman who lives to the south of Thelma runs all over the countryside, leaves her teenage kids unsupervised. Loud music, cars and motorcycles racing in and out, stuff like that."

"I take it she was no help on the Walsh case," Mitch said.

"Not really. She's got a view of the road where Walsh had to pass Friday morning. Brasfield too, if he was out there."

"I'm sure he was out there," Mitch said.

"Thelma did say she might have seen a dark-colored pickup go by early Friday morning, but it could've been Thursday."

"We know where Walsh parked," Virgil said, "but there's a dozen other places Brasfield could've parked and gone into the woods."

"Brasfield would have left his truck where it wasn't visible from the road," Mitch said. "He could have pulled it into the woods a ways. He could also have parked it near where we found Walsh's truck, where Walsh saw it. That could be why Walsh stopped in that particular spot."

"Makes sense to me," Duck said. "And now Brasfield is on the run."

"We'll find that out Monday," Mitch said. "If he doesn't come home, we start looking for him in earnest."

"What if he can prove he knows nothing about Walsh's murder?"

"Hell if I know," Mitch muttered. "I'm going home and watching a ball game on TV."

"What ball game?" Virgil asked.

"Any ball game. Call me if you need me."

13

Sunday after church, Mitch took Emily out for lunch. They spent the afternoon catching up on the laundry, and later that evening watched a TV movie. Both of them were yawning before the movie ended, at which point they hit the sack.

On Monday morning, Mitch drove by the Brasfield house before going to the station. The white Pontiac was still in the driveway, but no dark blue pickup. He didn't stop, thinking he'd give Brasfield time to get to the high school, where he'd phone him later.

But he had to investigate two minor accidents and it was noon before Mitch got back to the station. He found a message from Ken Pohl, the medical examiner. Mitch dialed the M.E.'s office and caught Pohl before he left for lunch.

"I autopsied your game warden this morning," Pohl said. Mitch heard papers being shuffled. "Let's see here," Pohl continued, then read, " 'palpation of skull revealed two fractures, one at the base, the other behind the left ear. Examination of ears showed signs of hemorrhage behind eardrums, confirming fracture through base of skull.' "

"In other words," Mitch put in, "he was beaten to death."

"That's about the size of it, Chief. There was epidural bleeding at both sites. Whichever blow came first would have rendered him unconscious and death would have resulted quickly, from severe compression of the brain from the hematomas caused by the bleeding. The man probably never knew what hit him."

For the benefit of Walsh's wife, Mitch hoped the death certificate was couched in gentler terms. "Anything else, Doc?"

"Well, he had bacon, pancakes, milk, and orange juice for breakfast. I'd call that a medium-sized meal, wouldn't you?"

"I guess. Does it matter?"

"Oh, yes. A light meal can take from a half hour to two hours to digest, a medium meal from three to four hours. Walsh's stomach contents were largely undigested. It's just a guess, but I'd say he died within an hour of eating. Can't get any closer than that."

Walsh would have eaten right before he left the house Friday morning. He was probably dead by eight o'clock. "Thanks, Doc."

"You're more than welcome, Chief."

Mitch hung up. He was about to phone the high school, but before he could place the call, Mrs. Brasfield phoned the station.

She identified herself, then said in a rush, "I want to file a missing person's report," as though she'd practiced the words several times before calling.

"Your husband didn't come back from Norman?" Mitch asked.

"No, he didn't. He isn't at school, either. I've talked to his secretary three times this morning."

"Mrs. Brasfield, I need to question your husband. He could be a witness in our investigation into the murder of a game warden. Are you sure you don't know where he is?"

"No!" She paused before she said, "Why would you think Vian knows anything about the warden's death?"

"I can't know if he does or not until I talk to him. More to the point, I can put the word out on that right away. As for the other, we normally wait forty-eight hours before we consider an adult a missing person. You know where your husband was over the weekend, so he's only actually been missing a few hours."

There was a long silence.

"Mrs. Brasfield?"

"Chief Bushyhead," she said in a strained voice, "that's not really the case."

"What isn't?"

"That Vian has only been missing a few hours."

"What does that mean, Mrs. Brasfield?"

"It's a long story," she said heavily.

"I think we'd better talk face-to-face. I'll be at your house in a few minutes."

"If you really think that's necessary," she said with clear uneasiness.

"I do," Mitch said, and hung up.

There were dark smudges beneath Nicole Brasfield's eyes, and the lines around her mouth and the corners of her eyes appeared deeper than when Mitch had seen her two days ago. She wore a loose-fitting cotton dress and loafers whose heels dragged across the floor as she walked.

Wordlessly, she led Mitch into the spotless living room, offered him a chair, and sank wearily into the gray velvet couch.

"First off, I need you to clarify something," Mitch said. "You told me Saturday that your husband left early that morning to go to Norman. He was due back home this morning at the latest. Is that right?"

Her head bobbed once. "That's what I told you."

"You must know where he stayed in Norman. Have you tried to reach him there?"

She stared at her hands as they smoothed her cotton dress over her heavy thighs. She took a deep breath and said, "To tell you the truth, I'm not sure he even went to Norman."

"So you think he lied about where he was going?"

"Not exactly."

Mitch was real tired of getting the runaround from this woman. "Will you stop going all around the mulberry bush and talk to me?"

She pressed back against the couch, startled by his burst of irritation. "What I meant is that Vian never told me he was going to Norman."

"What exactly did he tell you?"

"Nothing."

Mitch sighed. "We seem to be talking at cross-purposes here. Why don't you start at the beginning."

She gazed at him for a long moment, looking as if her thoughts were scattered in several directions at once and she couldn't decide which to give voice to. "I'm sorry. I didn't even offer you a drink. Would you like something?"

Why was she having so much trouble getting to the point? Silently Mitch counted to ten before he said, "No, ma'am. I want to find out what's going on here."

She glanced around the room, as if looking for something to dust, and a flush spread over her face. Then she seemed to gather herself together and said, "Vian hasn't been home all weekend."

"Since Saturday morning, you mean."

She shook her head. "I know I said he was here Friday night, but he wasn't. I'm sorry. I shouldn't have lied to you. . . ." Her voice trailed off and she stared at her hands clasped tightly in her lap. Blinking a few times, she glanced up again. "I was embarrassed to admit I didn't know where he was. I thought he was with someone. I was sure he'd be back in time for school today and the whole town wouldn't have to know."

She could not maintain eye contact and looked down at her hands again. As the import of what she was saying sank in, Mitch gripped the arm of the couch and bit back a furious retort. She'd lied because she was *embarrassed*. Meanwhile, her husband had been gone for more than three days. "You thought he was with Virginia Craig?"

She didn't speak.

"I asked if you thought your husband was with Virginia Craig."

"How did you—" Her voice was almost a whisper.

"I talked to Ms. Craig Saturday. She told me she'd received three phone calls from this house and she was concerned. She has caller I.D. on her phone, so that's how she knew. Frankly, she suspected it might be you and that's why she didn't take the last two calls."

Her face colored again, with anger this time. "You mean she was there all the time?"

"Until Saturday afternoon. That's the last time I talked to her, but I assume she never left town. Did you try to call her again on Sunday?"

"No." She met his gaze, but it was a real effort. "I thought she and Vian were together. When I talked to Vian's secretary this morning, she told me that Virginia had come to work at the usual time. But that didn't tell me where she'd been all weekend. I—I kept thinking that Vian would turn up soon. But he still wasn't there by noon, and that's when I called you."

"You say Ms. Craig was at the high school. Why didn't you just ask her if she knew where Vian was?"

She hesitated a second, then laughed, a nervous laugh. "That would feed the teachers' lounge gossip for a month. Besides, do you really think Virginia would tell me anything?"

"Well, she told *me* that she and your husband are just friends."

She mulled that over for a moment, but didn't seem convinced. "Frankly, I wouldn't believe anything that brazen woman says. She's been trying to break up my marriage for three years, ever since her divorce was final."

Virginia Craig had as much as told Mitch the same thing. He didn't respond, waited for her to go on.

"That's neither here nor there, at the moment," she added, then stopped and looked at him anxiously. "If Vian wasn't with Virginia this weekend, then where was he? Where is he now?"

"Have you checked friends, relatives?"

"Oh, yes. I called a couple of the Cherokee dancers. And I talked to his brother in Kansas City. None of them has heard from Vian in several days."

"There's no other place where he might have gone?"

She took a deep breath. "None I can think of."

Mitch pulled out a small spiral tablet and pen and jotted down a few notes. "When was the last time you saw or spoke to your husband, Mrs. Brasfield?"

"Friday night at the dance ground. I saw him leaving and tried to catch up with him, to talk to him. But when I got out to the road, his pickup was nowhere in sight. I thought he'd gone to the house, so I drove straight here. He never came home."

"Then you haven't actually talked to him since Friday morning?"

"No."

Mitch studied her. "Mrs. Brasfield, have you and your husband talked about a divorce?"

"No!" she said emphatically. "Vian hasn't left me, if that's what you're thinking."

"I don't want to offend you, Mrs. Brasfield, but if you can suspect your husband of having an affair with Virginia Craig, your marriage can't be too solid." What he really wanted to ask was why she wanted to stay married to a man she thought was being unfaithful, a man who told his colleagues he wished he had never married her. But, upon reflection, that wasn't so surprising. She probably had no job skills, couldn't support herself if her husband left.

"Our marriage," she said stiffly, "is nobody else's business. It might not suit other people, but it suits us." She glanced around her perfectly kept living room as if to convince herself. "I don't know what I'll do if . . ." She halted, squared her shoulders. "No, he wouldn't just leave. Years ago, I almost left Vian, but he begged me to stay. He promised me he would never leave me as other people had, and I made the same promise to him."

What an odd way of putting it, Mitch thought. Most women would talk about how much they loved their husbands and how that love was returned. Nicole Brasfield had never said the word "love." Instead she talked about promises made years ago. But people change. How could she be so sure her husband wouldn't break his word? And what *other people* had left her?

"Did your husband expect you to be at the dance ground Friday night?"

"Not really," she answered with a frown. "I don't go every time."

"Has it occurred to you that the reason he left early was to avoid talking to you?"

"Yes, that's possible," she said haltingly, as though it were a difficult thing to admit.

"You seemed pretty mad at him for missing dinner," Mitch pointed out. "Maybe he didn't want to get into an argument."

She gave an impatient shake of her head. "Vian doesn't argue. There was a time . . . but never mind that. I get angry and lash out. It makes me feel better to let off steam. But it just rolls off Vian like water off a duck's back."

Sounded like her husband had stopped listening to her years ago. She was right, the Brasfields' marriage wouldn't suit everybody. Mitch decided to pursue another angle. "Friday morning, when he left the house, did you notice anything different about him?"

"Different? How?"

"Did he seem worried or preoccupied?"

"No." She drew the word out reflectively. "No, he didn't seem any different than he always does."

"Yet he lied to you about where he was going."

"Well, that may be true. I did call a few cafés, but not every restaurant in town."

"Mrs. Brasfield, I have reason to believe that your husband went eagle hunting Friday morning."

Instead of another vehement denial, she said wearily, "Perhaps he did. I wouldn't know about that. But it doesn't explain why nobody's seen him since then."

She was watching Mitch now, with something like distrust. "On the phone, you said you wanted to question Vian about the game warden's murder. Surely you don't think Vian had anything to do with that."

"I don't know. That's why I want to talk to him."

"Oh, you're wrong if that's what you think. As a young man, Vian had a tendency to lose his temper when things didn't go his way, but he conquered that. He could never have stayed in public school administration if he hadn't. Vian wouldn't hurt a fly."

That seemed to be the opinion of everyone who knew Vian Brasfield. But then, every time a serial murderer was caught, you could count on the people close to him being more shocked than anybody. Why, he was such a nice man, they'd say. A good neighbor.

A good neighbor who just happened to kill people in his spare time.

"Can you remember what your husband was wearing when he left home Friday morning?" Mitch asked.

She told him and Mitch wrote it down. Then he asked for a description of the pickup and the tag number. She went to her husband's office and returned with a copy of the registration.

"We'll put the word out," Mitch said. "Meanwhile, you need to come down to the station and let one of my officers take your statement. Can you be there about two?"

"Yes, and you'll let me know immediately if you hear anything about Vian, won't you?"

Mitch left, thinking that if he'd learned anything about Nicole Brasfield in his weekend dealings with her, it was that she could lie without batting an eye. She'd lied to him repeatedly in the past two days.

Was she still lying?

14

Mitch had no sooner returned to the station than he got a call from Troy Reader.

He left, telling Helen that there was some kind of demonstration happening at the high school and he was going to check it out.

Reaching the school, he saw that the "demonstration" consisted of one man, Dane Kennedy, marching back and forth, carrying a sign, and shouting at Virginia Craig and Troy Reader, who'd come outside to stand in front of the glass entry doors.

Mitch climbed out of his car and walked toward Kennedy. The sign the old man carried said, DISCRIMINATION IS AGAINST THE LAW! Mitch found it bewildering how militant types could rave against unconstitutional laws, then turn around and appeal to law for their own interests.

"What's going on here, Mr. Kennedy?" Mitch asked as he approached.

"I'm protesting!" Kennedy yelled.

As Mitch reached him, the old man stepped back. "Keep your hands off me!"

"I'm not going to touch you, Mr. Kennedy," Mitch said in as calm a tone as he could muster. "What are you protesting here?"

"My son told me Brasfield's running an Indian club right out of this public school, which is paid for with taxpayers' money!"

In fact, Mitch remembered Emily saying something about the club. It had sounded okay to him. "You got a problem with that?"

"Damned tootin'! The school's sponsoring a religion. Ain't that against the law?"

Glancing toward the school building, Mitch saw students' faces pressed to the windows. "From what I know, they learn about various Indian heritages. That's not sponsoring a religion."

"Then it's political! When I wanted to distribute some of my literature at the school, they turned me down. That's discrimination, pure and simple!" He waved his sign in Mitch's face.

"I'm going to have to ask you to leave, Mr. Kennedy. You're disrupting classes."

"I ain't answerable to you!"

"When you cause a disturbance in this town, you are," Mitch said quietly. "I'll arrest you for disturbing the peace if you don't go."

Kennedy glared at him, his eyes like black holes burned in his face. Mitch thought Kennedy's ongoing rages might have burned a hole in his brain, as well.

Kennedy thought about his options and finally said, "I'll go, but this ain't the end of it!" He stalked to an old pickup, threw his sign in the back, got in the driver's seat, and roared away.

Mitch walked up to Virginia Craig and Troy Reader. "Thanks, Chief," Reader said. "We'd probably have ignored him, but he kept yelling out his crazy slogans. 'Down with oppressive governments,' stuff like that."

"Why didn't his son talk to him?" Mitch asked.

"He tried," Virginia Craig said, "but it seemed to make the old man angrier. He accused Hunter of conspiring against him, said he was Vian's dupe. Hunter went back inside, thinking Mr. Kennedy might calm down some if he was gone."

"He said Hunter told him about the Indian club."

Reader nodded. "Apparently Hunter tried to explain to him that all the Indian heritage teaching that goes on at school is simply the teaching of history. His father wouldn't listen."

Mitch gazed toward the road leading to the high school. Kennedy's pickup was nowhere in sight. "He's gone for now. If he comes back, give me a call."

Hunter Kennedy turned up at the police station Tuesday at noon, and Helen showed him into Mitch's office, where for the past fifteen minutes Mitch had been pedaling the stationary bike he kept in the corner. He climbed down to greet Kennedy, who was dressed in gray trousers and a white shirt, one of those collarless dress-casual shirts men were wearing with suits these days.

Mitch put his shirt back on over his undershirt and pulled out a handkerchief to wipe his moist brow. He sat behind his desk and leaned back in his creaking swivel chair. "Sit down. What can I do for you?"

Kennedy took a chair. "I'm on my lunch hour, so I don't have much time. I'm having to do two jobs with Vian gone." He gripped both chair arms tensely. "I want to apologize for my father—that protest of his at the school yesterday."

"He's a grown man. You don't make his choices for him."

He shook his head. "If only I could." He hesitated, then said, "I've got other things on my mind right now. There's a rumor at school that Mrs. Brasfield filed a missing persons report."

"That's true."

"Have you learned anything about where Vian's gone?"

"Nothing." Mitch's chair protested noisily as he sat forward to place his elbows on his desk. He couldn't seem to remember to bring the WD-40 from home to give the swivel mechanism a few squirts. He picked up a pen, fingered it idly. "I don't suppose you'd have any ideas on the subject?"

Kennedy shook his head dejectedly. "I . . ." He hesitated, looking unsure. "I went out to the farm last evening to talk to my sister about Dad's showing up at school yesterday and those phone calls to the Cherokee clinic. I didn't see Dad, but Dee said she'd talk to him."

"Appreciate it," Mitch said.

"Of course, it probably won't do any good. He'll do what he wants to do."

"At least he knows he's still our prime suspect for the anonymous calls."

Kennedy sounded unhappy. "Dee and I went for a walk around the farm, like we used to do when we were kids when we couldn't stand being cooped up in the house with Dad any longer. She was preoccupied—I got the impression it had something to do with her husband—and I hoped she might loosen up and talk to me. But she didn't." He glanced out the window, then at a police academy certificate on the wall, at the cracked ceiling, anywhere but at Mitch. He hadn't come here to talk about his sister, Mitch realized, and probably not even about the protest or phone calls. Mitch just watched him and waited.

Finally Kennedy said, "I wrestled with this all night. I couldn't be sure, you see, and . . . well, I guess I convinced myself I was wrong. . . ." His voice trailed off.

"About what?"

He leaned forward. There was tension in his shoulders and the grim set of his mouth. "While Dee and I were walking, I saw a truck—only the front end of it, actually, parked in some trees. It looked something like Vian's pickup, but it was all mud-spattered, so I couldn't tell. I know my father doesn't own a truck like that, and besides, he would park it near the house. I pointed it out to Dee. She hadn't noticed it before, but she can't see it from her trailer or from the house, and she's not over on that side of the farm often. So the truck could have been there awhile." He stopped, swallowed, and went on. "I didn't make anything of it with Dee, didn't want to worry her. And afterward, I convinced myself it wasn't Vian's."

"But now you aren't so sure."

"I just don't know. I thought about it all morning and decided I had to tell you."

"This truck you saw on your father's farm—"

"It's not on his property," Kennedy corrected him, "but it's just across the property line on the other side of the fence."

"Then it's on Brasfield's land?"

"Yes."

"You saw a pickup on Brasfield's land, but you decided it wasn't Brasfield's? Dammit, Kennedy!" Mitch exploded. "You should have reported this immediately."

He hung his head. "I know. I just—I mean, it was so close to my dad's place and I knew you'd think . . ."

"Exactly what you're thinking, apparently."

"Look, my father and I don't get along, but I didn't want to cause any more trouble for him than he already has. Frankly, I think Dee's starting to worry about him too. Also her husband, who's evidently been sucked into Dad's paranoia. And please don't tell Dad that I was in here talking about him."

Mitch struggled to control his temper. First Nicole Brasfield waits more than two days to report her husband missing. Then Kennedy vacillates almost twenty-four hours before reporting sighting a truck like Brasfield's. A young husband and father-to-be was dead, and nobody seemed to see any connection between the murder and the fact that the man who had almost certainly been in those woods with the game warden that morning was nowhere to be found. What was wrong with these people?

When Mitch could speak calmly, he said, "Tell me exactly where you saw the truck." After jotting down what Kennedy said, he preceded Kennedy from his office, throwing over his shoulder, "Thanks for coming in, Kennedy." Even if it was a day late, he added to himself.

As a subdued Kennedy left the station, Mitch saw that Duck was engrossed in paperwork and said, "Shelly, come with me. We've got a possible sighting of Brasfield's pickup."

Duck looked up. "No shit? Where, Chief?"

"Out at Brasfield's dance ground."

"You mean it's been there all the time?"

"I just told you all I know, Duck. It might not even be Brasfield's truck."

The pickup was dark blue with tinted windows, and the tag number matched the one Nicole Brasfield had given Mitch. It was Brasfield's truck, all right.

Mitch and Shelly had parked the patrol car and trudged through tangles of dead weeds and brush, following Hunter Kennedy's directions. The mud-splattered pickup had been backed in among several trees, with only the front of the cab visible. Obviously it had been driven there, but the Ford was a four-wheel drive and sat high off the ground. The patrol car might have bogged down if Mitch had tried to take the same route across the field.

The truck was unlocked and the keys were in the ignition. "Looks like he was in a hurry to leave it and get out of here," Shelly observed.

"On foot?" Mitch pulled himself up to kneel in the driver's seat and look at the floorboard between the front seats and the narrow back seat of the extended cab.

"Somebody could have picked him up. Virginia Craig, maybe."

The guidance counselor had seemed genuinely worried about Brasfield's whereabouts the last time Mitch talked to her, but she could be lying or not telling all she knew. That seemed to be true of everybody else in this case.

Mitch reached down to pick up the patchwork quilt piled on the floorboard. It was part of Brasfield's costume for the booger dance. Despite his own suspicions about Virginia Craig, he said, "You don't even know Virginia Craig, Shelly. How come you don't trust her?" Mitch had reported his conversations with the guidance counselor to his officers, but he didn't think Shelly had ever met her.

"I just know that a woman will lie for the man she loves."

Or for her meal ticket, Mitch mused, thinking of Nicole Brasfield. He threw the quilt into the front passenger seat, exposing a bow and quiver full of arrows like the one he'd found near the dead eagle, a gourd rattle, an eagle feather wand, and a red mask. He held up the mask. "Hey, look what I found."

"Yipes! What's that?"

"It's called a booger mask. Brasfield wore it Friday night in the booger dance, before he took off."

"And drove out here?"

Mitch turned around to sit sideways in the driver's seat. "I don't know. His wife said he left the grounds. She tried to follow, but didn't see the pickup. She assumed wrongly that he'd gone home."

"I guess he could have driven in here from the highway. It curves back around just east of Brasfield's land." Shelly was gazing across the barbed-wire fence toward a pond on Dane Kennedy's farm. "At any rate, he didn't go home Friday night. Somebody had to pick him up. And where did he go from here?" She pondered her own question for a moment. "Mrs. Brasfield could be lying when she says she doesn't know where her husband is. If Brasfield killed Arnett Walsh, his wife could have picked him up on the road and delivered him to wherever he's hiding out."

"I don't know, Shelly—"

"Look," she said sharply.

Mitch climbed down from the truck and walked over to stand beside Shelly at the fence. "What?"

"See that spot of white?" She pointed toward the pond. "Could be just a rag."

"Let's find out. Step on this wire so I can get it."

"Isn't that trespassing?"

He laughed. "It'll be our little secret."

She held a low wire down with her foot and pulled up on the wire above it, making an opening wide enough for Mitch to crawl through. He walked over to the pond bank where the piece of white fabric lay. It looked like a man's handkerchief. It wasn't beaten down as it would have been if it had been rained on, which meant it had landed there sometime after Friday morning's downpour.

He bent, picked it up by one corner, carried it to the fence, and crawled back through. Holding it by two corners, he shook it out.

"There's an initial!" Shelly exclaimed. "B." She looked at Mitch. "Brasfield."

"I'll see if Mrs. Brasfield can identify it."

Shelly gazed across the fence at the pond. "What was Brasfield doing on that side of the fence?"

Mitch didn't reply, assuming the question was rhetorical. They were silent for a moment. Finally Mitch said, "If this is Brasfield's handkerchief, you know what it means, don't you?"

Shelly didn't seem to be listening. Instead, she mused, "Okay, we know that Brasfield was on Kennedy's land Friday night. He parked his pickup and crossed over to Kennedy's property. To meet somebody?"

"Could be," Mitch agreed.

She sucked in a breath. "What if Brasfield never left here Friday night?"

"You're reading my mind. So now we're gonna have to drag Dane Kennedy's pond."

15

Mitch and Shelly took the handkerchief to the Brasfield house. Shelly waited in the patrol car while Mitch knocked on the door. Nicole Brasfield, still in the same cotton dress she'd worn on Mitch's previous visit, stepped out on her front porch.

"Have you found Vian?"

"No, ma'am." Mitch held out the handkerchief. "Just this. Can you identify it?"

She stared at the "B" embroidered in one corner of the handkerchief. "That looks like one of the handkerchiefs I gave Vian for his birthday." She glanced up at Mitch. "Where did you find it?"

"Near his pickup," Mitch said, "which we found on your husband's property west of town."

She looked dazed and then she paled. "But . . . why did he go back there? He's not hurt, is he?"

"No sign of him, ma'am," Mitch hastened to tell her.

"But if his truck's there, where is he?" A vein pulsed rapidly at the base of her throat. "I don't understand."

"We don't, either, but we'll conduct a thorough search of the property." Mitch turned away before she could question him further. "You'll hear from us soon."

Shelly watched him get in the car and start it before she asked, "It's Brasfield's handkerchief, isn't it?"

Mitch nodded. "We'll go out to Kennedy's farm now and try to get permission to drag his pond."

"Oh, sure, like that's really going to happen. Especially after you ran him away from the high school yesterday."

"If he'd give permission, it'd save the paperwork and hassle of trying to get a warrant. It's worth a try."

Nicole's bones were rubbery, like the fake bones they bought for the little rat terrier her daughters had had when they were very young. Jasper, they'd called him. Jasper used to slobber and chew on those bones for hours at a time. He'd keep on gnawing and gnawing until he'd reduced them to a sodden mess. Her limbs felt like those chew toys. If she moved too quickly or went too far, her bones would collapse.

She shuffled like an invalid down the hall, holding herself upright with a hand on the wall. She entered the kitchen. Everything looked different, as though she'd been transported to another house while she'd napped on the sofa, before the arrival of the police had awakened her. She'd been napping a lot the last couple of days, escaping the terrifying present.

She felt chilled. Moving to the counter, she poured a cup of leftover coffee and heated it in the microwave. But when she took the cup out and drank, it tasted bitter, nasty. She poured the coffee into the sink.

Sissy, the calico cat, wound between her legs, meowing. She'd forgotten to feed her. She got the sack of cat food from the cabinet and filled the cat's bowl, and Sissy began to eat greedily. Had she fed her yesterday? Nicole couldn't remember.

She was so cold her teeth were clacking. She'd already turned up the furnace, and it hadn't helped. She had to get warm. She stumbled back to the living room, where she'd left a crocheted afghan on the couch. She wrapped herself in the afghan and lay down. But it wasn't enough. She was still shivering.

Clutching the afghan around her, she shuffled to her bedroom, where she saw, to her surprise, that she hadn't made the bed since she'd gotten out of it early that morning. She always made her bed as soon as she got up. It was as automatic as breathing. But nothing was the same now. Her thoughts were sluggish and her reflexes weren't working. When she moved, she felt a resistance, as if she were trying to walk underwater.

She crawled into bed and pulled the sheet and coverlet up over the afghan. She curled into a tight, round ball and closed her eyes.

She longed for a living, breathing body beside her, a warm body to wrap herself around. But Vian hadn't been in her bed for ages, and now he was gone. Would anybody ever warm her bed again?

Vian wouldn't hurt a fly. That's what she'd told the police, because he had never hit her. She couldn't even remember when he had last touched her. She had never feared that Vian would hurt her physically. He had rarely even raised his voice. Instead, he had used quiet, cruel words, which fell from his lips like slivered ice, destroying her with frozen malice.

Sleep tugged at her and she let it pull her into a cocoon of nothingness. When she slept, she didn't have to think.

At the Kennedy farm, Mitch got out of the patrol car, opened the gate, and drove through. Hearing the car, Kennedy's hounds started barking. Mitch jumped out again to close the gate, then ran back to the patrol car as the three barking, mangy-looking hounds barreled down the lane. He slammed the door just as the dogs reached the car, and drove on up to the house. The hounds followed, throwing themselves at the car, their teeth snapping, managing with the agility of long practice to keep clear of the tires.

Dee Bregman heard the hounds barking and went to the window of her mobile home. A police car was coming down the drive.

Her seven-year-old daughter, Cindy, wandered out of her bedroom and saw Dee at the window. A frown creased her little brow. "Why are the dogs barking, Mommy?" Lately Cindy seemed anxious too much of the time. Dee suspected her daughter's anxiety was caused by her grandfather's frequent harangues about how people were out to get them. Now Hank was starting to say things like that too. Dee had wanted to send Cindy to school in town to expose her to other kids, a different environment, but Hank had insisted Dee home-school the child, saying he didn't want her being brainwashed.

Just the other day, Dee had remembered a similar argument between her own parents, before her mother left. Her father had wanted to take her and Hunter out of school and let their mother teach them at home. It was one of the few times her mother had stood up to him and refused to give in. After she'd left, her father had told her to quit school and stay home to keep house for him and Hunter. Remembering her mother's courage, she'd said no, said that if he kept after her about it she'd run away.

Funny, that she hadn't remembered that until just recently. She was always telling Hunter that things hadn't been as bad as he remembered when they were growing up, but lately she'd remembered other unpleasant incidents. When she tried to talk to Hank about it, he said she'd been listening to Hunter too much. She was like all those people who claimed they'd been molested by their fathers as children, Hank had said, only, according to them, they'd repressed it until some psychologist messed with their heads and convinced them they'd been abused.

Hank was getting as bad as her father, and ever since Hunter had told her about that incident at the high school and those phone calls to the Cherokee clinic, she was worried sick. Her father had staged protests before, but that didn't worry her as much as the phone calls. When Hunter had told her about them, a terrible suspicion had come into her mind.

But what could she do? Whenever she suggested that they move to town, now that Hank had had a job for several weeks, he said they had to get caught up on their back bills first. Dee was afraid that whenever the bills were paid, Hank would come up with some other excuse.

Maybe Hunter had been right all along. She should never have agreed to move out to the farm. Yet her father had sounded so lonesome when he'd suggested they come. Even knowing that he'd driven Hunter and their mother away, she still felt sorry for him.

Cindy stood on tiptoe to peer out the window. "They're policemen, Mommy. Are they going to arrest us?"

"No, sweetheart. They won't hurt you." Damn her father and Hank for filling Cindy's head with their cops-are-out-to-get-you bull. "Come away from the window now." Dee led the child to the kitchen. "How about some milk and graham crackers?"

Cindy glanced once more toward the window before she climbed into a chair at the table. "Okay," she said without enthusiasm.

Giving her daughter a hug, Dee wondered for the hundredth time whether she should go to the police with her suspicion. Would they keep her name out of it?

But Hank would find out, and then what would become of her family? Could she support herself and Cindy? It was frightening even to consider it.

Hank might even try to get custody of Cindy. And if she left the farm, her father might just back him up. Did she dare chance it?

As always, when she asked herself these questions, Dee decided to keep quiet and hope for the best.

Mitch parked in the graveled drive between the old house with the peeling white paint and a neat-looking mobile home. A woman with short brown hair and a little girl had watched them approach, but she'd left the window now without acknowledging the visitors in any way.

He honked the horn several times before Dane Kennedy opened the front door of the house and stepped out on the porch.

Mitch rolled the car window down a couple of inches. "Call off your dogs, Kennedy," he shouted. "We need to talk to you."

In overalls and a plaid cotton shirt, and with his full beard and bright, burning eyes, Kennedy looked like a cross between a mountain man and an Old Testament prophet.

"I got nothing to say to no dupes of the federal gov'ment!" Kennedy yelled.

"What's he talking about?" Shelly asked.

"He's a little nuts."

One of the dogs jumped and tried to jam his nose through the window opening, leaving saliva on the glass. Mitch wished he had something to bang against the hound's nose. Instead, he cranked the window up an inch. "I think you'll talk to me after you hear what I have to say," he hollered. He didn't believe a word of it. He just hoped it would buy him a few minutes with the old man. If he could appeal to Kennedy's humane side—if he had one—maybe he'd give permission to drag the pond.

While the hounds barked and jumped, snarling, at the windows of the patrol car, Kennedy stood, shading his eyes against the light to glare at the car, wondering perhaps if he should just shoot the officers and be done with it. Finally, he called the dogs and led them around the house, where he confined them to a pen. Mitch and Shelly got out as Kennedy returned to the porch, opened the front door, and stalked inside.

He left the door open, so Mitch and Shelly entered into what had once been the living room, now an office. There were two desks, their ends shoved up against opposite walls along with four-drawer file cabinets and several old wooden folding chairs. Against one wall were four cardboard boxes. One of them was open; it was full of crudely printed booklets. Mitch wasn't close enough to read the titles, but he had a good idea what kind of material the booklets contained.

Kennedy stood next to the larger of the desks, his hands in his overalls pockets. "If you're here about my protest yesterday—"

"No," Mitch said.

"Then if you've come to try to coerce me into paying my property taxes, you made a trip for nothing," he said combatively. Before Mitch could respond, he snatched a book from the desk and held it up. The title was *Never Pay Taxes Again.*

"The gov'ment people taxed me and all other property owners at a meeting where we didn't get to vote," he ranted, waving the book around. "Common law, constitutional law says taxation without representation is illegal."

Shelly looked at Mitch with a bewildered expression.

"Sir—" Mitch began.

Kennedy threw the book on the desk with a loud bang. "You people try to force me off my land, I'll bring in reenforcements. I can raise an army if I have to. We'll fight to the last man."

Exactly the sort of thing Mitch worried about in the middle of the night. "This isn't about your property taxes," he said.

Kennedy stared at him. "Oh, I get it. It's about them phone calls that Cherokee doctor claims I've been making to her clinic." He took a threatening step toward Mitch, who let his hand fall on the butt of his gun in its holster and stood his ground. "My daughter told me all about that. Well, I didn't make no phone calls!"

"Sir—"

Kennedy raised his voice another notch and steamrollered over Mitch's protest. "But I sure sympathize with whoever did! The Constitution and Bill of Rights empowered white men. *White men,* you hear me?" His eyes glittered with the same kind of madness Mitch had seen only in psychotics and extreme fanatics. They raked Mitch's Cherokee face with contempt. "All the rest of the laws the gov'ment enacted—the so-called amendments putting in income taxes, forbidding racial segregation, giving women the vote—all them things violate the organic Constitution. They're illegal!"

Shelly sucked her breath in at the mention of women and the vote. Her jaw grew rigid, but she kept her mouth shut.

"We're not here to argue constitutional law with you, Mr. Kennedy," Mitch managed to insert.

Kennedy took another step forward and shook a finger at Shelly. "Listen here, gal! You're a white woman, and you don't even know what danger you're in."

"Danger?" Shelly queried, glancing around the room uneasily.

"With all the mixing of the races that's going on and the way the gov'ment pampers minorities, America's white population will perish sometime in the next century!" He stomped to the open box against the wall and snatched a booklet from it. "The proof's in here!" He tried to push the booklet into Shelly's hand. She put both hands behind her back and shook her head. Kennedy threw the booklet back into the box. "Now they've put in the damned Brady law to try to take away our guns." He glared at Shelly. "Don't that scare the bejesus out of you?"

"Well, uh, all the Brady law does is require a waiting period before the purchase of a firearm."

"You're blind, gal! Brainwashed! They've banned the manufacture of assault weapons too."

"Only a small number of them, sir," Shelly said. "And why on earth do private citizens need assault weapons, anyway?"

"It's an infringement on our constitutional right to bear arms! And it's just the beginning. Mark my words, they're gonna try to disarm the country. Gun control is for only one thing: people control! That's why people like me are trying to get the word out before the whole country's as defenseless as a bunch of sheep. The New World Order is on the move!"

Mitch stepped in front of Shelly. "Mr. Kennedy, could we talk about this later? A man has disappeared and we just found his truck next to your fence and his handkerchief across the fence near your pond. We need your permission to drag the pond."

Kennedy froze, his mouth half open. "*My* pond?"

"Yes, sir."

Kennedy's gaze darted around the room, as if he were trying to get his bearings. "Who's this man that's disappeared?"

"The principal of Buckskin High School, Vian Brasfield."

"You mean that Injun who's been holding savage rites on the place next to mine?"

"They're Cherokee dances," Mitch said.

"They're un-Christian! The noise from over there sounds like a bunch of African cannibals getting ready to boil a white man!" Kennedy swiped at a trickle of saliva that ran down his chin. His face was red. Kennedy seemed able to work himself up into a real frenzy with lightning speed.

"If Brasfield's gone," Kennedy sputtered, "good riddance, I say. Maybe they'll hold their barbaric ceremonies somewhere else now."

"About the pond—"

"Hell, no!" Kennedy waved both arms. "You're already trespassing on my property. You ain't dragging my pond. Now git out! Before I get my shotgun and shoot you full of holes. Git!" He was practically nose to nose with Mitch now.

"Go, Shelly," Mitch said quietly without looking around. This old man was crazy enough to actually attempt what he threatened, and Mitch might have to shoot him in self-defense. Which would give the militia types all over the country more fodder for their fires of hate. That was the last thing he wanted. When he heard the screen door bang shut behind Shelly, he backed away, felt for the door, and let himself out.

Kennedy followed him as far as the porch. "You can tell that tax assessor he'll get the same treatment if he comes on my farm. In the Bible, God says, 'The earth is mine'! Your laws don't apply to God! I ain't paying taxes on God's land, neither!" When they drove away, Kennedy was still waving his arms and yelling.

"Good Lord!" Shelly breathed as they cleared the gate. "It's like a parallel universe out here."

"Yeah," Mitch agreed, "a real scary one."

"So what now?"

"We see if Judge Walters will issue a search warrant."

"Kennedy will try to stop us, warrant or no warrant."

"We'll cross that bridge when we get to it."

16

Two hours later, Mitch and Shelly returned with Duck and a couple of divers. Since it was cheaper to pay two divers for a few hours, Mitch had decided to try that first before calling in the heavy equipment. They only had a couple of hours before dark, but the pond was small.

Mitch's patrol car was in the lead, followed by Duck and Shelly in another car and the divers in a truck. Not wanting to get into a confrontation with Kennedy before they even reached the pond, Mitch sped past the house without stopping, heading straight for their destination.

The divers weren't even in the water yet when Kennedy's old GMC pickup plowed across the field and clattered to a halt beside Mitch's car. The woman Mitch had seen in the mobile home, evidently Kennedy's daughter, a little girl about seven or eight, and a man in his mid-thirties, probably the daughter's husband, were with him. All of them got out. The woman held on to the girl and stayed beside the pickup with the passenger door open.

Kennedy was carrying a shotgun. The younger man took a few steps, then stopped, but Kennedy stormed straight for Mitch.

The woman gasped. "Daddy, don't!" Kennedy ignored her.

"Mommy," the little girl queried, "what's wrong with Grandpa?"

"Shhh," her mother cautioned.

Mitch, Duck, and Shelly pulled their guns and spread out to cover Kennedy from three directions. One of the divers said, "Oh, shit!" and they both ducked behind their truck.

"Are they gonna shoot Grandpa?" The child's voice quavered.

"You watch this, Cindy girl," the old man yelled. "This is how the police treat citizens on their own property!"

The child started to cry.

"Get back in the pickup, Cindy," her mother said urgently. Cindy climbed in, but her mother remained standing behind the pickup's open door.

"Drop the gun, Kennedy," Mitch ordered.

"Git off my land!"

"We got a search warrant," Mitch said. "Drop the gun!"

Kennedy's gaze traveled from Mitch to Duck to Shelly. Three handguns against one shotgun didn't look like very good odds to him. "You got no damned right—"

"We don't want anybody getting hurt here, Kennedy!" Mitch cut in. "And you're scaring your granddaughter."

"She damn well oughta be scared!" Kennedy snarled. "You people are always talking about obeying the law, but it's different when they apply to you. I've declared this farm an independent nation, and you can't come on it without I invite you!"

Mitch released the safety catch on his gun. "Drop that shotgun!"

The younger man snarled, "You shoot Dane and you'll be sorry that you were ever born."

"Shut up, Hank," the woman cried shrilly. "You're just making it worse. Daddy, do what they say," she pleaded. "Let 'em do what they came to do and leave."

Kennedy didn't move for what seemed forever to Mitch. Evidently he was considering the pros and cons of becoming a martyr for the cause. Finally, he let the shotgun slide to the ground. Mitch pulled the search warrant from his shirt pocket and handed it to Kennedy, who frowned fiercely and scanned the warrant briefly.

Then he cursed and threw it at Mitch. It landed at Mitch's feet. "This is illegal! I ain't under your laws!"

"We'll get out of your way as soon as possible," Mitch said.

"I'm gonna watch you from the truck." Kennedy bent to pick up the shotgun. "You do your bizness and git out!"

"Leave the gun!" Mitch ordered.

Kennedy straightened up. Stiff with rage, he stalked back to his pickup, a stream of curses flowing back to Mitch. All three adults got into the single seat, the woman holding the little girl on her lap.

Mitch picked up the shotgun, unloaded it, and laid it beside the patrol car where he could keep an eye on it. "You got any more guns in your truck, Kennedy?" Mitch yelled.

When the old man didn't answer, the woman thrust her head out the truck window. "There're no more guns in here."

Cautiously, the divers came out from behind their truck. "You can go to work now," Mitch told them. He glanced back at the pickup. "Duck, keep an eye on Kennedy."

Duck walked around and leaned on the back of the patrol car, facing Kennedy's pickup, gun in his hand. After a while, Kennedy got out of his truck again, leaned against the hood, his glittering eyes following every move the divers and officers made.

"I thought we were going to have a shoot-out there for a few minutes," Shelly said to Mitch. They were wandering over the pond bank, waiting for the divers to surface. Even though the pond wasn't large, the divers were slowed by the fact that the water was muddy; they had to feel their way over the bottom.

"Kennedy's just trying to intimidate us," Mitch said.

Shelly shivered. "It's working, Chief. That old man scares the crap out of me. He's got crazy eyes. You notice that?"

"Yeah," Mitch said, "but Duck's watching him. Don't let him get to you."

She hugged herself, running her hands up and down her arms in the long-sleeved khaki shirt. "No wonder his wife left him."

"Too bad she didn't take her kids with her."

"The son seems to have turned out all right, in spite of being raised by a certified lunatic. Don't know enough about the daughter to have an opinion. The fact that she's living on the farm, keeping that child around the old man, doesn't say much for her, though."

"Her brother said they had to move the mobile home out here when her husband lost his job."

" 'Home is the place where when you have to go there, they have to take you in,' " Shelly murmured.

"Huh?"

"It's a quotation," she clarified, "from a Robert Frost poem."

"Thought it sounded familiar."

Dusk was falling by the time one of the divers surfaced and swam toward the bank. He pulled off his mask. "I found something," he said. "Can't see my hand in front of my face in that muddy water, but it sure feels like a body. It's caught on an old log or something, and I couldn't pull it loose. I'll go down and try again." His anxious gaze left Mitch and Shelly to focus on Dane Kennedy for a moment. "It'll be dark soon, and I sure don't want to have to come back out here tomorrow."

Shortly, the other diver surfaced and the two went down together. Moments later, they came up, dragging between them a body covered with mud and weeds. The divers laid the body on the pond bank.

Dane Kennedy ran past Duck, who followed, and up to Mitch. "What the hell did you pull out of my pond?"

"My best guess, it's Vian Brasfield," Mitch told him.

"Geez, what a mess," Duck said.

Mitch peered toward Kennedy's pickup, where his daughter, granddaughter, and son-in-law still sat waiting. The woman's head was bowed, as if she were praying—or crying.

Mitch pulled out a handkerchief, knelt beside the muddy, bloated body, and wiped the worst of the debris off the face. It was too swollen and discolored to make a positive I.D. But even with mud and weeds all over the trousers and shirt, Mitch could tell they matched the description of the clothes Brasfield had been wearing when he left home Friday morning. To be absolutely sure, they'd have to get dental records.

Mitch unbuttoned a hip pocket in the man's trousers and found a wallet. The driver's license was protected by plastic laminate, and the name on it was Vian Brasfield.

Kennedy's daughter and son-in-law got out of the pickup, leaving their daughter inside, and walked toward them, halting a few feet away. Kennedy paced like a prowling beast and waved his arms. "How in hell did he get in there?"

"I thought maybe you could give me a clue about that," Mitch responded.

"I don't know nothing about it!" Kennedy yelled. "You try to accuse me, I'll sue you for slander!"

Mitch was tempted to comment on the illogic of Kennedy's willingness, when it suited him, to use the laws that he said didn't apply to him. Instead, he ignored Kennedy's agitation, went to his patrol car and called for an ambulance.

Kennedy's daughter watched Mitch fearfully. "Daddy?"

Kennedy walked over to her and continued to rant and rave. She looked from her father to her stone-faced husband and began to sob.

"Shelly, see if you can get some decent prints off him, then wait here till the ambulance comes. Duck, you come with me." Mitch picked up the shotgun. "We have to ask you all a few questions, Mr. Kennedy. Can we go back to your house?"

"I ain't got nothin' to say!" Kennedy protested.

"We didn't know that body was here," Kennedy's son-in-law said. "We sure don't know how it got there."

"You're Kennedy's son-in-law, I take it," Mitch said.

He gave a curt nod. His wife composed herself and said, "I'm Dee Bregman and this is my husband, Hank."

"Well, Mr. Bregman," Mitch said, "if you all know nothing about this, then you won't mind answering a few questions."

He frowned and his wife put her hand on his arm. "Hank, Daddy, let's go back to the house. We're going to have to do this, so let's get it over with."

It was dark by the time they got to the house. Mitch asked the Bregmans to return to their mobile home while he talked to Kennedy. Bregman didn't like it, but again his wife intervened and they left the house. Mitch sent Shelly back to the station and directed Duck to question the Bregmans—separately, if possible.

Kennedy had flipped on an overhead light. He took a combative stance in the center of the living room/office. Mitch leaned the shotgun against the wall and stayed near the front door, his hand in easy reach of his gun.

"You want to sit down, Kennedy?"

"No. Just ask your questions and git outta here."

Mitch shrugged. Let the old coot stand there all night if he wanted to. "Where were you last Friday night from about ten P.M. on?"

"Right here," Kennedy snorted. "Where I am every night. You saw me yourself, when I was out walking, after I locked the dogs in the barn. Those drums was driving 'em crazy."

"How long were you outside?"

"I don't remember. Fifteen minutes maybe."

"Did you walk in the direction of the pond?"

"Hell, no!"

"Friday night," Mitch said, "did you hear any noises from the direction of the pond, or see anybody going or coming?"

For an instant, he looked uncertain. Then he demanded, "How could I hear anything over those heathen drums?"

"Do you remember what time you went to bed?"

"I always go to bed right after the TV news goes off at ten-thirty, except that night I didn't bother. Them damned Indians was just getting started when the news went off, kept that hooplah going all night."

"Did you ever complain to Brasfield about the noise?"

"Hell, yes! Plenty of times. He'd give me this shit-eating grin and promise they'd keep it down. But they never did. Never intended to. Damned Injuns think they own the whole county."

"What about last Friday night when I saw you walking around? Did you complain to Brasfield that night?"

He sneered. "Knew it wasn't no use. I came inside, turned the TV on to try to drown out those drums, then went to bed and put a pillow over my head and tried to sleep, but I couldn't on account of the drums. Finally got up and addressed some envelopes. I got a mail-order business here."

"Were your daughter and son-in-law at home Friday night?"

"Dee was. Hank's been working nights at a service station in Grove." He walked over to one of the desks and sat down. "I'm finished answering your questions. I cooperated. Told you everything I know." He touched a drawer as if to open it, then changed his mind and put both hands on the desk.

"Let's speculate for a minute," Mitch said. "How do you think that body ended up in your pond?"

He favored Mitch with a stare of exasperation. "Injuns trespass over there when they have them dances. I seen footprints. Found some beer cans once. Likely it was some of them put the body in my pond."

He couldn't be sure the trespassers were people who attended the dances. "They're not allowed to bring alcohol to the dances," Mitch said.

"Don't mean they don't do it anyway." He grinned suddenly, showing a couple of missing teeth from the bottom row in front. It was the first time Mitch had seen him smile, and it wasn't a pretty sight. "That's probably why they come over on my place. To drink," he said, "or get a little Injun pussy." He spread out his bony-fingered hands. "Maybe they'll quit now."

Now that Brasfield was dead, he meant. Was he just taking up Mitch's assumption about the identity of the dead man, or did he know that was Brasfield? And if the latter, how could Mitch prove it?

The farm was fairly isolated. Kennedy could have been all over it Friday night without anybody knowing; even Kennedy's daughter in her mobile home. After Mitch saw him outside, he could have come back in the house and left again by the back door.

They hadn't gotten any good evidence from Brasfield's pickup, either. Not wanting to mess up any fingerprints, Mitch had decided not to drive it to town, but had had it towed to the police station while they waited for the judge to decide about the search warrant. Duck had dusted the interior of the cab for fingerprints. The steering wheel and door handles had been wiped clean.

If Kennedy had been at the pond Friday night, waiting, how had he known Brasfield would drive out there? By pre-arrangement? Would Brasfield have agreed to meet Kennedy

in the middle of the night, out in the country with no wit-
nesses?

"Thanks for your cooperation," Mitch said curtly.

Kennedy didn't speak or move as Mitch walked out, went
over to the mobile home, and tapped on the door. Hank
Bregman opened it.

"I'm looking for Officer Duckworth," Mitch said.

Bregman nodded toward the back of the mobile home.
"He's in the kitchen, talking to my wife."

Mitch didn't wait for an invitation to step inside. "I need
to ask you a few questions, then."

Bregman grunted and backed away from the door. "Keep
it down, will you? My wife already put my daughter to bed."

"You shouldn't have brought a child out there," Mitch said.
"Your father-in-law frightened the daylights out of her."

Bregman stared at him stonily. "She knows Dane won't
hurt her. It was you and your officers pulling your guns that
scared her." He was perhaps five feet ten inches tall, weighing
in at one eighty or so, looking more solid than fat. His jeans
and T-shirt showed a few dark streaks of what looked like
motor oil, and his butter-colored hair could have used a
shampoo several days ago. Not the cleanest guy in the world,
but there was intelligence in his green eyes, along with distrust.

Mitch was tempted to tell him that he was lucky his father-
in-law decided to put down his gun, or his daughter might
have seen her grandfather get shot. But he didn't want to add
to the man's defensiveness. "What can you tell me about last
Friday night?" Mitch asked.

"Not a thing. I wasn't even here. I was at work. I got the
night shift at the Texaco station over in Grove."

"What're your hours?"

"Ten to six. It takes about fifty minutes to get there, so I leave at nine, get home around seven in the morning." He looked at his watch. "I have to be there a little early tonight, so I need to be out of here in the next thirty minutes."

"This won't take long," Mitch said. "You aren't home when they're dancing at Brasfield's place?"

"Not since I started this job. That'd be about six weeks ago."

"Before that, you were here?"

"Usually."

"Were you disturbed by the noise?"

He snorted. "Does a duck quack?" He made a sweeping gesture with his hand. "These walls are about as thick as a tin can. You can hear a coyote walk by half a mile away." His lip curled. "I hate this damned trailer. I'd move into the house with Dane, but Dee won't hear of it. She's wants to move to town."

"Mr. Kennedy says he has a mail-order business. Are you involved in that with him?"

His face closed up. "I help him address envelopes once in a while, when he gets behind."

"I noticed some boxes of pamphlets over at the house. Does he publish them himself?"

He nodded. "Types 'em up on an old typewriter and takes 'em to Muskogee to get 'em run off and the covers put on."

"You agree with your father-in-law's . . . uh, political views?"

His thick brows shot up. "Political views? What do you mean by that?"

"His anti-government paranoia."

He thought about it. "It ain't paranoia if it's true, is it? Sure makes sense to me," he said sullenly.

At that moment, Duck and Dee Bregman walked out of the kitchen. She was a petite woman, dressed in jeans and a sweatshirt. Her short hair was badly cut, and she wore no makeup. She looked at her husband anxiously.

"I've already talked to Mr. Bregman," Mitch told Duck. "You ready to go?"

"Yep."

Mitch thanked the Bregmans. He and Duck walked silently to the patrol car and got in.

"Mrs. Bregman tell you anything?" Mitch asked.

"Not much. She was at home Friday night. Didn't leave the mobile home after seven or so. Saw nothing. Heard nothing except for the dances at Brasfield's place. Oh, and she said her husband was at work."

"That's about all I got out of Kennedy and Bregman too."

"She acted real nervous," Duck said. "She's scared, Chief."

"Don't blame her, the way her father acted out at the pond."

"No, I think it's more than that."

"What's she scared of, then?"

"You got me, Chief."

"Could be she's afraid her husband or her father is responsible for that body in the pond."

"Could be. How'd Bregman act?"

"Resentful, but not really worried."

"Then I guess he's sure of his alibi—he really was at work Friday night."

"I'll check with his boss first thing tomorrow," Mitch said. "Right now we have to tell Mrs. Brasfield what we found."

Duck sighed. "I hate doing that. Haven't got over telling Mrs. Walsh about her husband yet."

"You can wait in the car," Mitch told him.

"I'm not waiting in the car," Duck said, offended at the suggestion. "I'll go in with you."

17

"I want to see him," Nicole Brasfield insisted. She had taken the news with such amazing calm that Mitch wondered if she was on tranquilizers. She remained dry-eyed and stoic.

The three of them were standing in the Brasfield living room. Duck shifted uncomfortably and glanced at Mitch.

"They'll have taken him to the morgue in Tahlequah," Mitch said. "It'd be closed by the time you could get there." Mitch had known the medical examiner to perform autopsies at night, but he sure didn't want Mrs. Brasfield walking in in the middle of that. "Your husband, if it is your husband—"

"What do you mean, *if*?" she asked shrilly. "Don't you know?" The first thing he'd told her was that they hadn't made a positive I.D., but evidently she hadn't absorbed that.

"If it's your husband, Mrs. Brasfield, he—he doesn't look like himself."

Her eyes closed and her hand covered her mouth as the import of what Mitch was telling her finally sank in. She turned away, struggling for composure.

"Why don't you wait until we get his dental records for comparison," Mitch suggested. "Then, if it's a match and you still want to see him, I'll take you to Tahlequah myself."

"All right," she murmured without turning around. "Thank you for coming by."

"I'll need the name and address of his dentist, ma'am."

"It's Dr. Chambers here in Buckskin. His office is on the main street."

"I know where he is. Thank you."

Duck practically bolted for the door and Mitch followed, pulling the door closed behind them.

"She didn't act too torn up, did she?" Duck inquired, as soon as they were off the porch. "Not like Mrs. Walsh. She went all to pieces."

"People react in different ways."

"Yeah, I guess," Duck said doubtfully.

Since it was past quitting time, Mitch dropped Duck off at his house and drove home.

Emily met him at the front door. "Well, finally. I was getting worried about you."

"That's usually my line, sugar," Mitch said, kissing her cheek. "How does it feel on the other end?"

She swatted his arm. "Awful. You could've called me."

"I'm sorry. I got busy."

"Doing what?"

"Routine stuff." He wasn't going to spoil her evening by telling her they'd found a man's body that had been submerged in muddy water for a while. She'd find out soon enough.

"I made potato soup," she said. "I've already eaten, but I'll fix you a bowl."

Mitch tried to push thoughts of corpses from his mind, but the image of the swollen body on the pond bank lingered, and he had little appetite. "Sounds great. I'll shower and change first. Won't take fifteen minutes."

"Okay. Kevin's coming over at eight so we can study for our geometry test."

"Uh—where are you going to study?"

She rolled her eyes. "I know the rules, Daddy. We'll study at the kitchen table."

Mitch stayed downstairs long enough to say hello to Kevin Hartsbarger before going upstairs to his bedroom. It wouldn't hurt to remind the boy he was in the house, he theorized. If Emily could have read his thoughts, she'd have accused him of not trusting her. Which might be partly true. What he didn't trust were teenage hormones, especially those of testosterone-crazed seventeen-year-old boys. His memories of his own teen years were still vivid, and what he remembered most was an almost constant preoccupation with sex. For Mitch, until he was out of high school, his sex life had consisted mainly of fantasy. But times were different now and kids seemed to grow up faster than in his day.

Like most fathers, he pretended he had some control over his daughter's behavior. Shortly after Ellen's death, he'd had a talk with Emily about the virtues of waiting to have sex until she was old enough to make a long-term commitment. Then he'd brought up sexually transmitted diseases, adding that the only absolutely safe sex was no sex. That little talk was one of the hardest things he'd ever done, but he'd felt compelled to make the effort. He'd been embarrassed by the whole thing and, finally, Emily said, "Daddy, don't worry. We have sex education at school." He hadn't brought it up again, but he didn't think Emily was sexually active. If she was, he preferred being left in his ignorance.

He stretched out in the lounge chair in his bedroom and tried to read his *Outdoor Life*. It was the fishing issue, and it reminded him he hadn't enjoyed a fishing trip in a good long while. Maybe he could take a couple of days off after he wound up the investigations into the deaths of Walsh and the man in the pond. He went back to his magazine.

This evening, the murmur of voices from the kitchen below was more reassuring than distracting. As long as they were talking, his imagination didn't run wild. What kept diverting his thoughts from his reading was that body they'd dragged out of Dane Kennedy's pond. Before long, he tossed the magazine aside, laid his head back, and closed his eyes, letting his mind go where it had been trying to go all along.

Behind his closed eyelids, the image of the muddy, weedy, bloated corpse was sickeningly vivid. He was ninety-nine percent sure it was Vian Brasfield. Waiting for the dental match was a mere formality. Had Brasfield drowned? Mitch could concoct a couple of possible scenarios. Brasfield had been sick or drunk, left the dance ground Friday night, took a wrong turn, and ended up in that field, from where he wandered onto Kennedy's farm and fell in the water. But Troy Reader had said that he'd known Brasfield to drink to excess only once in all the years he'd worked for him. Furthermore, Mitch didn't think Brasfield would break the rule about no alcohol on his own dance ground.

So that possibility seemed less likely than the second scenario: Somebody had forced him into the pond, one person strong enough to hold him under till he drowned, or two men—like Hank Bregman and Dane Kennedy.

A third possibility: Brasfield had been drugged or knocked unconscious, and then dragged under the fence and into the pond.

Or he hadn't drowned at all.

Was Brasfield's death connected to the murder of Arnett Walsh, and if so, how? If Brasfield had killed Walsh, how was Mitch going to prove it, with his suspect dead?

He deliberated these questions until he fell asleep. When he awoke abruptly after midnight, his neck was stiff and his right foot was asleep. Groaning, he got out of his chair and hobbled across the room, a thousand needles stabbing his foot as he made his way down the hall. From the lighted hallway, he assured himself that Emily was safely asleep. Then he stumbled back to his room, stripped down to his briefs, and fell into bed.

Mitch picked up Vian Brasfield's dental X rays Wednesday morning and delivered them to the medical examiner's office in Tahlequah.

"When can you get to the autopsy, Doc?" Mitch asked.

"Did it last night," Pohl said. "I was about to call you when you walked in." He took the X rays from Mitch, went around his desk, and picked up the X rays he'd taken during the autopsy. He walked to a viewer, clipped the X rays on it, and studied them closely. Finally, he slid one over the other. "It's a match," he said.

"I was already sure it was Brasfield," Mitch said, taking one of the padded chairs in front of the desk. "Can you tell me how he died?"

Pohl sat down at his desk and linked his hands behind his head. He had a habit of running his hands through his dark hair, so that usually, as now, it stood up in spikes at strange angles. Mitch had concluded long ago that Pohl never looked in a mirror after he left the house each morning. In his fifties, the doctor wore thick-lensed glasses that made him look bug-eyed. Even in his office, which was down the hall from the morgue and autopsy room, he habitually wore a long white lab coat and smelled of disinfectant.

"When a body has been underwater, we start by assuming drowning. It isn't always easy to prove otherwise."

"Are you saying you're leaning in that direction?" Mitch said. "To otherwise, I mean?"

"There were multiple cuts and abrasions on the face," Pohl went on as if Mitch hadn't spoken. The medical examiner didn't like being hurried to a destination before he laid out the route he'd taken. "That doesn't necessarily mean the wounds occurred before death. When a person drowns, the body always assumes a facedown position, with the arms, legs, and face dragging against the bottom. The face may scrape against the bottom, which forces weeds and sand into the nose and mouth, and this may cause abrasions of the face and forehead. After three days or so, it'll fill up with gases and rise to the surface."

Mitch was getting impatient. "So you're saying he drowned, after all."

Pohl pushed his glasses up his nose. "Patience, Mitch," he reprimanded. "I'm getting there. According to the para-medics, the body was in a muddy pond with lots of rocks and weeds. If I'd found weeds or mud inside the lungs, I could say with assurance that the man had drowned. I did find bits of weed and dirt in the mouth and nose, but none in the lungs. More telling than that, though, were the wounds on the back of the head. One of them fractured his skull and there was extensive damage to the lining of the brain. I don't think that could have been caused by falling into the pond, and it's my educated guess that one of the head wounds is what killed him, and that he was dead when he hit the water."

"These wounds . . . would you care to hazard a guess what caused them?"

"They were nonpenetrating," Pohl said, "therefore made with a blunt instrument." He chuckled. "Beyond that I can't go, Mitch. I certainly can't draw you a picture of the murder weapon. Dead men do tell tales, but they don't fill in all the details."

This wasn't the first time Pohl had told him that. "Okay. What about time of death?"

"Hard to say. The water was cold, which, as you know, slows down postmortem changes. The body was considerably swollen from interior gas formation, enough to cause the body to surface, but the paramedics said the clothing was snagged by something on the bottom. For that much gas to have formed, the man must've been dead about four days, could be longer. It's remotely possible it could have been a little less than four days if he was kept in a warm place for a day or two before being dropped in the water. But let's assume he was put in the water shortly after death. You found him late Tuesday, so I'd say he died Friday or early Saturday. Could've even been Thursday. Alas, forensics is not always as exact a science as we'd like it to be."

"He was seen Friday night," Mitch said, "so it must've happened shortly after that." Which was what he'd thought all along.

"Something else I might mention," Pohl said. "The head injuries were similar to those inflicted on the game warden I autopsied last weekend." As Mitch sat forward alertly, Pohl held up a hand. "Now, don't read too much into that, Mitch. I said they were similar. I didn't say they were made by the same instrument. Since I was not present at either death, nor am I psychic, it's impossible for me to make any such determination."

Mitch sighed and stood. "Okay, Doc. I won't jump to that conclusion. And thanks for doing the autopsy so quickly."

"I've sent the stomach contents and some other samples off for analysis. I won't have that report for a few days. If there's anything unusual in the findings, I'll call you."

"Good."

"Wait a minute, and I'll get you his belongings. The family might want them." He opened a cabinet drawer and pulled out a brown paper sack. "That's his clothes and everything he had on him."

Mitch took the bundle. "Thanks again, Doc. Next time you're in Buckskin, Doc, I'll buy you lunch."

"Don't think I won't hold you to that, Mitch."

18

"Sorry to have to bother you again, Mrs. Brasfield," Mitch said. He'd come directly to her house from the medical examiner's office. Wearing makeup and with her hair brushed smoothly into place, she looked a little more rested today.

"It's all right. Come in."

Mitch stepped inside. Taking note of her dark green suit and white blouse, he asked, "Were you going out?"

"In a little while. They've released the body. I have an appointment at the funeral home in about an hour, to make arrangements for the service."

"I brought your husband's things," Mitch said, offering her the sack.

She took the bundle and held it out in front of her for a moment, as if she didn't quite know what to do with it. Then she went into the living room, sat down on the couch, and opened the sack.

Mitch followed, watched her reach in and take out a folded pair of dark blue trousers, a cotton plaid shirt, jockey briefs, dark socks and boots. The mud had dried along with the clothes, and as she placed the items on the floor, a few chunks fell to the carpet, which looked as pristine as the day it had been installed. Nicole Brasfield was such a dedicated house-keeper that Mitch doubted dried mud had ever marred her carpet before.

Finally, she pulled out Brasfield's wallet and car keys and laid them on the coffee table. The keys reminded Mitch of the pickup, which was still parked behind the police station.

"We're finished with your husband's truck. I could bring it over later this afternoon, if you want."

"That'll be fine," she said distractedly, still staring at the clothes on the floor beside her feet. "I've made a mess on the carpet. I'll have to run the vacuum sweeper again when I get back."

She sounded almost disinterested, detached. "I'll leave the keys under that mat I saw on the porch," he said.

She nodded, but she was still staring at the clothes, and he wondered if she'd really heard him.

"Mrs. Brasfield?"

She looked up. "Where are the other boots?"

"What other boots?"

She pointed to the mud-smeared boots at her feet. "These are Vian's old boots."

Mitch walked over, squatted down, and picked up one of the boots. They looked about as you'd expect them to look after being submerged in a muddy pond for a few days. Mitch didn't know how anyone could tell if they were new or old until he noticed that the heels were worn down. He set the boot down and stood up as he remembered something she'd said at the dance ground.

"I remember now. You told me Friday night that your husband had bought new boots that day."

"That's right. I got a good look at the toes when he was dancing. They were a much lighter color than these." She touched her hand to her forehead for a moment, half covering her eyes. "It seems so trivial now. I—I was angry with Vian because he'd worn new boots to dance in." She dropped her hand and looked at Mitch. "But they aren't here."

The boots weren't in Brasfield's pickup, either, Mitch thought, and suddenly his view of the case jumped out of the rut where his thoughts had traveled repeatedly and veered in a new direction. Was it possible Nicole Brasfield was mistaken and Brasfield had not danced at all Friday night?

But wait a minute. Mitch pulled his thoughts back from this stunning new road. Nicole Brasfield had seen her husband leaving the dance ground in his pickup.

"Mrs. Brasfield," Mitch said, "are you absolutely sure you saw your husband at the dance ground?"

She looked up and focused her gaze on him, as if returning from a far place. "Why, of course I saw him. He was in the booger dance."

"In costume, yes. But didn't you say you didn't see him before he put on the costume?"

"Yes, but—"

"What about when his pickup left the dance ground? Did you actually see him then?"

She frowned. "Yes. So did you. I pointed him out to you."

"You pointed out the pickup, but I couldn't see the driver through those tinted windows. I couldn't even tell how many people were inside. When you ran toward him, did he roll the window down so that you could see his face?"

She was silent for a long moment, as though trying to fathom what Mitch was driving at. "No, he speeded up when I shouted at him."

"So you didn't actually see him?"

"No," she said slowly. "I don't guess I did. But it was Vian. Who else would have been driving his pickup?"

"I don't know, ma'am. I'm sure we'll figure it out. Don't worry about it. I have to get back to the station now."

She was still sitting there staring at the boots when Mitch left.

At the station, Mitch called Shelly and Duck into his office and related his conversation with Nicole Brasfield, adding, "I don't think Brasfield was ever at the dance ground Friday night. That was somebody else wearing his costume."

"Why would somebody put on his costume and dance?" Duck asked.

Shelly's expression was suddenly animated. "To make everybody think Brasfield was there."

"What would be the point?" Duck asked.

"If people saw Brasfield, or somebody they assumed was Brasfield," Mitch said, "then obviously we'd all think he was alive Friday night."

Duck sat forward in his chair, which groaned with his weight. "You mean he *wasn't* alive Friday night?"

"I don't think so," Mitch said.

"Then whoever it was," Shelly said, "he's about the same size and height as Brasfield. How tall was Brasfield?"

"Five-nine or -ten," Mitch said.

"Even so," Duck inserted, "he'd have to have more guts than a slaughterhouse to masquerade as Brasfield."

"He may have killed two men," Mitch said. "That's pretty damned gutsy."

"Two?" Duck looked bewildered. "But we've been going on the assumption that Brasfield probably killed Walsh, and then somebody killed Brasfield. Two murders, two killers."

"We do know that Brasfield was in the woods Friday morning," Shelly said, frowning, "because the thumbprint on that arrow matches his."

"I don't get it," Duck said, scratching his head. "How'd one man kill two men with a pipe or whatever it was? He could have taken one by surprise, but not both of them."

"Yes, he could have," Shelly said, "if the second one didn't arrive till after the first one was dead. And if the newcomer didn't see the body right away, the killer could've surprised him too."

"There was no prior connection between the two victims," Mitch said. "They didn't even know each other. The only reason the killer would have to kill the second man was to keep him from talking and putting the killer in the woods that morning."

Duck rolled that around in his mind before he said, "You're saying the murderer meant to kill only one man."

"Right," Mitch said. "It makes sense out of a lot of things that seemed unrelated before. One killer, one intended victim. The question is, which one?"

19

Long after Emily had retired for the night, Mitch gave up trying to sleep, pulled on jeans and a T-shirt, and went quietly downstairs. In the kitchen, he considered heating up the coffee left in the pot from dinner, but rejected the idea because the last thing he needed was more caffeine. He was cutting down, he reminded himself.

He dipped a bowl of strawberry ice cream and sat down at the kitchen table. While he ate, he tried to follow the circuitous routes his thoughts had been taking through his brain all evening. When he finished the ice cream, he found a pen and tore off a sheet of paper from the pad attached to the message center by the phone, where he and Emily left notes for each other. Back at the table, he stared at the blank piece of paper for a moment and pondered.

Before the meeting in his office had broken up that afternoon, Mitch and his officers had agreed that, if the murderer had gone to the woods Friday morning, planning to kill one man, and had killed the second man to keep him quiet, the original target was more likely Vian Brasfield than Arnett Walsh. Walsh hadn't been in the area long enough to know many people, certainly not long enough to have made any enemies. Of which his wife and sister-in-law swore he had none, anyway. Brasfield, on the other hand, had lived in Buckskin for almost thirty years and, at an early time in his life at least, had had a quick temper.

But so as not to miss anything, they decided to investigate both men's backgrounds and find out what they did and who they interacted with during the last few weeks of their lives. Virgil and Roo had arrived for the evening shift just as the meeting in Mitch's office was breaking up, and Mitch brought them up to date. Then he assigned the check of Walsh's background to Virgil and Roo. He, Shelly, and Duck would concentrate on Brasfield.

Who might have wanted to kill Vian Brasfield? Mitch began to jot down names as they came to him, censoring nothing for the moment.

Dane Kennedy was first on the list. He'd had several run-ins with Brasfield about the noise from the all-night dances on Brasfield's land. He was a white supremacist to boot, and though Brasfield was only one-eighth Cherokee, Kennedy had referred to him as an Indian. Kennedy had written numerous letters to the editor criticizing the Cherokee Nation. He had demonstrated against the Indian club that Brasfield had started at the high school. The fact that Brasfield continued to ignore his protests infuriated Kennedy.

Hank Bregman was the second name on the list. Mitch had checked with Bregman's boss Wednesday morning and learned that Bregman had, indeed, been at work Friday evening. But if Brasfield was killed Friday morning instead, then Bregman had no alibi. But what was the motive? Mitch wrote "Motive?" beside Bregman's name.

Nicole Brasfield was next. The Brasfield marriage was evidently an unusual one and, from what Mitch had sensed, not happy. In spite of Nicole's assurances to Mitch that her husband had promised never to leave her, Brasfield could have changed his mind and asked for a divorce. Nicole was in her early fifties and, it appeared, had no particular skills to qualify her for a job away from home. A divorce would have been financially devastating for her. But there could well be life insurance proceeds if Brasfield died. Mitch made a mental note to check into it.

Virginia Craig had been close to Brasfield, perhaps was even in love with him. According to Nicole, Virginia had been trying to take Brasfield away from his wife for three years. Virginia herself had made it clear that she was romantically interested in her boss. Given that, Brasfield might finally have realized Virginia's feelings were more than friendship and made it clear to her that he would never leave his wife. Was it possible Virginia had been so humiliated and angered by the rejection that she'd killed him? Mitch could almost imagine her striking out in the first flush of rage. After all, she'd spent three years listening to the man's troubles and providing sympathy, in hopes that the relationship would develop into more than friendship. But Brasfield's murder had been premeditated. Unless Mitch was way off track, someone had gone to the woods intending to find Brasfield and kill him.

Beyond that, could a woman have killed two men with a blunt instrument? Both Nicole and Virginia were good-sized women, close to five feet eight inches tall, which would have allowed them to pass for Brasfield in the booger dance costume. But Nicole had been sitting in the bleachers during that dance, so if she was involved, she had an accomplice. As for Craig, she was middle-aged and didn't appear particularly fit. But that afternoon, as Duck and Mitch left the station— Duck to follow Mitch to the Brasfield house with the pickup, then drop him at home—Duck had insisted that a woman scorned was capable of anything.

Mitch had trouble believing that either Nicole or Virginia, scorned or not, was physically equal to the task of killing two men. Still, he wouldn't cross them off just yet.

From what Mitch had seen Friday night, few dance steps were required for the booger dance. It wasn't so much a dance as a comedy act. Each booger seemed to be pretty much on his own as long as he clowned around. Chances were the boogers never performed in exactly the same way twice. Conceivably, if the killer had seen the booger dance once or twice, he could wing it.

Both Nicole Brasfield and Virginia Craig had seen the dance several times. Dane Kennedy and Bregman hadn't admitted to seeing the dances, but they easily could have. There were places on the Kennedy farm that provided a view of the dance ground, so they wouldn't even have had to leave the property.

In addition, there were several young male staff members at the school, including Hunter Kennedy, who'd reported to Brasfield, any one of whom could, with surprise on his side, physically overpower another man—two men, provided he didn't have to take them on at the same time. Brasfield had invited all the teachers to attend the dances and most of them had taken him up on it at least once. The dance ground wasn't brightly lit and the boogers constantly moved around, jumped, stooped, sat. Under those conditions, even someone as tall as six feet could probably pass for Brasfield. But if Hunter Kennedy's attitude toward his boss was shared by the others, none of them would seem to have a reason to kill Brasfield.

With the single exception of Troy Reader, who had been passed over for the vice-principal's job in favor of Hunter Kennedy, after Brasfield had let him think he had a good chance of getting the job. According to Virginia Craig, Reader had wanted the job, despite his words to the contrary, had even gotten angry and yelled at Brasfield when he hired Hunter Kennedy. It must have rankled to see an outsider brought in. Reader, who was older and more experienced than the young Kennedy, would have thought he had the job in the bag and been humiliated when he didn't get it.

Mitch added Troy Reader's name to the list. It seemed that Brasfield had gotten drunk and begged Reader's forgiveness, but Mitch wondered if, instead of mollifying Reader, that had merely added fresh fuel to his anger. He'd better have another talk with Reader.

Leaving Troy Reader for the moment, Mitch went back to Dane Kennedy and Hank Bregman, still his two best suspects. He would have to bring both men into the station for questioning. He didn't relish the thought, particularly in the case of the older man.

Mitch got to the high school the next morning fifteen minutes before the start of classes. Students were already milling around in the multi-purpose room through which Mitch passed to get to the principal's office. Stopping at the secretary's desk, he asked to see Troy Reader. The secretary called Reader out of the teachers' lounge.

Reader's equable smile wavered a little when he saw Mitch. "Hi, Chief."

"Can we talk in private?" Mitch asked.

Reader led him through the multi-purpose room, past the principal's office, and into a small room containing cold drink and snack machines.

As soon as they were out of sight of the students in the multi-purpose room, Reader said, "I hear you're the one who found Vian's body." He pressed his lips together. "What a terrible thing."

"Yes, it is. I know some of the teachers were worried about his absence, but I'm sure you were all surprised when you found out he was dead."

"Surprised! I was in shock. We all—everybody here, I mean—were stunned. It's incomprehensible."

"I'd like to clarify something you told me the other day," Mitch said.

He smoothed his mustache with one finger. "Yes?"

"You said you didn't want the vice-principal job."

His trying-to-be-helpful expression closed up and he looked blank. "That's right."

"You didn't apply for it, then?"

"Well, yes, I did apply, but only because Vian asked me to."

"Since our talk, I've heard otherwise. I heard that you were furious with Brasfield for passing you over for an outsider, that you went to Brasfield's office and yelled at him."

Reader's face reflected sudden comprehension and he examined Mitch with a frowning distrust. "Where did you hear that?"

"I can't say, but your confrontation with Brasfield was overheard by more than one person."

"Oh, well—I guess my feelings were hurt." Reader's voice was clipped, very defensive now. "If Vian hadn't practically told me I had the job, that would have been one thing. But he did, and naturally I expected it to be offered to me."

"The job you didn't really want."

"I might not have accepted it, but it was humiliating not to even be given the chance." Reader's voice bristled with defensive irritation and his eyes narrowed. "Chief Bushyhead, the bell will ring any second. You'll have to excuse me. I should be in my classroom."

Mitch, who was standing in the door of the vending machine room, didn't move. "Give me another minute or two, please."

Reader's hostile gaze raked him. "Okay."

"Had you gotten over feeling humiliated by the time you went to the conference in Oklahoma City, when Brasfield got drunk and apologized for passing you over in favor of Hunter Kennedy?"

Again he smoothed his white-blond mustache with one finger, looking reflective. "I didn't want to out-and-out contradict Hunter that day in the teachers' lounge, but I doubt that's what Vian meant."

"What was he talking about, then?"

He lifted his shoulders. "I don't know, but he wasn't looking at me when he said it."

The bell clanged loudly.

"I really must go, Chief Bushyhead."

Mitch stepped aside and let him pass.

20

Dee Bregman and her daughter watched her husband and father leave the farm in the back seat of the police car. After arguing a few moments, her husband had agreed to accompany the officers, but her father hadn't gone without a struggle. Dee had watched, horrified, as the two officers manhandled and handcuffed him and forced him into the car.

Fortunately, Cindy was at the kitchen table eating her breakfast, and hadn't realized anything unusual was happening until she heard her grandfather shouting threats. By the time the little girl reached the window, he was inside the car with the door shut.

The car drove away.

"Why are Grandpa and Daddy going with the policemen?" Cindy asked.

"It's nothing to worry about, sweetheart," Dee told her.

"The officers just want to talk to them. Have you finished your breakfast?"

Cindy craned her neck to catch a last glimpse of the police car. "No, but I'm not hungry."

"Then get dressed and we'll start on your schoolwork."

Cindy left obediently, but Dee stood at the window for a long time after her daughter was gone. She didn't know why the police had taken her father and Hank to town, but she couldn't allow herself to believe they'd had anything to do with that body in the pond. Although her father had complained often and bitterly about the noise from Brasfield's dance ground, she couldn't accept that he'd commit murder in order to stop the dances.

She wasn't so sure, however, that both men were above committing minor crimes. Whatever they'd done, though, it was all her father's fault. Hank would never get involved in criminal activity except to win Dane's approval, and Hank did seem to want that very much. Hank's recent interest in her father's books and pamphlets was the first thing Dee thought of when Hunter told her about those phone calls.

But she wasn't going to let Hank take all the blame for whatever stupidity he'd gotten involved in to get her father's attention.

Maybe it was time she had a talk with the police herself. But the thought of her father or Hank hearing about it scared her. Lately it was hard to predict what either of them might do.

Again, she procrastinated. She'd wait and see what came of their trip to the police station.

Dane Kennedy was telling Mitch that he was a victim of storm-trooper tactics and false arrest, and he wasn't going to take it lying down.

They were in the small interrogation room next to Mitch's office, with a wood table, two chairs, and a tape recorder. "You aren't under arrest, not yet," Mitch told him for the fourth time. "You are merely being held for questioning."

"I was hauled out of my house, forced into a police car, brought here, and put in this room with you standing in front of the only door. If that ain't arrest, what is it?"

"I'm asking you to cooperate in the investigation of the murder of Vian Brasfield."

"Murder? Why, that weren't nothing but an accident. That Injun got drunk as a skunk, fell in the water, and drowned."

"According to the medical examiner, he didn't drown. He was attacked and beaten to death. The killer caved in his skull. There was a lot of hate and rage behind that blow, Kennedy. Brasfield was dead before he ever hit the water in your pond."

Kennedy stared at him sullenly. "I told you I don't know nothing about it."

"I'm not accusing you—not yet, anyway. But sometimes people know more than they think they do. I need to go over a few things with you. Will you cooperate, Mr. Kennedy?"

Kennedy's face got red. "I already answered too many questions!" he stormed. "I don't feel like cooperating. You keep cooperating with the government, one day you find out you ain't got no rights left!" He folded his arms across his chest, glaring at Mitch. "If I ain't under arrest, then I can walk out of here anytime I want to, right?"

"I'll take you back home after you've made an official statement."

"If I can't walk out of here right now, then I'm under arrest and you're a liar!"

"If you try to leave before we have our talk," Mitch said, "I would have to exercise my legal right to detain you temporarily."

Kennedy banged on the table with both fists. "Detain, arrest! Words! It's the same thing."

Mitch was tired of arguing in circles with Dane Kennedy, who only became more firmly fixed in his twisted logic. "You have the right to have a lawyer present for the questioning, if you want."

"Any lawyer in this town would be in your hip pocket!"

Kennedy had an answer for everything. After some mumbling, he said, "Oh, hell, just get on with it so I can get out of here!"

Mitch walked to the table and pushed the on button of the tape recorder. "This is Mitch Bushyhead, chief of police, Buckskin, Oklahoma. It's Thursday, March tenth"—he glanced at his watch—"ten-twenty A.M. I'm here at the Buckskin Police Station with Dane Kennedy of Rural Route 2, Buckskin. Mr. Kennedy, I will be asking you some questions related to the police investigation into the homicide of Vian Brasfield of Buckskin. You have not been formally charged with any crime at this time. Do you wish to have an attorney present?"

Kennedy mumbled a few curses, but finally said, "I don't know nothing about Brasfield's death, so I don't need no shyster lawyer telling me to admit to something I didn't do. I know a few things about the law myself, and I want to say for that recording machine there that I am here under protest. My constitutional rights are being trampled underfoot. I don't know how that Injun got in my pond, but he had to break the law to get there. I got my place posted."

Trying to get Kennedy on the matter at hand, which was not about whether Brasfield had trespassed on Kennedy's land, but instead this investigation into a brutal double murder and attempted cover-up, Mitch said, "You have stated that you went to Vian Brasfield and told him the Indian dances on his property were disturbing your sleep and asked him to stop them."

"Wasted breath. He never meant to stop them dances."

"Did you and Brasfield argue?"

"Some people might call it that. I told him he was infringing on my right to privacy and peace in my own home. He said I was infringing on his right to practice his religion. Religion! You believe it? That's the kind of people we've got running our public schools. I'm thankful my granddaughter won't be exposed to such. Dancing all night in masks and wild garb and chanting in a foreign tongue ain't got nothin' to do with religion, to my way of thinking."

And a really weird way of thinking it was too, Mitch told himself. But he hadn't missed the reference to masks, which meant Dane Kennedy *had* seen the booger dance. "So you argued, and Brasfield didn't stop the dances. How did you feel about that?"

"Mad as hell! That's how I felt about it."

"What did you do about it?"

"Do? Nothing I could do. Knew coming to the cops wouldn't help. You're one of 'em, and you Injuns got the feds on your side too."

Mitch had a hard time imagining Dane Kennedy getting no satisfaction from Brasfield and doing nothing about it. The man was an overreaction just waiting to happen. "How many times did you complain to Brasfield?"

Kennedy rolled his eyes toward the ceiling. "Four, five. I lost count."

"Did these arguments ever escalate into a physical fight?"

He cackled. "Oh, he'd've liked that, he sure would. Made him mad, me calling him a savage ignoramus. The truth hurts, don't it? But he had to stand there and take it 'cause I was smart enough to have my shotgun with me every time I talked to him."

"Did you threaten him with the gun, point it at him?"

"No. Just held it down at my side. A little reminder to keep his distance, that I wasn't gonna take no guff from the likes of him. Once or twice, he got so worked up, I thought sure as hell he'd jump me anyway." He leaned closer to the recorder. "Wish he had. I'da blowed his brains out without a second thought."

His picture of Brasfield, so angry he came close to attacking a man with a gun, did not jibe with anybody else's description of the late principal. "According to Mrs. Brasfield—"

"That bitch pervert!"

"—Vian Brasfield never lost his temper." Of course, if anybody could have made Brasfield lose his cool, it would be Kennedy.

"Lying whore!" Kennedy was suddenly so agitated he could hardly sit still.

Mitch watched him in amazement. He'd sure punched one of Kennedy's hot buttons. "You don't seem to have a very high opinion of Brasfield's wife, Kennedy."

He scooted forward in the chair, planted his elbows on the table, took them off again, sat back, and stared at Mitch's chest. "Long as she keeps away from me, we'll do fine."

"What are you saying? Has she refused to keep away from you in the past?"

"Didn't say that."

"But I wasn't even aware that you knew the woman."

"That ain't what I call a woman!" He spat the words, then clamped his lips together and ran both hands over his face; he appeared to make a supreme effort to control himself. "I don't know her very well," he said sullenly, "but I seen her around."

"And concluded from that that she's a whore and a pervert?"

His eyes held a feral glitter. "I—I heard things. . . . Besides, she married an Injun, didn't she?"

"Not that it has any bearing on anything, but Brasfield was only one-eighth Cherokee."

"It's tainted blood, whether it's a bucketful or a drop!" He suddenly seemed to realize that he wasn't helping himself by saying these things to an Indian who conceivably had the power to arrest him. Briefly, judgment overcame irrationality. "Don't get me wrong. I ain't got no bones to pick with a red man as long as he keeps with his own kind. It's the mixing of the races that's wrong. If God hadn't wanted us to stay separate, he wouldn't have made us different colors."

Let's get off this before he pops a blood vessel—or I do— Mitch thought. "What do you think will happen to the dances, now that Brasfield's dead?"

"I hope it stops 'em."

"That would please you, would it?"

"Durn tootin'! It'd mean I could get a good night's sleep every night, like I used to before Brasfield started the dances. I ain't a young man no more. I need my rest."

Mitch took him over the same territory several times, but his answers didn't vary significantly. He talked to Brasfield about the dances four or five times, they argued, but neither man ever laid a hand on the other. Not that Brasfield, who was a few years younger and a lot heavier, wouldn't have tried it if Kennedy hadn't been carrying his shotgun—the great equalizer, Kennedy called it.

Mitch suspected Kennedy kept that gun within easy reach most of the time and that being confined in a room at the station without it made him feel naked and vulnerable to dangers on all sides. The fact that neither victim had been shot was the biggest problem Mitch had with trying to pin the murders on Kennedy. Another problem: How had Kennedy known Brasfield would be in the woods Friday morning?

"Did you know," Mitch asked, "that Vian Brasfield had been killing eagles illegally, to get the feathers for the dances?"

Kennedy studied Mitch with calculating eyes. "Don't surprise me none. Like I said, Injuns think they own the county."

"That doesn't answer my question. Did you know Brasfield was hunting eagles?"

"No. Never thought about it. Ain't no skin off my nose if he was."

"Can you remember where you were and what you were doing last Friday?"

"I already answered your questions about Friday night."

"Before that, I mean. Let's take it from, say, six-thirty Friday morning."

"That's about when I wake up, so I reckon I got up, made some coffee, and ate breakfast."

"Do you remember what you ate?"

"Hell's bells! What's that got to do with anything?"

Mitch forced a smile. "Humor me, and let's get through this, Kennedy. I want out of here as much as you do."

"Shit. I guess I ate cornflakes. That's what I have for breakfast five or six days a week."

"What did you do after breakfast?"

"I don't remember. Probably addressed envelopes. I've always got pamphlets to mail out."

"Do you come to town to mail your pamphlets?"

"There's too much to leave in the box and the mail carrier won't come up to the house and get my stuff," he huffed. "That's a federal employee for you." Mitch didn't blame the mail carrier in the least.

"Did you take mail to town last Friday?"

He heaved a put-upon sigh. "How am I supposed to remember that?"

"I should tell you that we have a witness who saw your truck in town Friday morning."

"Then I guess I was here. I usually get a big bunch of envelopes addressed and take 'em to the post office on Fridays."

"What time were you in town Friday?"

He sighed again. "Midmorning, I guess. Ten, ten-thirty." That was about the time the clinic had received the anonymous call.

"Did you make any phone calls while you were here?"

"Phone calls? I got a phone at home if I want to make any calls." His brow furrowed and his eyes narrowed. "I ain't stupid, Bushyhead. You can't pin a murder on me, so you're trying to say I made those phone calls to the Cherokee clinic. I told my daughter and I'm telling you, I didn't make no calls to that clinic!"

"Any idea who did?"

"No."

"Is there anyone who can verify that you were at home until late Friday morning?"

He thought about it. "That's the morning Dee and Hank and Cindy left real early."

"Where did they go?"

"Didn't ask. All I know is they took two cars. Dee and Cindy came back with a trunk full of groceries. Hank got home just about suppertime."

"In other words, neither you nor your son-in-law has a verifiable alibi for Friday morning."

"I ain't Hank's keeper. You can talk to him. As for me, I didn't do nothing wrong, so I don't need no alibi."

Just for the hell of it, Mitch asked him a final question. "How can I get in touch with your wife, Kennedy? Or is she your ex-wife?"

He leaned on the table as he came to his feet. "I don't know where that bitch is, and I don't care."

"When was the last time you heard from her?"

"The day she walked out of my house, left two half-grown kids without a mother. No decent woman does a thing like that. As for me, I was glad to be shed of her. That was seventeen years ago, and I ain't never seen or heard of her since."

"What about your children? Has she been in contact with them?"

"Not that I know of. Never even sent 'em a Christmas card."

"That must've been real hard on them."

"Way I look at it, it was just as well she didn't make contact. She was a piss-poor example for the kids, anyway. They were better off without her."

Mitch doubted that his children thought so. "Your son suggested that she might have left because she disagreed with your political activities."

He snorted. "Hunter don't know nothing about it. He was just twelve when she lit out."

"Didn't you ever try to find her?"

"Never. She left *me* for some—" His face twisted, as though he were in pain. It was the first sign Mitch had seen that he might have regretted his wife's desertion, at least in the beginning.

"For some what?"

He shook his head. "Some wild notion or other," he said vaguely. "Finding herself, some such damned fool nonsense. Probably got that from one of those women's magazines she was always reading." His eyes glittered as he looked at Mitch. "She walked away from her *responsibilities*."

21

Hank Bregman was even less helpful than his father-in-law. Hearing that Brasfield had probably been murdered Friday morning, rather than Friday evening when Bregman was at work, didn't seem to faze him. He said that he had gone to Muskogee Friday morning to hook up with a friend who introduced him to men at a couple of companies who were currently hiring and training factory workers. The service station job didn't pay enough to support a family, Bregman said, and besides, he didn't like working nights.

Bregman was unclear about what time he'd left home. When Mitch informed him that his father-in-law had said he left quite early, Bregman agreed that could be the case. His wife and daughter were leaving, and he didn't like staying in that "tin can" by himself, so he headed for Muskogee, stopped at a roadside café for breakfast en route before going to his friend's house. He gave Mitch his friend's name and phone number, and after Bregman left the station, Mitch called the number.

Bregman's friend's recollection was that Bregman had arrived at his house about ten-thirty Friday morning. Muskogee was close to an hour's drive from Buckskin. Even with the breakfast stop, Bregman had had time to commit the murders before leaving town.

But Mitch still couldn't come up with a motive. The dances at Brasfield's place had disturbed Bregman's sleep too, prior to his taking the night job. But he'd left it to Kennedy to lodge a complaint with Brasfield.

Bregman had been working Friday nights for the last six weeks. Even if having his sleep interrupted, before he started working nights, was enough to spur him to commit murder, why wait six weeks to do it? Furthermore, Bregman denied any knowledge of Brasfield's eagle hunting, which, if true, meant he couldn't have known Brasfield would be in the woods Friday morning. Unless he'd followed Brasfield when he left his house, which Dane Kennedy or anyone else could have done.

Bregman was looking less and less like a suspect, not that he'd ever been a really viable one.

After the interrogations, Mitch sent Duck to take the men back home, then went to his office to write up the reports for the case file. When he opened a drawer to find a pen, he saw the picture of the young woman in its small circle holder. He'd tossed it in the drawer after several people he'd asked could not identify the woman, deciding it wasn't relevant to the murder investigation anyway.

Taking it out now, he held it up to the window to study it. The picture was a real mystery in itself.

How *had* this picture ended up in the gravel where Walsh and probably Brasfield had parked their trucks Friday morning?

Mitch studied the young woman's thin, unsmiling face. Something about the eyes seemed unutterably sad. Who was she? Mitch was certain he'd never seen her before. He took the picture out to the dispatcher's desk. Shelly was out on a call, and Helen had the common room to herself.

"Helen, you given any more thought as to who this might be?"

Helen took the picture and looked at it again. "Hard to tell," she mused. "This is awful small. I might have seen her somewhere, but if I did it wasn't lately."

"This could be an old picture. Could she be somebody you went to school with?"

She thought about it, then shook her head and handed the picture back to Mitch. "I really can't be sure one way or the other. It drives me crazy to try to place a face or think of a name that I should remember, but can't."

"I know the feeling," Mitch said. "I threw this in my desk and had forgotten it. No evidence it's connected to either Walsh or Brasfield, but I'd still like to know who she is so I could put it out of my mind for good. Loose ends bug me. I think I'll show this to a couple more people." If he came up blank again, he'd accept that the picture had no relationship to the murders.

"I'll hold the fort here till Duck or Shelly gets back."

"When you get time, could you help us out with some transcribing? Do whatever you can and Shelly can finish it up."

"Kennedy's and Bregman's statements?"

"Yes."

She stood. "I'll get right on it, Chief. This ought to be interesting."

"That's one word for it," Mitch told her.

"All the time you were questioning Bregman, that old man paced around in here like a caged bear, muttering to himself. It was downright eerie."

Mitch pulled up in front of the Walsh house. Three cars were parked in the driveway. He'd read the funeral notice in the morning's weekly edition of the *Buckskin Banner*. Arnett Walsh's service had been held Tuesday in Yukon, where Walsh was buried. Mrs. Walsh would probably be moving soon, to someplace where she would be closer to relatives.

The woman who came to the door was about thirty-five, medium tall with a trim figure and a thick mane of red hair. "I'd like to see Mrs. Walsh."

"I'm her sister. Come on in. I'll get her for you."

Another youngish woman hovered in the hallway behind the sister. She was taller and heavier, with a pretty face. Both women left Mitch in the living room and went to get Arnett Walsh's wife.

A few minutes later, a third young woman entered the living room alone. She had blond hair, but Mitch could see a resemblance to the redhead. Same blue-green eyes. Mrs. Walsh wore a loose-fitting dress to accommodate her pregnancy. "Hello. I'm Linda Walsh."

"Mitch Bushyhead, ma'am. Thank you for seeing me. I know this is a rough time for you."

"You have no idea," she sighed.

"I lost my wife a couple of years ago."

"Oh, I'm sorry. Then you do know how it is." She struggled to smile and placed a hand on her stomach, as if to protect the child within. "In a way. But your wife probably wasn't murdered."

Mitch shook his head and wondered if that could really be much worse than watching the woman you love go through months of pain before dying of cancer.

"I'll get through this," she said. "I have to for the baby."

"Yes, ma'am."

"If it's a boy, I'll name him Arnett. We had a disagreement about that, you know, as much as Arnett would disagree about anything. I wanted to name our first son after his father, but Arnett hated his name. Now—well, I don't think he'd mind, do you?"

"No, ma'am."

She glanced around the room. It was neat, but there was nothing on the walls, no little homey touches. Evidently the Walshes hadn't lived there long enough for Linda Walsh to put her stamp on it. Now she never would.

"I couldn't live in this house by myself," she said, "but my sister and cousin are staying with me a few days. They'll help me pack and get ready to move."

"Back to Yukon?"

"Yes. I have a couple of cousins there and a lot of friends, and my sister—the one who answered the door—lives just thirty minutes away. We—I haven't lived here long enough to have made any close friends in Buckskin. I couldn't stay, anyway, not where Arnett was killed." She moved toward the sofa and sank down wearily. All at once, she looked a little frightened. "Have you come to tell me something about the murder?"

Mitch took a chair facing her. "I don't have anything solid yet, but we're working full-time on your husband's case along with the murder of the high school principal."

"I heard about that," she murmured. "You don't think about things like this happening in a small town, but I guess violence is everywhere. I didn't know the principal, but the paper said he had a wife and two daughters. I feel so sorry for them. I know what they're going through."

"Did your husband ever mention Vian Brasfield?"

She studied Mitch. "That's the principal's name, isn't it?" He nodded. "No, I don't recall ever hearing that name before I read it in the newspaper. Do you think Arnett knew him?"

"I don't know, but one of the avenues of investigation we're following is that Vian Brasfield was the eagle killer your husband was looking for."

Her blue-green eyes widened. "But he was the high school principal. Everybody seemed to like him."

"He was part Cherokee and sponsored eagle dances on property he owned in the country. We think your husband and Brasfield may have run into each other in the woods Friday morning."

Her brow furrowed. "I don't understand. The paper said Mr. Brasfield's body was found in a farm pond."

"It's possible he was taken there after he was killed. These are all just possibilities at this point, ma'am. I came by to ask you to take a look at something." He took the picture from his shirt pocket. "This was found in the area where your husband parked his truck at the edge of the woods." He handed her the picture.

She studied it gravely.

"Do you recognize it?"

She shook her head. "I've never seen this before."

"And you don't know the woman?"

"No." She fingered the smooth disk. "This looks like it came off a chain of some kind, doesn't it? It's like a memento. Somebody's probably sad about losing it." She handed it back.

"Thank you. I wanted to be sure. Frankly, good leads are pretty scarce at this point. We're following up on anything and everything."

Without warning, tears filled her eyes and trickled down her cheeks. She seemed to take no notice, made no effort to wipe them away. "You will catch the person who killed Arnett, won't you?"

"Yes, ma'am. It may take a while, but we'll catch him."

Mitch left, still hearing the promise echoing in his mind. He hoped he could live up to it, but at that moment the words sounded empty to him.

Nicole Brasfield leaned against the high back of a chair to look out the bedroom window. Outside, sunlight slanted through the big, leafing oaks in the backyard, the rays so bright that, even at this distance, she could see individual blades of grass. Maybe they wouldn't have another really cold snap, after all. Spring was her favorite time of the year; when the green of grass and trees was fresh and rich, not rain-starved as it would be later in the summer, and her favorite flowers bloomed—daffodils, tulips, irises, and forsythia. In spring, new beginnings seemed possible, though less and less so for Nicole these last few years.

Spring was not the time for funerals. This morning at the cemetery, the open grave had seemed to her a desecration of nature. She had glanced at the casket suspended over the gaping hole only once, and the most excruciatingly raw twist of suppressed pain had gone through her, and she'd had to grab hold of her elder daughter's arm to keep from falling. She had known, in that moment, even while fear of the future gripped her, that she felt no regret over Vian's death. She would never be his victim again.

Nicole, what's done is done. We will not discuss it, ever. We will forget and go on.

But she had not forgotten. She had tried to live for her daughters, but even that had left her empty. She knew that Vian hadn't forgotten, either. The few times she had tried to discuss it with him, he'd gone pale and ordered her not to speak of it, as though the mere words threatened him. So she had kept the words inside, like sores festering in the musty dark, away from the healing air.

She went to the bed, lay down on top of the coverlet on her side, and stared into the sunlit yard, the grass, trees, flowers suddenly blurred. As though she viewed it through a pane of cheap, wavy glass that separated her from the world. Even at those times when she had lost her temper and given Vian a piece of her mind, she went so far and no farther, never beyond the glass barrier. Her anger had seemed almost manufactured, as if she were an actor in a play.

The barrier had been there for so long that finally, when a time came that she no longer cared what Vian wanted and could have spoken of the things that Vian wouldn't hear, it was too late. The sores inside her had dried up and scarred over and had been shoved into the bog of forgetfulness. The thought of reaching into the morass and poking around in the old wounds, *feeling* again, terrified her.

22

The white Pontiac was parked in the Brasfield driveway. Mitch knocked and a small, white-haired woman whom Mitch didn't recognize came to the door.

"I'm Mitch Bushyhead with the Buckskin police."

"Yes, I know who you are." She opened the storm door. "I'm Pearl Anderson, Nicole's neighbor. I came over to sit at the house during the funeral this morning."

Mitch had forgotten they were burying Brasfield that day. "I'm sorry. It slipped my mind. I guess Mrs. Brasfield isn't back yet."

"Oh, yes, she's been home a little while. The daughters are here, too. They're all lying down for a rest. I insisted on it, said I'd stay and fix lunch for them." She lowered her voice and added in a confidential tone, "Usually people from church provide a meal after the funeral, but the Brasfields never went to church."

"I wanted to talk to Mrs. Brasfield, but if she's resting . . ."

She gestured with a small, blue-veined hand. "Come on in. I'll have lunch ready in a few minutes and then I'll let her know you're here." Mitch followed her quick, birdlike steps down the hall to the kitchen. "I'd rather not disturb her until it's time to eat, if you don't mind waiting. Would you like a cup of coffee or a glass of iced tea?"

"Tea would be nice, ma'am." Mitch pulled out one of the stools at the breakfast bar and sat.

She placed a glass in front of him. "How about a piece of pie? I made cherry and apple, and there's only the four of us for lunch." She was whispering now. "The daughters told me there was just a handful at the funeral, mostly people from the high school, but no one wanted to come back to the house." She made a clucking sound. "Now that I think about it, the Brasfields never had many visitors at the house, either. It's a shame not to have any more friends than that." She picked up a ladle. "Which do you prefer, cherry or apple?"

"Apple," Mitch said, thinking about the sparse turnout for Brasfield's funeral. He was surprised that the Cherokees who took part in the dances with Brasfield hadn't attended the service. He suspected they knew Brasfield's wife would not appreciate their presence.

As she placed a piece of apple pie on a plate and carried it to the bar, she said, "Nicole told me that some Cherokees wanted to bring a medicine man to the house to do some kind of cleansing ceremony. You'd know about that, I suppose."

"Actually, ma'am, I don't know much more about it than you do. I think the medicine man spreads cedar branches around and says a prayer."

She looked sad. "I think Vian would have liked that, but Nicole turned them down in no uncertain terms."

Mitch took a bite of pie. It was delicious. Reminded him of the apple pies his mother used to make. "How is Mrs. Brasfield holding up?"

Pearl Anderson perched on a stool, facing him. "A little too well, if you ask me. The daughters came home from the service with eyes nearly swollen shut from crying, but Nicole was as calm as you please. Didn't look like she'd shed a tear. Some people just can't give in to grief. I don't know if it's pride or what."

Mitch didn't know, either. In this case, it could just be that Nicole wasn't grieving. "This is the best apple pie I've had in a long time, ma'am."

She looked pleased, but waved away the compliment. "I raised four kids, Chief Bushyhead, so I've made plenty of pies in my time. Would you care for another piece?"

Mitch pushed his plate aside. "Thanks, but I couldn't."

She got up to check something in the oven. "I'll give the casserole another couple of minutes," she said, coming back to the bar. "I'm worried about Nicole, you know. The girls will be all right. Tears are healing. But when a person holds in their grief like Nicole does, they're bound to break sooner or later."

"Pearl?" There was the sound of muffled footsteps in the hall. "Who are you talking to?" Nicole Brasfield, in a chenille robe and house slippers, came into the kitchen. "Oh, it's you, Chief Bushyhead." Her face, without makeup, was pale and drawn, and a crease ran down her right cheek where she'd lain on that side.

Mitch stood. "Sorry to disturb you, Mrs. Brasfield."

"I was going to let you rest as long as possible," Pearl put in. "Chief Bushyhead said he didn't mind waiting."

Nicole went to the sink and got a glass of water, which she brought over to the bar. She remained standing. "I wasn't able to really rest, anyway. There's so much to do. Have you learned something about Vian's death?"

Studying her face, Mitch decided that the neighbor was right. Nicole did look as cool as a cucumber. Her face was almost too still, masklike, except for faint tension around her mouth.

"Nothing definite yet," Mitch said, "but I'd like to ask you a couple of questions, if you feel up to it."

"I'll just wait in the living room," Pearl Anderson said, and left the kitchen. Her footsteps faded so quickly that Mitch wondered if she was standing in the hall, eavesdropping.

"What is it you want to know?" Nicole asked.

"I need some information for the case file. Did your husband have life insurance?"

If the question fazed her, she didn't show it. "Yes, through the state education association."

"Do you know how much coverage he had?"

She frowned and set her glass on the bar. She wiped her mouth with the back of her hand, then clutched the edge of the bar with both hands. "Two hundred thousand dollars," she said tightly.

Enough to provide a nice nest egg for a woman whose husband wanted a divorce—*if* Brasfield had wanted one. Nicole said they hadn't talked of divorce, and Mitch had no way of proving otherwise.

"That should be helpful," he said.

She looked at him coldly. "It won't go very far. This house isn't paid off, nor my car."

Mitch fished the picture of the unknown young woman from his shirt pocket. "We found this near the woods, where we think your husband parked his pickup Friday morning. We're trying to identify her." He held the disk out to her.

She didn't take it, but she looked at it for a long moment, and her jaw seemed to tighten, but maybe that was Mitch's imagination.

"Do you recognize her?"

She looked at the picture for another moment, then shook her head. "No. Are you saying this belonged to Vian?" Did she think it was an old girlfriend, or maybe a not-so-old one?

"No, ma'am."

Without warning, the little color left in her face drained away and, before Mitch could get around the bar, she slid to the floor, knocking over a stool, which clattered loudly, like gunshots.

Pearl Anderson ran into the kitchen. "What happened?"

Mitch was kneeling beside Nicole Brasfield. "She fainted. Get a damp cloth."

Pearl opened a couple of drawers, found a dish towel, and wet it at the sink. Mitch folded it and laid it across Nicole's forehead. She moaned, already coming around.

"It's all right, Mrs. Brasfield," Mitch said. "You fainted."

She struggled to sit up, dislodging the towel, which fell to the floor. Mitch helped her to her feet, her weight heavy against him. Nicole Brasfield was a substantial woman. "Let's get her to the couch so she can lie down."

With Pearl holding one arm and Mitch the other, they led

her into the living room. "I—I feel so foolish," Nicole murmured.

"Nonsense," the neighbor said. "You've been under a great amount of stress."

They helped her to lie down and Pearl arranged an afghan over her. She clutched it beneath her chin and shivered.

"I'll go now and let you rest," Mitch said. "I'm sorry to have bothered you."

Nicole had closed her eyes and didn't respond. Pearl Anderson followed Mitch to the door. "Didn't I tell you?" she whispered as Mitch opened the door.

He glanced back. "What?"

She nodded solemnly. "I told you she'd break sooner or later."

"Yes, I guess you did."

"Nicole's always been standoffish, never even had any women friends that I know of. She kept to herself, minded her own business. You could never know how she felt about anything. But it's not natural for a wife not to cry when she loses her husband."

"No, ma'am," Mitch said.

The neighbor was probably right, he mused as he drove away from the Brasfield house. Nicole had kept a stiff upper lip for days, held it all together so that she could get through telling her daughters about their father's death, and then the funeral, and finally it had all been too much for her.

23

The investigations into Walsh's and Brasfield's backgrounds did not turn up a single clue pointing to other potential suspects. Except for Brasfield's obsession with his Cherokee culture and his tendency to confide in a woman other than his wife, both men had led ordinary lives. Outwardly, at least. Walsh would be grieved and missed for a long time by a loving wife, as would Brasfield—by his daughters and Virginia Craig, if not his wife.

Out of sheer frustration, Mitch made an appointment with Brasfield's daughters Friday afternoon. When all else failed, you turned over every rock. They came to his office at three o'clock, as scheduled, introducing themselves as Martha and Kate. Martha was tall and sturdily built and looked a lot like her mother. Kate was smaller and quite pretty, with dark hair and eyes, a genetic throwback who looked more Cherokee than her father. Both appeared to be in their early to mid-twenties, and neither was married.

After establishing that this trip was the first time either young woman had visited her parents since Christmas, Mitch asked if they were in frequent contact with their father.

"He or Mother wrote or called us every week," Martha said.

"Which one contacted you more often?"

Kate glanced at her sister. "Usually it was Mother. She had more spare time than Dad. I'd call Dad at school if I didn't hear from him for a few weeks. He was always full of information about the Cherokees and I enjoyed hearing him be so enthusiastic about something."

"Did you notice a difference in him when he started researching the Cherokees?" Mitch asked.

"Definitely," Kate said, and Martha nodded in agreement. "Before that, I couldn't find much to talk to Dad about. I'd tell him about myself, my job and friends, and ask what he had been doing. He usually said 'Just working' or 'Same ol', same ol',' and that would be the end of it."

"Your mother was more forthcoming, then?" Mitch asked.

"In some ways, yes," Martha responded. "She never talked about anything important, just chitchat. Sometimes she complained about Dad, mostly about his being gone so much doing research. But at least there were none of those awkward silences we used to have with Dad. It was like he was . . . well, depressed, I guess."

"Would you say your parents had a good marriage?"

They looked at each other, each apparently waiting for the other to speak. Finally, it was Kate who said, "I don't know. It was the only marriage I knew much about, so I had nothing to compare it to. In the last few years, I've realized that there was a lot of silence in our house." She cast a smile in her sister's direction, as if asking forgiveness for revealing family secrets. "Mother is a very private person, not at all demonstrative. They didn't talk much. Really talk, I mean. While we were at home, most of their conversation seemed to revolve around Martha and me, our activities and friends. Beyond that, they'd talk about what Mother was fixing for dinner or what time she could expect Dad home, things like that."

"Do you know if they ever considered divorce?"

The question seemed to make Martha uncomfortable. "Not that I know of," she said.

"I never heard anything about that, either," Kate agreed.

"In your recent conversations with your father," Mitch said, "did he give any indication that he had any enemies? Did he have a problem, or a confrontation, with anyone? Maybe somebody at work?"

"He never mentioned anything like that to me," Martha said.

Kate looked more pensive. "He said once that the man who lives on the farm west of Dad's property had complained about the Cherokee dances. Can't remember his name."

"Dane Kennedy?"

Her expression cleared. "Yes, that's the name. Dad said this Dane Kennedy had made veiled threats, but Dad thought he was kind of nuts, so I don't think he paid much attention."

"He didn't seem worried about what Kennedy might do?"

"No," Kate said, and Martha agreed that her father had never indicated to her that he was particularly worried about it.

"Did he ever mention hunting eagles?"

Kate expelled a breath. "Mother told us that you think

Dad was killing eagles. If he was, he didn't say anything to her, or to Martha or me about it."

Mitch could see that this was going nowhere. "How is your mother doing?"

There was a silence, and finally Martha said, "She was doing fine until the last day or two."

"She fainted when I was there yesterday," Mitch said. "I hope I didn't upset her."

Kate shook her head. "No, I think it just finally hit her that Dad is really gone. Mrs. Anderson, the neighbor you met the day of the funeral, says it's a good thing, that she has to grieve and get beyond it. Mother's been spending a lot of time in her room. She says she's resting. Otherwise, she just seems distracted."

"She's started to think about everything she has to do now," Kate went on. "Dad always paid the bills, handled tax returns, took care of business things. I think Mother feels overwhelmed."

Martha gave a sad little smile. "It's odd, but I always thought of Mother as being so capable. She never seemed to get very emotional about anything. It took Dad's death to break down her defenses."

"She wasn't always so . . . well, reserved," Kate said suddenly. "I can remember, until I was eight or nine years old, she was very loving. She used to read to us a lot and give us hugs." She shook her head. "Gosh, I'd forgotten that until now. I can remember her squeezing me so tight that I'd have to tell her to stop."

"That was just a phase she went through," Martha corrected. She looked at Mitch. "I'm older than Kate, and as I remember it, she acted that way for several months when I was about eight. Before that, she was pretty reserved, and after a few months she reverted to type. She'd probably read a book or something that made her feel guilty, feel that she wasn't a good mother. So she tried to change, but it didn't last."

Kate was staring at her sister. "You almost sound like you resent her."

"Maybe I do," Martha said with a toss of her head. "I feel like I don't know Mother. She keeps everything to herself. Face it, Kate, neither one of us opens up to people easily. I think that comes from being raised by our mother."

Kate looked down at her hands.

"May I ask how old you both are?" Mitch asked.

"I'm twenty-five," Martha said, "and Kate's twenty-three."

If the "phase" Nicole went through occurred when Martha was eight; that would make it seventeen years ago. Mitch had heard that figure before in this investigation.

He thanked the Brasfield daughters for coming in and escorted them out of the station. Returning to his office, he got out the Brasfield case file. According to his notes, there had been some trouble in the Brasfield marriage sixteen or seventeen years ago. The same time that Nicole's behavior toward her daughters had changed. She became more attentive, more loving for several months. Was she afraid of losing them in a divorce?

That didn't seem likely. Nicole would have had to be judged unfit to lose custody of her children, and there had never been the slightest hint that she had ever neglected or abused them, unless you could call being a cold fish abuse.

Saturday morning, Emily told Mitch that she and Kevin were going to a party at a school friend's house that night.

They were doubling with Temple and her current boyfriend, and after she assured him that the classmate's parents would chaperon, he agreed to add thirty minutes to Emily's curfew.

Then he phoned Rhea at the clinic. It had been a full week since he'd talked to her, which he thought showed a lot of restraint on his part. She seemed pleased to hear from him. He explained that he'd just learned his daughter would be gone until late that night and asked if she'd like to go out for dinner and a movie.

She sighed. "This has been one hellacious week. I'd much rather cook dinner at home. You could pick up a video on the way over."

"Even better," agreed Mitch, whose own week had not been exactly a day at the park. "What kind of movies do you like?"

"Something lighthearted. I see enough tragedy at work. I'd rather not have to witness more in the guise of entertainment."

"I knew we were kindred spirits," Mitch said. "I couldn't agree with you more."

She met him at the door with a glass of champagne in one hand. She handed him the glass at the same time that he caught her around the waist and pulled her against him for a kiss. A few drops of champagne spilled on them, and she was laughing when his lips covered hers.

The kiss was sweet and full of longing—on her side as well as his, Mitch sensed.

Eventually she broke away, saying, "We're giving the neighbors a show." She wore flowing silk pants and a matching tunic, soft green with big yellow flowers. Her hair, parted on one side, fell loose and shining around her shoulders. She smiled at him with her head cocked to one side and tucked her hair behind her ear. She was the loveliest thing Mitch had seen in a long time.

He grinned and shut the door. "It'll give them something new to talk about."

She had set up a card table in the den at the back of her house, beside a bay window that looked out on a patio and yard surrounded by a privacy fence. He could make out the fence in the light from two outside wrought-iron pole lamps. The table was spread with a white cloth. Beside each white, ivy-ringed plate was a linen napkin in a silver ring.

The den was paneled in ash with a brick fireplace on one side. Brass andirons gleamed and the hearth had been swept clean now that the wood-burning season was past.

The curving sectional sofa that was placed facing the fireplace was a rich, deep wine color. An open bottle of champagne in an ice bucket sat on a low table between the couch and the fireplace. A couple of books lay on the small table at the end of the sofa, as if Rhea sat there to read. An ancient rifle and two handmade bows hung on the wall. They'd belonged to her grandfather, Rhea explained. On another wall was a large photograph of a Cherokee couple in their fifties, Rhea's late parents. Brass pots of greenery sat on the hearth and on a stand beside a side window. Mitch remembered from a previous visit that Rhea had several green plants in her kitchen as well.

"Make yourself at home," she said, picking up their plates, "while I get dinner."

Mitch settled with a satisfied sigh against the curving arm of the couch and drank his champagne. It pleased him to

know that she must have bought it especially for this occasion.

After a few minutes Rhea returned to the den, set their full
plates on the table, and went back for the bread basket. Dinner consisted of cucumber and onion salad, grilled tuna
steaks, and a medley of new potatoes, broccoli, squash, and
carrots sautéed in buttery sauce. The whole wheat rolls were
feather-light and still warm from the oven.

The food was better than anything they could have gotten
in a Buckskin restaurant. "I didn't know you were such a good
cook," Mitch remarked. "When did you have time to learn?"

A teasing sparkle lit her dark eyes. "It's a natural talent,
darlin'," she told him, mimicking Mitch's response when she
had complimented his kissing, and they laughed.

"Is this your birthday or something?"

She looked perplexed. "No, why?"

He touched his glass. "The champagne."

"Oh, that. I'm just celebrating getting through this week."

"A tough one, huh?"

She nodded. "I found cancer in two patients, both of them
in their forties. It's too far advanced for either of them to be
saved. About all I can do now is make their last months as
comfortable as possible." She got up to get the champagne
bottle and refilled both their glasses. "I know your week
couldn't have been good, either, with two murders to investigate. Have you made an arrest yet?"

He shook his head. "Evidence is scarce as hen's teeth."

"Would it help to talk about it?"

"No. My officers and I have talked until we're sick of hearing each other. I'd rather talk about anything else."

"Good, and I don't want to talk about my work, either. What movie did you bring?"

"*Throw Mama from the Train*. Billy Crystal and Danny DeVito. I've seen it twice and laughed till my stomach hurt both times. Have you seen it?"

"No."

After dinner, they moved to the couch. Rhea inserted the video into the VCR, turned it on, and came to curl up in the curve of Mitch's arm with her head on his shoulder. The film was the perfect choice. Rhea found it as funny as he did, and when she laughed, her breath was sweet and warm against his neck.

As the closing credits scrolled across the screen, Rhea stretched, as languidly as a cat, then twisted around, facing him, and wrapped her arms around him as they kissed. This time she didn't pull away until they were both breathless and trembling with desire.

"I want you," she murmured.

Mitch was afraid to believe his ears. "What did you say?" His lips brushed her brow.

"I want you in my bed."

He needed no second invitation. He lifted her and carried her to the bedroom with the queen-sized bed covered by a puffy white comforter. Pale light fell through the open doorway from the hall and they undressed, watching each other with hungry eyes. The loving was wild and greedy the first time. The second time it was slow and savoring.

Afterward, Mitch pulled her back against him, spoon fashion. "You surprised me," he murmured. "I didn't expect this."

"Are you complaining?"

"No, *ma'am*."

"In my rare idle moments this week, I thought about you and hoped you'd call again."

He chuckled. "Honey, you'll never know how hard it was for me to wait a week so I wouldn't seem too pushy. You said not to rush things."

"Hmm, I did say that, didn't I? Maybe being reminded twice in recent days that life is uncertain changed my mind. Whatever it was, tonight everything felt different. All through the movie, I was thinking about making love with you."

"Honestly?" Mitch had had the same thoughts, but he'd been sure she was totally engrossed in the movie.

"It's true."

He laughed. "I was having the same fantasy. We could have skipped the movie altogether."

"No, the anticipation was delicious."

He buried his face in her hair. "Tell me something. What would you have done if I hadn't called and asked you out tonight?"

"I'd have called you, of course—eventually."

Later, they fell asleep, wrapped in each other's arms, the comforter and sheets tangled beneath them.

Later still, Rhea stirred and lifted her head to look down at him.

He opened his eyes to find her smiling. "You're beautiful," he murmured.

She chuckled. "You're not so bad yourself, babe. But could you move off the comforter. I'm getting cold."

He sat up, held his arm up so that the light from the hallway illuminated the dial of his wristwatch. He longed to crawl under the comforter with Rhea and lose himself once again in the soft, sweet smell of her. But it was a few minutes after midnight. He groaned. "I can't believe it's so late. Emily will be home in half an hour."

Turning on her side, she snuggled into the comforter and ran her fingers caressingly down his arm. "You should probably get home ahead of her."

"Yeah."

She watched him dress, her eyelids growing heavy. "Be sure the door locks behind you," she said.

He bent to kiss her. "Good night, sugar. Thank you."

"Mmmm," she mumbled. "It was my pleasure."

24

Gus was sweeping the common room Monday morning when Mitch got there. "Hey, Chief. How was your weekend?"

"Superb."

Helen, who was working a crossword puzzle at the dispatcher's desk, looked around, both her heavily lined eyebrows rising a half inch higher than usual. "That sounds intriguing. What was so special about it?"

Mitch grinned at her. "Mind your own business."

"Ah-ha, there's a woman in the picture."

"You got you a new girlfriend, Chief?" Gus asked. He leaned against the broom handle, deposited a plug of tobacco in his cheek, and chewed contemplatively.

"Gus," Mitch said, ignoring the question, "prisoners are not supposed to be in possession of tobacco products."

"Heck, I know that. But I ain't a prisoner right now. I'm an employee of the city."

"Excuse me if I don't see the distinction," Mitch muttered.

"I ain't got any tobacco in my cell," Gus said defensively. "Helen keeps it in her desk for me and lets me have a chew while I'm working."

Mitch looked at Helen. "What is wrong with this picture?"

She lifted her shoulders in a negligent shrug.

"This isn't the Holiday Inn, in case you hadn't noticed. Gus's little stay with us is supposed to be punishment for all those unpaid traffic citations."

"He's locked up when he's not working around here," Helen said. "That's punishment enough."

Mitch threw up his hands. Actually, he knew Gus was enjoying his thirty-day sentence. He bellyached about the iron cot in his cell, furnished with a paper-thin mattress, claimed he hardly got a wink of sleep, but Mitch heard snores from Gus's cell several times a day. Furthermore, Gus was warm and dry and Helen or an officer brought him meals from one of Buckskin's cafés three times a day. In fact, on average Gus was eating better than Mitch was. Now he had Helen holding his tobacco for him.

Gus shifted his cud to the other cheek and gave Mitch a snaggletoothed grin. "Don't you worry, Chief. I'm learning my lesson."

Mitch had no doubt that he was learning a lesson, but he wondered if it was the one the city intended. "Are Duck and Shelly on patrol?" he asked Helen.

"Yes," she said, "and I finished transcribing all the interviews on the Walsh and Brasfield cases. I put them on your desk."

"Good." Mitch helped himself to coffee from the common room urn and headed for his office. He closed the door and glanced through the stack of typed pages Helen had left there, wondering if somewhere in the morass of words there was a clue that would break the murder cases wide open. If so, he didn't find it.

Helen buzzed him and he picked up the phone. "There's a Dee Bregman here to see you, Chief."

What could Dane Kennedy's daughter have to say to the police? "Send her in." Mitch hung up and went around the desk to open the office door.

Dee Bregman, in jeans and red T-shirt, sidled in, looking as if she already regretted whatever impulse had brought her there.

"Have a seat, Mrs. Bregman," Mitch greeted her. "What can I do for you?"

She took the nearest chair and waited for Mitch to sit down behind his desk before she confirmed Mitch's first impression. "I really don't know what I'm doing here," she said. "It seemed like a good idea earlier."

Mitch laid both arms on the stack of transcribed interviews and gave her what he hoped was a disarming smile. "What can I do for you?" he repeated.

She combed her short, shaggy brown hair back with her fingers. "My husband told me that you think Vian Brasfield was murdered Friday morning instead of Friday night. I thought—well, I wanted to tell you that Hank couldn't have had anything to do with that."

"You can give him an alibi?"

She looked unhappy and shook her head. "No, but I know Hank. He may be getting sucked into Dad's anti-government beliefs, but he would never kill somebody just to get Dad's approval."

It was a thought that had never occurred to Mitch, but evidently it had occurred to Dee Bregman, her denials to the contrary. "Your husband isn't under arrest, ma'am."

"I know, but he wouldn't tell me what all you questioned him about, and I was afraid . . ." Her voice trailed off. She drew in a breath of air before continuing. "I realize now it was silly of me to expect you'd believe me. I'm his wife, I'm supposed to take his side. But Hank is not a murderer, Chief Bushyhead."

Mitch fingered the top page of the typed interviews. "What about your father? Would he kill a man for disturbing his sleep and trespassing on his property?"

She hesitated, then lifted her shoulders wearily. "I honestly don't think so."

"Frankly, ma'am, you don't sound too sure."

"Dad's gotten real strange the last couple of years. Now he thinks he's making some kind of stand for freedom by refusing to pay his property taxes. And I won't deny he's fired off a few shots to scare off trespassers. But he just fired into the sky, he wasn't trying to hit anybody. I don't think he's stupid enough to kill somebody."

Mitch tried to look encouraging, to keep her talking.

After a moment, she asked, "Do you think my father killed Brasfield?"

"We're still investigating. If you really want to help your husband, tell him if he knows anything he hasn't already told us, he should come and see me right away."

She looked alarmed. "What is it you think he hasn't told you?"

Mitch attempted to be cagey. "I'm not at liberty to reveal that, ma'am."

She twisted her hands together nervously and blurted, "If Hank made those phone calls, he did it because my father nagged him into it."

It was a moment before Mitch realized what phone calls she was talking about. "Your husband is the anonymous caller who's threatening the employees of the Cherokee clinic?"

"I didn't say that! I just said *if* he did it, it wasn't his fault."

She *did* believe her husband made the calls. "He's over twenty-one and in possession of his mental faculties, isn't he?"

"You don't know my father," she said miserably. "He can drive you so distracted with his tirades you'll do almost anything to shut him up. I'd forgotten how bad it could be until we moved out to the farm and were around him all the time."

Mitch felt sorry for her as well as disgusted with her misguided attempts to protect her husband. "I'll keep that in mind, Mrs. Bregman." He wheeled his chair around and extracted the Walsh and Brasfield folders from the file cabinet. Separating the typed transcripts, he began arranging them in the appropriate folders. Dee Bregman hadn't moved. He glanced up at her. She was staring gape-mouthed at his desk.

"Is there anything else I can do for you, ma'am?"

"Where . . ." She swallowed. "Where did you get that?"

Mitch was still holding the last few pages of transcript, which was what she seemed to be staring at. "What?"

She pointed at his desk. "That."

He raised the sheaf of paper higher, exposing the plastic disk with the picture of the unidentified young woman. He'd left it lying on the desk and Helen had put the transcripts down on top of it. He picked it up. "You mean this?"

She nodded, her eyes fixed on the picture.

"It was"—Mitch improvised quickly—"found lying in the road and someone turned it in here." He placed the disk on the desk in front of her. "Nobody's claimed it, though. Of course, it's not valuable, except as a keepsake."

She nodded numbly, reached for it, looked at it more closely. In fact, she couldn't seem to stop looking at it. "You said it was found on the road. What road? Where?"

"Out by the lake, I think. You recognize her?"

"Yes." She put the disk back on the desk almost reverently. "It's my mother. Her name is Mary."

Stunned, Mitch stared at her. "Are you sure?" The woman in the picture looked younger than Dee Bregman.

"Yes," she said, her voice barely above a whisper.

"Then it's an old picture."

"At least twenty years. As I remember, that's pretty much how she looked when she left us."

Mitch touched the disk. "Have you ever seen this before?"

"No. I don't even remember that picture. When Mother left, Dad went on a rampage, gave all her clothes and personal belongings to a church rummage sale and destroyed all the pictures. I managed to save four or five snapshots of her, hid them at the back of my dresser drawer."

"This isn't from one of the snapshots you saved?"

"I don't think so. I still have them, I can check."

"Would you do that, please, and call me back as soon as possible?"

"All right."

"Mrs. Bregman, have you heard from your mother since she left?"

She shook her head. "At first I was sure she'd call or write. I mean, I knew she wanted to get away from Dad. I used to lie in my bed at night and listen to them argue. Or rather, listen to Dad. He'd pace the floor and yell at her, say terrible things, call her awful names. So it was no big surprise when she left. But I couldn't believe she wanted to cut all ties with me and Hunter. I guess I was wrong. Except for the letter she mailed right after she left, we never heard from her."

"There was a letter?" Interesting that Dane Kennedy hadn't mentioned it.

"Yes, the date on the postmark was the day after she moved out. She mailed it from Tulsa. She wrote it on some hotel stationery. I guess she stayed there a day or two before she moved on. I tried calling her there the next week, but she wasn't registered."

"Do you still have the letter?"

She gave the question some thought. "I think it's with the snapshots. I'll see if I can find it."

"I'd like to read it."

"Why? It's been so long. It can't possibly have anything to do . . ." She glanced at the disk again and didn't finish. "I—I have to be going. You won't tell Hank or my father that I was here, will you?"

"No," Mitch assured her. "Don't forget. Call me if you find that letter."

When she was gone, Mitch picked up the disk and studied the picture again. How in God's name had it ended up out at the edge of the woods where Walsh and Brasfield had parked the day they were killed? He'd dismissed that as coincidence, but now that he knew who it was, it stirred up more questions. Had Brasfield or Walsh dropped it? He rejected Walsh right away. But Brasfield had lived in Buckskin when Dane Kennedy and his wife were together. Had Brasfield known Mary Kennedy?

Mitch grabbed the Brasfield case file, opened it, and leafed through the interview with Kennedy until he found what he wanted.

25

MITCH: *How can I get in touch with your wife, Kennedy? Or is she your ex-wife?*

KENNEDY: *I don't know where that bitch is, and I don't care.*

MITCH: *When was the last time you heard from her?*

KENNEDY: *The day she walked out of my house, left two half-grown kids without a mother. No decent woman does a thing like that. . . . That was seventeen years ago, and I ain't never seen or heard of her since.*

Kennedy had lied. The letter to Mary Kennedy's children had arrived several days after she left her husband. Mitch paused to gaze out the window.

Seventeen years ago. That number kept cropping up. It was about seventeen years ago when the Brasfields had some "problems" and when the daughters noticed a change in their mother's behavior that lasted several months. Was it mere coincidence that the problems in the Brasfield marriage occurred during the same period of time when Mary Kennedy left her husband and children?

Mitch read more of the interview.

MITCH: *What about your children? Has she been in contact with them?*

KENNEDY: *Not that I know of. . . . Way I look at it, it was just as well she didn't make contact. She was a piss-poor example for the kids, anyway. They were better off without her.*

MITCH: *Your son suggested that she might have left because she disagreed with your political activities.*

KENNEDY: *Hunter don't know nothing about it. He was just twelve when she lit out.*

MITCH: *Didn't you ever try to find her?*

KENNEDY: *Never. She left me for some—*

MITCH: *For some what?*

KENNEDY: *Some wild notion or other. Finding herself, some such damned fool nonsense.*

But even at the time, Mitch had sensed that wasn't what Kennedy had started to say. *She left me for some . . .* what? Other man? Injun?

It could be. In Kennedy's worldview, the only thing worse than his wife leaving him for another man would be her leaving him for a man with "tainted blood." Vian Brasfield? It didn't appear, though, that she had left him for Brasfield, who had stayed with his wife. But Mary Kennedy may have thought he would leave Nicole if she, Mary, were free.

Mitch closed the case file, picked up the picture of Mary Kennedy, and took it out to the dispatcher's desk.

"I found out who this is," he said.

Helen, who'd just hung up the phone, turned around and saw what he was holding. "The woman in the picture?"

"Yes. Does Mary Kennedy ring any bells?"

She gasped. "That's it! That's who the picture reminded me of. Dane Kennedy's wife. No wonder I couldn't remember. She left years ago and as far as I know hasn't been back to Buckskin in all the time since."

"Seventeen years, to be exact," Mitch said. "Except for one letter, mailed the day after she left, she hasn't even contacted her children."

Helen's full lips compressed into a line of disapproval. "I can't imagine a woman leaving her kids with a man like that and not even calling to check on them. It's like she just threw them away."

Mitch glanced around and saw Gus standing in a corner, listening with his mouth slightly open, absorbing every word to pass along to his cronies down at city hall when he got out of jail. "Damn it, Gus," Mitch fumed, "get out of here. This is police business."

Gus threw him a hateful stare, grabbed his broom, and went back down the hall toward the cells.

"Helen, how well did you know Mary Kennedy?" Mitch asked.

"Not very well. I'd see her around town occasionally. She was always friendly enough, she'd speak and all, but she never stopped to chat for more than a minute or two. Maybe her husband didn't want her getting too friendly with other people, I don't know."

"Or maybe she already had—gotten too friendly with someone, I mean—and Dane was on to her."

"What do you mean?"

"Before she left, do you remember any gossip going around about Mary Kennedy and another man?" It was almost impossible to conduct an extramarital affair in Buckskin without someone finding out.

Helen gazed at him for a moment, then frowned thoughtfully. "That was a long time ago, about the time I was divorcing my second husband, so I had enough of my own business to worry about without getting into somebody else's. But let me think." She closed her eyes and tapped her fingernails on her desk. "You know," she mused, "I do seem to recall a story like that making the rounds. It wasn't long before she left, I think. I never put much stock in the stories, though."

"Do you remember hearing the man's name?"

She opened her eyes and looked at Mitch. "If I did, I can't think of it now. It's possible I heard it then but didn't know the man, so I forgot it."

"Could it have been Vian Brasfield?"

"Is *that* who it was?"

"I don't know, but it has occurred to me. If so, I guess she expected they'd both leave their spouses to be together, but Brasfield didn't go along."

She tucked her bottom lip beneath her top teeth, thinking. Finally, she shook her head. "No. I don't remember hearing Brasfield's name. There was probably nothing to the stories, anyway. I can't imagine Mary Kennedy having an affair with another man while she was still under Kennedy's roof. He'd have killed her."

"Maybe he did," Mitch said.

*   *   *

Some time later, Helen buzzed Mitch in his office. "Dee Bregman's on the phone, Chief. Wants to talk to you."

Mitch picked up the phone. "Mitch Bushyhead here."

"I found that letter, Chief Bushyhead. The snapshots too, and I'm sure none of the ones I saved is missing."

"I'd like to come out and get the letter right now, if that would be all right, Mrs. Bregman."

"Well, I guess it's okay. Come on out. I'll be here."

Mitch hurried out of his office and across the common room. "Wait a minute, Chief," Helen said. "Do you really think Dane Kennedy killed his wife?"

Mitch turned around at the door. "Don't repeat that to anybody, Helen," he said sharply. "I don't even know Mary Kennedy was having an affair. Or, if she was, whether Vian Brasfield was the man involved. I sure don't know that Kennedy killed her." Nor how he would ever find out unless Kennedy suddenly broke down and confessed. Yeah, right. They'd have snow in July before that happened.

Helen glanced toward the hallway leading to the cells. "I wonder how far down the hall Gus went? Do you think he heard everything we said?"

Sweet Lord, Mitch hoped not.

Kennedy's hounds met the patrol car at the gate again and followed Mitch all the way to the mobile home, yapping their heads off. Dee Bregman heard them and came out. She called them over to her, petting them and talking to them until Mitch could get to the door of the mobile home. Then she followed him inside.

"I let Cindy go to town with Hank," she said. "I'd rather she didn't hear this. I've never talked to her about Mother for fear she'd say something to Dad and he'd get mad and tell her that her grandmother was a bad woman. What would that accomplish?"

"Nothing good," Mitch agreed.

She went to the kitchen, returning in a moment with five faded snapshots and the letter. Two of the snapshots showed Mary Kennedy alone and Mary Kennedy with her husband. Three of the snapshots were of Mary with her two children. She had been a pale, pretty woman, the kind of dewy, fragile prettiness that was dependent on youth and didn't hold up well over time.

"I hadn't thought of Mother much for ages until this morning," Dee said. "I came home, after talking to you, and dug out the snapshots. Seeing them made me feel all those old feelings again. Sadness and the longing to see her. The anger too, because she never came back for me and Hunter."

Maybe she couldn't, Mitch thought but didn't say. He unfolded the letter. It was written in flowing script on Williams Hotel letterhead. Mitch had never heard of a Williams Hotel in Tulsa.

Dee went to a window and gazed out as Mitch read the letter.

Dearest Dee and Hunter,

I'm sorry I didn't tell you I was leaving. I didn't know what to say. Please forgive me. Your Dad and I haven't been happy together in such a long time, and you know how much I hate the farm. Your father has changed from the man I married—or from what I thought he was. And I've changed, too, probably more than he has.

I just couldn't stay there another day. You may not be able to understand now, even if I could explain, but you will when you're older.

So much has happened in my life the last few months, in ways that I could never have imagined. I needed to get away so I could think—figure out who I am and what I want now. None of this has anything to do with you two.

Please, please believe me.

I love you both so very much. I don't know where I'm going or what kind of job I can find. But as soon as I get settled I'll write or call you. Maybe your father will let you come and visit me.

With all my love,
Mother

Mitch glanced at Dee Bregman's back as he refolded the letter. "May I take this and make a copy?"

She turned around. "Sure." She sat down on the couch.

"She said she'd be in touch, that she wanted you to come and visit her," Mitch said.

She bowed her head and fingered the nubby arm of the couch. "Maybe she knew that's what we wanted to hear. She said she loved us too, but obviously not enough to pick up the phone."

Mitch tucked the letter into his shirt pocket. "Mrs. Bregman, before your mother left, is it possible she was seeing another man?"

She looked down at her hand resting on the couch arm. "I don't know, but to tell you the truth, I've wondered about that—because of what she said in the letter, about her life changing in ways she couldn't have imagined." She looked up.

"Whatever it was that changed her life made her question everything, even who she was."

"Did you suspect she was having an affair—before you got the letter, I mean?" Mitch asked.

"No," she said. "I knew she had a lot on her mind. She was quieter than usual. Sometimes she didn't hear when I spoke to her. But I thought it was because she and Daddy were fighting so much. The way she was acting worried me, but I tried to pretend everything was fine for Hunter's sake. He adored Mother. As hard as it was for me when she left, I think it was doubly hard on Hunter. Before you got here, I called him at the high school and told him about that picture you found. I didn't want him to hear about it from somebody else."

"Did he have any idea where that picture might have come from?"

"I described it to him and the little holder it was in. He couldn't remember ever seeing anything like that. I think it upset him, though. He's never really gotten over Mother leaving. He even hired a private detective a year or two ago to try to find her."

"What came of that?"

Her mouth twisted. "Nothing. The detective searched public records on the computer—for driver's license, social security number, things like that. He said if she was driving a car or working, he should be able to track her to somewhere. She might not still be there, but it would be a place to start. But he found nothing. He said if she was still alive she must be using another name."

"Why would she do that?"

"The only reason I can think of is that she didn't want us to find her."

"Do you believe that?"

She thought about it. "I know she wouldn't want to hear from Dad, but then he doesn't want to hear from her, either. It's hard to accept that she wouldn't want to hear from Hunter and me, though."

"Do you think she's dead?"

"I don't know what to think." She gazed at him with sad eyes. "But I've wondered about that myself."

26

"I keep thinking about that handkerchief," Shelly said as she strolled into Mitch's office the next morning, carrying a cup of coffee.

Mitch had been studying the picture of Mary Kennedy in its plastic holder, trying to imagine her married to Dane Kennedy, even a much younger Kennedy. It was a stretch. Now he tossed the disk on his desk and leaned back in his swivel chair. "Brasfield's handkerchief?"

Shelly tested her coffee with the tip of a finger, then took a cautious sip. "Yeah. The way it was out there in plain sight on the pond bank bugs me. According to Doc Pohl, the body was most likely put in the pond sometime during the day Friday. We've been assuming the handkerchief fell out of Brasfield's pocket while the killer maneuvered the body into the water. But if it was in daylight, how could the murderer have missed seeing it?"

"He was probably so desperate to get out of there, he took off as soon as the body hit the water. Didn't think of looking around for something like a handkerchief."

"It just doesn't seem like he could've missed it, even if he wasn't looking for it. I spotted it the first time I glanced that way." She took another swallow of coffee.

"Obviously he *did* miss it, unless . . ."

"Yeah, unless he left it there on purpose, placed it there to be found by us."

"So we'd have a reason to drag the pond?"

"And find the body, yes. He'd parked the pickup as close to the pond as he could on Brasfield's side of the fence. But maybe he figured that wasn't enough of a clue for us, and he couldn't stand the suspense of waiting for the body to surface and be found by somebody who happened to be near enough to see it."

"That could've been weeks, even months. I get your point. But if that's what happened, it wasn't Dane Kennedy."

She wandered over to a framed certificate hanging on the wall and straightened it absentmindedly. Turning around, she said, "Yeah. Kennedy's weird, but surely not crazy enough to deliberately implicate himself in Brasfield's murder. So. If we follow this thread, that the handkerchief was planted by the killer, it sure knocks our case against Kennedy into a cocked hat."

"Mmm," Mitch said.

The phone on Mitch's desk rang. They waited silently while Helen answered at the dispatcher's desk, then buzzed Mitch. He said hello and then listened in silence, frowning more deeply every second the hysterical female voice bombarded his eardrum. The caller didn't identify herself and it took a few moments for him to realize who she was.

"Are you there alone? Don't touch anything. We'll be right out."

"That was Dee Bregman," he told Shelly, hanging up the phone. "I think she was saying her father's been shot."

They saw Cindy Bregman peering out a window of the mobile home, her nose pressed to the glass, as she anxiously watched her parents, who were in the front yard of Kennedy's house. Hank Bregman walked over to the patrol car as Mitch and Shelly got out.

"I'm trying to get Dee to take Cindy away from here for a while. She doesn't know what's happened, but she heard her mother scream, so she knows something's wrong."

"Is your father-in-law dead?"

"Uh-huh."

"Your wife found him?"

"Yeah, a few minutes before she called you."

"About nine o'clock, then?"

He nodded. "She went over to the house to check on Dane because we hadn't seen him this morning. He's usually out and about by seven-thirty or eight. If we're up, he'll come over for coffee. Cindy was doing her arithmetic assignment and I was out back working on the lawn mower and heard Dee yelling. I ran to the house and caught her as she came out the door like a bat out of hell. She just kept pointing toward the house, but I couldn't understand what she was trying to say. So I went in and there he was, slumped over his desk. He was shot. With his own gun, the one he kept under his bed. I could tell there wasn't any hope of saving him. The blood had dried. Dee finally got ahold of herself and came in behind me. She called you from Dane's phone. Didn't want Cindy to hear."

"Did you hear a gunshot earlier this morning?"

"No."

"Your mobile home is close enough, you should have heard the shot, unless it happened when nobody was at home."

"I had last night off and we went to Muskogee to play cards with some friends. Left Cindy with Dee's brother in Buckskin. I guess it could've happened while we were gone."

"What time did you get back?"

"It was late. One o'clock by the time we picked up Cindy. One-thirty by the time we got home. Dane's lights were out, so naturally we figured he was in bed."

Dee Bregman, in a blue terry-cloth robe, still stood in the front yard, her arms wrapped around herself, and looking wretchedly abandoned.

"I better go and get Cindy away from that window," Bregman said.

Mitch and Shelly walked over to Dee Bregman. She had been crying. Her face was blotchy and bloated. "Now, Mrs. Bregman," Mitch said, "it's probably not necessary for you to go back into the house with us."

Her eyes filled with fresh tears. "Hank says Cindy and I should leave until Daddy . . . until he's gone."

"That's probably a good idea," Mitch agreed, "but I have to ask you a few questions first. Your husband says your father was seated at his desk when he saw him. Is that how you found him?"

She choked back a sob. "Yes."

"You didn't try to move him?"

"Oh, no," she said, horrified. "There was so much blood. I know you're not supposed to move an injured person. But then Hank came in and said he was dead."

"And you didn't touch anything else, like I told you?"

"Not after I talked to you."

"What did you touch before that?"

"The telephone, and I—well, the note was on the floor beside the desk. I picked it up and read it. You couldn't expect me not to read it, could you?"

"Your father left a note?"

She nodded miserably. "He typed it on his old typewriter. He must have lost his mind, just snapped. That's the only explanation I can think of."

"Where is the note now?"

She hesitated, touching the pocket of her robe. Mitch held out his hand. She reached into the pocket and drew out a crumpled piece of white paper. Mitch could see that it was cheap bond, the kind you could buy in any drug or variety store.

He took the crumpled paper, straightening it by holding on to diagonally opposing corners, even though any fingerprints it contained had probably been blurred by Dee Bregman's handling it. Shelly moved closer and looked over his shoulder.

The words had been typed on a manual machine that needed cleaning. The impressions weren't uniform, the o's were clogged with built-up ink, and there were a lot of strikeovers.

"To the Police," it said.

I can't go on this way any longer. I tried to be civil to Vian Brasfield. I told him to do something about the noise from the dances, but he wouldn't. I ain't slept more than two or three hours on a Friday night in months. A lot of Saturday nights, too. I told him something had to be done. But I didn't mean to kill him when I went out there to the woods that morning. I just meant to talk to him again. I realized after I got there that I didn't have my twelve-gauge. I took it in the house to clean it and forgot to put it back in the pickup. So I grabbed a tire iron in case I needed to protect myself. I came up on Brasfield right after he'd shot an eagle. I said I wouldn't tell what I saw if he'd do something about the dances. He laughed at me, called me a nut case and a lot of worse things that made me see red. I hit him before I knew I was going to do it. He yelled and grabbed me around the neck. I had to keep hitting him to get him to let go. I would have left him there, but that game warden showed up and I had to kill him, too. I drug the warden into a cave and Brasfield back to his pickup. I drove the pickup to Brasfield's place and left it in amongst some trees and put him in my pond. I walked the two miles back to where I'd left my pickup and came home. I want to say that Dee and Hank had nothing to do with this. I don't think they even knew I was gone.

Dane Kennedy

Mitch handed the note to Shelly, who took it by one corner and carried it to the patrol car and put it in one of the evidence bags that were in the glove compartment.

"Did your husband touch the note too?" Mitch asked Dee Bregman.

"Yes. We were both so shocked when we read it, we weren't thinking straight. After Hank read it, I stuffed it in my pocket, out of sight." She wiped her eyes on the sleeve of her robe. "I've messed up evidence, haven't I? I'm sorry."

"Did you suspect your father of killing Brasfield and Walsh?"

"No. I still can't believe it. Like I said, he must've snapped." She glanced toward the open door of the house. "Oh, God, now I've got to go call Hunter."

"I'd rather you'd wait until the ambulance removes the body," Mitch said. "Another half hour shouldn't matter."

"All right," she said, "it would probably be better if I told him in person, anyway."

"One more thing. Your husband said your father was shot with his own gun."

"That's right. He's had that gun for years. He always kept it under his bed where he could get to it if he heard somebody trying to get in the house. I recognized it right off." She glanced toward the house and shivered. "Can I go now?"

"Yes, ma'am."

"I'll get dressed and take Cindy to town for an ice-cream cone or something before we go to the high school. I can leave her with the secretary while I talk to Hunter." She turned and walked slowly toward the mobile home, her head down.

Shelly came back, carrying the department's camera and fingerprint kit, and she and Mitch entered the house. Dane Kennedy was seated at the larger of the two desks, the one nearest the door, his upper body slumped forward, the left side of his head resting against the edge of the desktop. He was dressed in overalls with no shirt. Both arms hung at his sides. A handgun lay on the floor beneath his right hand. Thirty-eight-caliber Smith and Wesson revolver. The right side of his head was a mass of pulp, and blood had wet his beard and dripped on his bare feet and the floor.

"Looks like he's been dead awhile," Shelly said.

"The Bregmans didn't hear the gunshot. They were gone last night until one-thirty. I'd guess it happened then, but we'll wait and see what Doc says." He pointed at the phone that sat atop the filing cabinet. "Call the ambulance."

While Shelly was doing that, Mitch walked around the room. It looked the same as it had the last time he was there, except that three of the four cardboard boxes against the wall were empty. The fourth, which was open, was full of booklets entitled *Last Call, White America!*

With a grunt of disgust, Mitch folded the box's flap down and revealed a hole in the wall a few inches above the box. He bent down for a closer look. It was a bullet hole.

"Look here," he said as Shelly hung up the phone. "I didn't notice this when I was here earlier, did you?"

"No, but I was too busy keeping both eyes on Kennedy to notice much of anything else. I'll go outside and see if I can find the shell."

Mitch looked through the rest of the house while Shelly was gone. He found Kennedy's old Royal typewriter in the bedroom, on a little typewriter table with wheels. A few sheets of white paper lay beside it. He rolled one into the machine, found a clean undershirt in a dresser drawer, stretched it over an index finger, and typed several o's. The holes were filled in with ink.

Continuing through the remaining rooms, Mitch found a dozen guns—all rifles or shotguns in a closet in a second bedroom.

Shelly returned some ten minutes later with a .38-caliber shell. "I'll bet it's from the same gun," she said. "Wonder when he shot the wall?"

"No telling. Bregman might know."

"You find anything else?"

"The typewriter. Same one used for the note. You can dust it and the gun for fingerprints after you get some pictures."

She walked over to the box of pamphlets and pulled up a flap. "Great literature here," she muttered. Positioning the camera, which was strung on a strap around her neck, she began snapping pictures of the victim from various angles. After a few moments, she said, "I guess I was wrong about that handkerchief. Kennedy obviously overlooked it."

"Maybe."

She looked around abruptly. "What?"

"There are some things here that don't make sense to me. That note, for one thing."

"Don't you think the note is genuine?"

"It's typed, even the signature."

"Looks like he used the typewriter all the time. Doesn't seem too unusual that he'd use it for his suicide note."

"I could buy that, except for one thing. Does that note sound like Dane Kennedy to you?"

"Well."

"It sounds too thought-out to me, too logical. And the grammar's nearly perfect."

"He must write better than he talks, or else why would he be putting out those pamphlets? And there was an 'ain't' in the note. That sounds like Kennedy."

"One. Like somebody threw it in at the last minute to make it sound like Kennedy. And he doesn't strike me as the type to kill himself. Playing the poor victim of an evil government, a martyr for the cause, yeah, but not a suicide. Another thing: How did he know where to find Brasfield that morning?"

"I wondered about that. And also why he didn't use the suicide note to make some anti-government statement. He probably knew this would make a lot of news reports. Would Kennedy let an opportunity like that pass?"

"Good point," Mitch said. "And look at the way he's dressed. Just the overalls. No shirt, no shoes, like he was getting ready for bed, or was already there and got up again. Did he suddenly decide to shoot himself in the midst of retiring? Or did he get up to answer the door?"

"You're saying he was murdered?"

"I'm just saying there are a lot of unanswered questions in my mind." Mitch shook his head. "We'll see what Doc Pohl has to say."

"Mrs. Bregman and her daughter are leaving," Shelly said, glancing out the front window, and Mitch heard the sound of a car engine start. He walked over to stand in the open door. As Dee Bregman's car cleared the gate, he heard the ambulance.

Mitch and Shelly stepped into the yard, leaving the body to the paramedics. When they carried the body from the house in a bag, Hank Bregman came out and stood beside the mobile home to watch. Mitch walked over to him. Bregman didn't look at Mitch, kept staring, trancelike, at the ambulance.

"We found a bullet hole in the north wall of Kennedy's living room. You know anything about that?"

Bregman came out of his trance, pulled his gaze from the retreating ambulance, and settled it on Mitch's face. "Where on the north wall?"

"About midway, a couple of feet above the floor. Right over a box of pamphlets."

"Dane never said anything about a bullet hole, and I never saw one, either. I'm pretty sure it wasn't there the last time I helped him stuff envelopes for mailing. I think I'd have noticed."

"When was that?"

With a weary groan, he rubbed both hands over his cheeks where the night's growth of beard bristled. "Jeez, I don't know. With all that's happened lately, I've lost track of time. Four or five days ago, I think."

27

Mitch spent much of the afternoon fielding calls from members of the city council and citizens wanting to know if it was true that Dane Kennedy had killed himself. Some wanted to know if Kennedy had killed Walsh and Brasfield. The word had already gotten out about the suicide note, probably via Hunter Kennedy or somebody else at the high school.

During a break in the phone calls, Mitch went out to the common room. Gus, the lamb's-wool duster sticking out of the back pocket of his trousers, was peering out the window as a Channel Six News van from Tulsa parked in front of the station. Shelly had just stepped outside to read the carefully worded statement Mitch had written for the media. He'd given strict instructions that no reporters were to be allowed inside the station and, beyond reading the official statement, no police department employee was to answer any of their questions.

"Hey, Chief," Gus greeted Mitch as he emerged from his office. "We got us a regular media circus going here. They ought to talk to me. I could tell 'em a few things about Dane Kennedy myself."

Mitch paused as he reached for a coffee cup. "I didn't know you knew Kennedy, Gus."

Gus nodded gravely. "We weren't close or nothing, but I knew him for years. Always thought he was strange, and he got worse after his wife left."

"You knew Mary too?"

"Oh, yeah. She used to come into the hardware store where I worked. Seemed like a nice lady. Too good for Dane."

"Why didn't you say something before? You could probably have identified that picture I was showing around town."

"Whut picture?"

Mitch went into his office and got the plastic disk. He showed it to Gus.

"Why, sure, that's Mary." He shot Mitch an offended look. "I heard you talking about a picture, but how was I to know who it was? Nobody bothered showing it to *me*."

Mitch glanced at Helen, who was biting her lip to keep from smiling. "You don't seem to grasp your role here, Gus," Mitch said. "We don't discuss police business with prisoners."

"Well, maybe you oughta try it," Gus huffed. "Might learn something."

"He's got you there, Chief," Helen commented.

"You oughta make me a police informant," Gus said, totally serious. "I know just about everything that's gone on around here for the past sixty years." He cackled. "You might say I know where all the bodies are buried."

Mitch hid the smile tugging at his own lips by turning his back while he poured himself a cup of coffee. "I guess you remember when Mary Kennedy left town, then."

Gus settled his skinny rump against the edge of Shelly's desk and folded his arms. "Sure do, Chief. It was pretty much the talk of the town."

"Did you hear any rumors before Mary left?"

"What kind of rumors?"

"Oh, that maybe she was running around on Dane."

Gus looked suddenly cagey. "I might know something. What's it worth to you?"

Mitch groaned. "I won't *pay* you for information, Gus."

Gus tilted his head back and sniffed. "I ain't asking for money, Chief."

"What, then?"

"Let's exchange information. Did I hear right? Dane Kennedy killed hisself?"

Mitch sent a sidelong glance in Helen's direction. There was only one place Gus could have heard that. "He was shot with his own gun, Gus. And there was a suicide note."

Gus worked his mouth around, ruminating. "Don't sound like Dane, but like I said, he was strange." For a moment he stared out the window at Shelly's back as she read the statement Mitch had written.

"About Mary Kennedy," Mitch said.

Gus returned his attention to Mitch and tried to look perplexed. "What was the question again?"

"Was Mary Kennedy involved in hanky-panky with another man?"

He gave a slow shake of his head. "That ain't the way I heard it."

"She wasn't having an affair?"

"Didn't say that." Gus's eyes gleamed now, as though he were getting ready to deliver a punch line. "What I meant was I never heard nothing about another man."

Mitch rolled his head back and looked at the ceiling. Gus was trying to drive him crazy. "So, she was having an affair, but there wasn't another man. What was she doing, Gus? Getting it on with a ghost?"

"Way I heard it," Gus said, glancing at Helen and lowering his voice, "it was a woman."

That evening, the news of "militant activist" Dane Kennedy's "suspicious death," along with a rehash of the Walsh and Brasfield murders, was reported on the NBC national news by Tom Brokaw. More lengthy versions made all three of Tulsa's local news shows. One of the network affiliates referred to the situation as a "reign of terror." Another dubbed Buckskin the "killing fields of Cherokee County."

Mitch had the house to himself, as Emily had gone to a cheerleaders' meeting at the high school. He sat in front of the television set, flipping from one of Tulsa's TV stations to another, and managed to catch part of each of the reports. After the news anchors signed off, he flipped off the set and picked up the Walsh and Brasfield case files, which he'd brought home with him.

At first he'd dismissed Gus's little bombshell as just another way for the old man to draw attention to himself, basking briefly in the limelight. Nevertheless, he'd ushered Gus into his office and questioned him further. But Gus knew, or would say, nothing more. He'd heard Mary Kennedy had "turned homo," that's all—she had a girlfriend. But as to the girlfriend's identity or where she lived, Gus claimed ignorance.

After Gus returned to his cell, Mitch had gone through the Walsh and Brasfield case files again. In the light of what Gus had said, a couple of things he'd given little weight to before jumped out at him.

During his questioning of Dane Kennedy, Kennedy had started to expand on why Mary had left him. *She left me for some* . . . he'd said, and finished by saying she'd left him for some notion of finding herself. Mitch had felt all along that Kennedy had almost let something slip, something that continued to enrage and embarrass him when he thought of it. Still searching for a motive for Brasfield's murder, Mitch had immediately thought of Vian Brasfield, one of the "tainted bloods" Kennedy so despised.

Now he reread the interview more closely, and something else Kennedy had said struck him with more impact. When Mitch had mentioned Nicole Brasfield, Kennedy had called her a "pervert." When Mitch had asked why Kennedy considered Nicole Brasfield a pervert, Kennedy had countered with, "She married an Injun, didn't she?" Knowing of Kennedy's white supremacist views, Mitch had accepted the answer—then. The only thing worse than Kennedy's knowing his wife was involved with another man, he'd thought, would have been knowing she was involved with an Indian. But he'd been wrong. To Kennedy's way of thinking, Mary's being engaged in a lesbian affair would have been worse yet.

He closed the case file. In light of what Gus had said, several things in the interviews pointed to Mary Kennedy's having a lesbian lover. Kennedy's extreme reaction to the mere mention of her name pointed to Nicole Brasfield. It sure gave him a new perspective on Nicole Brasfield's fainting spell when he showed her Mary Kennedy's picture.

He dialed her number and let it ring several times. She wasn't home. He'd have to wait till tomorrow to talk to her.

The news about Dane Kennedy came on Nicole's favorite Tulsa station the next morning. It was the first time she'd turned on the television set since her daughters had left. For two days she'd been drifting through the house, shades drawn, like a great, lumbering ghost. Last night, getting ready for bed, she'd stood naked in front of the full-length mirror on her bedroom door and did not recognize herself.

Who is that lumpy old woman? she'd wondered. And then, Where did my life go?

She'd pulled on her nightgown and lain in the still, dark house, thinking about the woman in the mirror. She was fifty-one years old, and she had spent the prime of her adult life in a state of self-imposed numbness. So much of what she felt and thought was unacceptable, therefore painful, and so she had learned to remove herself from such feelings and thoughts. But the trouble with that was that you ended up being an observer of life without ever really getting involved in it, growing more anesthetized and removed from those around you as the years passed. Until, finally, you felt no more connection to your own children than to people you might pass on the street in a strange town without ever making eye contact.

Before she fell asleep, she had made the most difficult and terrifying decision of her life. She would not live that way any longer. It might be too late to fully repair her relationship with her daughters, but she could begin by being kind to herself. Wherever that led her, she would not draw back into the shadows for fear of what others would think. She would live whatever was left of her life honestly and unflinchingly, on her own terms.

She slept through that night, waking only briefly when the telephone rang. She let it ring and went back to sleep. It was the first good night's sleep she'd had since Vian had left the house to go eagle hunting. When she'd awakened, she'd dressed and gone through the house opening shades, flooding the house with spring sunlight. Then she'd gone to make pancakes, and had turned on the small TV set she kept on the breakfast bar, just to dispel the silence as she moved about the kitchen.

She was standing at the stove, thinking of venturing out of the house—going somewhere for the day, to Muskogee or Tulsa, anywhere away from Buckskin, for lunch and a visit to a museum. Then she heard the TV commentator say, "Buckskin activist Dane Kennedy was found dead in his home yesterday."

Nicole turned off the burner under the griddle and went to stand at the breakfast bar where she could see the television screen. A dark-haired young woman in a yellow jacket was saying, "A source who asked not to be identified told this reporter that Kennedy left a note confessing to two recent killings in Cherokee County, the murders of game warden Arnett Walsh and high school principal Vian Brasfield."

The reporter moved on to another story and the phone rang. It was Nicole's neighbor, Pearl Anderson.

"Do you have your TV on? They're talking about Vian."

"Yes, I just heard it."

"They said that Kennedy person killed himself night before last. It must have been on the news yesterday too, but I've been a little under the weather. Didn't watch TV or read my newspaper. I noticed you didn't even take your paper in yesterday."

"No, and I haven't had the TV on until this morning," Nicole said.

"Do you know Dane Kennedy?"

"Not really," Nicole said. "I wonder if what they said is true."

"Of course it's true," Pearl said. "They wouldn't put it on TV if it wasn't, would they?"

"I suppose not." Disconnected thoughts swam in Nicole's brain. She had to think. "I have to go now, Pearl. Thanks for calling."

Nicole hung up the phone, turned off the TV, but continued to stare at the blank screen as she tried to make some sense of the news report. She had had only two or three conversations with Dane Kennedy in her life, and that had been seventeen years ago. He was an angry, frightening man even then.

Back then, she had half expected him to kill *her*. But she hadn't been afraid because she had thought she'd never see Kennedy again, that she would leave this town and never come back. Not only had she had to come back to Buckskin, to this house and Vian, but to do it broken and deserted and in humiliation. And Vian had told her how it would be from then on. After that, whenever she saw Dane Kennedy on the street, she looked the other way. And he had never spoken to her or even indicated that he was aware of her existence.

She would have thought Kennedy would rejoice at Vian's death. What complicated chain of reasoning had led him to take his own life?

That's when a new thought hit her. What else had Kennedy revealed in the note? Oh, God, would it never end?

And then she remembered Martha and Kate. She had to call them before they heard the news from somebody else. But as she started toward the phone, she heard a car pull up out front. Going to a window, she saw Chief of Police Mitch Bushyhead getting out of a patrol car.

Her earlier feeling of freedom, of embarking on a new road, drained right out of her. Watching Bushyhead come up to the door, she felt the past dragging her back into the shadows again where she didn't have to feel or think too much. No, she told herself. She was through with hiding.

She knew why Bushyhead had come and she was almost relieved.

28

"I've been expecting you," Nicole said as she ushered Mitch into the house.

Surprised by her welcome, Mitch seated himself on the velvet couch, waited for Nicole Brasfield to take an armchair facing him, and went straight to the point. "Tell me about Mary Kennedy."

She didn't seem surprised by the question. "What about Mary?" she asked softly.

"Start with why you fainted when I showed you her picture."

She took a deep breath. "I guess it was seeing her after so many years—she looked exactly as I remember her. It brought it all back, everything. It just overwhelmed me."

"Her daughter said it's an old picture. It was probably taken when you knew her."

She lifted her head and met his gaze then for the first time. "It was Dane Kennedy's, wasn't it? He'd kept it all those years."

"We're still trying to work that out," Mitch said. "Did Kennedy know about you and Mary?"

She looked at him for a long moment before she nodded an acknowledgment. "Vian found out and told him."

"How did Vian find out?"

"He followed me one night when I went to meet Mary at a motel in Tahlequah. When I got home, he told me that he knew about me and Mary and that he'd told Kennedy to keep his wife at home and he'd do the same."

"So you stopped seeing her."

Slowly, she shook her head. "Nothing Vian said could have made me stop. I felt alive for the first time in my life, and I could no more give that up than I could stop breathing." She looked down at the blue-veined hands that rested in her lap. "I know it makes me a terrible mother, but I couldn't stop even for my children. I was raised in a very conservative religious home, Chief Bushyhead, and I suffered agonies of guilt over Mary. But even that didn't make me stop."

"So you continued to meet until Mary Kennedy left town?"

She glanced up. "Mary and I were going to run away together." A faint smile lifted one corner of her mouth. "It sounds silly and childish now for two grown women to be talking about running away, but that's how we thought of it. We planned to meet in Tulsa, at a hotel. Mary went ahead a day before I was to meet her. Once Dane found out about us, she was afraid he would kill her if she didn't get out. She was supposed to wait for me at the hotel. I couldn't just disappear, like Mary. I knew I had to summon the courage to be honest with Vian. I told him I was leaving with Mary, where I was meeting her, everything. But I stayed here one more day because it was a Friday and there was no one to stay with the girls. Vian needed the weekend to make arrangements for a baby-sitter. I spent the evening with the girls, talking to them and reading their favorite books. When I put them to bed, I told them I had to go away for a while, but that I loved them and I'd see them again as soon as I could. Then I packed and early that Saturday morning I went to Tulsa." She gazed at the clear, bright day beyond the window and blinked, as though blinded by the sunlight. "When I got to the hotel, Mary was gone. I couldn't believe it. She hadn't left a note or anything."

Odd that she would write her children from the hotel, but not leave a message for Nicole. "What did you do then?"

"I came home." Her gaze returned to him. "I had nowhere else to go. By the time I got back to Buckskin, I'd figured out what must have happened. After I told Vian I was leaving, he left the house and didn't come back for hours. I became convinced that he'd talked to Mary, that somehow he'd made her leave without me."

"And had he?"

"He denied it at first, but I wouldn't let up. I badgered him until he finally admitted that he'd gone to Tulsa that Friday night and had convinced Mary that if she took our daughters' mother away from them, she'd never be able to live with herself. Martha and Kate were younger than Mary's children, babies, really—especially Kate—and I was the only one who'd ever cared for them. Vian convinced Mary that whatever she and I had together would be poisoned. He told me that he got the feeling Mary was confused about her own sexuality and was looking for a way out, anyway. At first I didn't want to believe him. Mary had never indicated to me that she had mixed feelings about our plans."

The words seemed to be spilling from some deep well inside her, as though, once started, she couldn't stop talking. She continued, " 'What did you do to her?' I kept asking him, over and over. 'What did you do?' I thought he'd threatened Mary, frightened her into going without me. In those days, Vian could fly off the handle at the drop of a hat. But he insisted that he hadn't, that he'd just talked to Mary, made her see the consequences for our family if we went through with our plans, even though she seemed to care nothing for what it would do to her own children. Mary told Vian she could never go back to Dane, but that she'd leave without me, she wouldn't be responsible for destroying my family as well as hers. I told Vian I didn't believe a word of it. But when the weeks went by and Mary didn't call or write, I began to accept Vian's version of what happened."

"You didn't hear from Mary ever again?"

"No." Even now it seemed to be painful for her to accept. "I finally stopped expecting a letter or a phone call. I—I devoted myself to the girls, tried to lose myself in caring for them. Vian said that he forgave me, that we would stay together for the children's sake. And that we would never speak of Mary Kennedy again." Her hands gripped each other tightly. "We didn't speak of Mary, but he never really forgave me. We had separate bedrooms after that. Vian said if I ever tried to leave him again, he'd take the children away from me." She rubbed the pad of her thumb over the prominent veins on the back of her hand. "I agreed to everything. Without Mary, I just didn't have the strength to fight. I learned not to care, even when I suspected Vian of being with other women. He was always discreet. None of the women he saw lived in Buckskin—until Virginia Craig."

"Ms. Craig swore to me that she and your husband were only friends. She even gave your husband the credit for that. She was the one who wanted more than friendship."

She lifted her shoulders carelessly. "I always knew she wanted Vian for herself, from the way she acted when he was around, but it doesn't matter now. Mostly I was worried and upset over the fact that Virginia and Vian worked together and that the other teachers had to be talking about them— and feeling sorry for me."

Mitch studied her drawn, sagging face. "You must have asked yourself what you'd do if your husband wanted a divorce, how you'd support yourself."

"I won't deny it crossed my mind. Seventeen years ago, I agreed to stay with Vian and make the best of it. I wasn't about to be pushed out to try to support myself at the age of fifty-one."

"What if your husband had insisted? How would you have prevented it?"

She considered the question for a long moment and finally said, "I don't think he would have."

"But suppose he had," Mitch persisted.

"I'd have thought of something."

She'd have thought of something, Mitch mused, as he returned to the station. Like what? Killing her husband?

Vian Brasfield was responsible for Mary Kennedy's leaving town without Nicole. In spite of what Nicole said, that knowledge must have festered below the surface for seventeen years. Had she really come to believe his version of what happened? Regardless, she and Vian had come to an agreement that they would stay together for the children. A marriage of convenience, which had its perks for both sides. Vian got a housekeeper and cook and a mother for his children. Nicole got support, security, and respect for her husband's position in the community.

And then Virginia Craig entered the picture. Maybe nothing *had* happened between Craig and Brasfield, but how could Nicole be sure of that? For the first time, Nicole had to live in the same town with a woman Vian showed signs of being interested in, had to see her from time to time and know that she and Vian were together five days a week. After agreeing to Vian's terms seventeen years ago, had Nicole become convinced that Vian meant to break their contract and put her out to fend for herself in late middle-age?

It gave Nicole Brasfield the best motive for murder Mitch had conjured up yet. Even the picture of Mary Kennedy could have been Nicole's. It made more sense for her to have kept the memento than Dane Kennedy, who'd destroyed all reminders of his wife, except for the few snapshots his daughter managed to hide. Nicole could have kept the memento in her purse, on a chain or a key ring. Mitch could imagine her driving to the lake, getting out of her car with the keys in one hand and a wrench or tire tool in the other. She'd come there to kill her husband, she'd have been nervous and scared, probably shaking with terror at what she was about to do. She could easily have dropped the keys. The chain breaks, keys and the plastic disk fly in all directions. She gathers up the keys, but can't find the memento and can't spend any more time looking, has to leave it and go in search of her husband.

Mitch had already convinced himself that an enraged Nicole Brasfield could have had the strength from an adrenaline rush to kill her husband, and then the game warden who happened on the scene. But why kill Dane Kennedy and leave a bogus confession? Because she feared Mitch was beginning to suspect *her*?

It sort of hung together. Except for the Kennedy killing. Would Nicole have coldly come up with such a plan, driven to Kennedy's, made sure Kennedy was alone on the farm, roused him from his bed, gone inside, somehow gotten her hands on his gun, killed him, then typed the suicide note?

Mitch had a real problem envisioning it. Would Kennedy even have let Nicole Brasfield in the house? And if he had, would he have stood by and let her get her hands on his gun?

Not in this lifetime.

It was harder for Mitch to believe than that Kennedy had killed himself, being overcome with remorse for committing two murders. There were smeared prints on the typewriter, but all the identifiable ones were Kennedy's. If somebody other than Kennedy typed that note, he or she wore gloves. Kennedy's fingerprints, and only Kennedy's, had been identified on the gun. But those prints could have been placed there after the gun was fired.

Back at the station, Mitch found a message on his desk. Ken Pohl had called. He had a report on Dane Kennedy's autopsy. Mitch called Pohl's office and caught him in.

According to Pohl, the gun that killed Kennedy had been fired at very close range. At most, the gun had been held a few inches from Kennedy's head. Though most suicides held the barrel against the head, it wasn't unheard of for it to be held a couple of inches away. The bullet's angle of entry didn't rule out suicide, either. The bullet had traveled virtually straight into the head and lodged inside the skull. Most telling of all, there were powder burns on Kennedy's right hand, proof that he had fired the gun.

Mitch was shaking his head in disbelief when he hung up. He called Shelly and Duck into his office and told them Pohl's findings. Finally, he said, "In spite of the doubts I still have, we may have to put it down to suicide, after all. Kennedy obviously fired that gun."

Shelly's expression was riddled with doubt. "But Chief, did Kennedy fire the gun only once?"

"What're you talking about?" Duck asked. "He was only shot once."

Mitch sat straight up in his chair. "But there *was* a second shot. One shot went into the wall. Two shots were fired in that room, and they could both have been fired in close succession."

Duck looked baffled. "I still don't get it."

"If you shot somebody and wanted to set it up to look like suicide, supposing you knew enough to know the victim's hands would be checked for powder burns, what would you do?"

Duck frowned for a moment, and then his face cleared. "Yeah, I see what you mean. I'd shoot him first, then put the gun in his hand and fire it again. That'd put his fingerprints on the gun and powder burns on his hand."

"And then," Shelly said, "you'd put something over the bullet hole in the wall, hoping the police wouldn't see it. Remember, Chief, that carton of pamphlets had been opened and the flaps were standing up."

"Exactly," Mitch said. It tracked, all right, but without a suspect, could they convince the D.A. that Kennedy was murdered?

*　*　*

Two days later, Mitch still had serious doubts about that question. He took the case files on all three deaths home with him that evening, intending to go over them carefully one more time. He didn't expect it to help much. He'd pored over the files so often he practically had them memorized. He just didn't know what else to do.

The phone rang as he closed the folders. It was Virgil Rabbit, calling from the police station. A man had turned in a camera he'd found while hiking in the woods across the road from Vian Brasfield's dance ground. Virgil had run it by the high school journalism teacher's house. He'd identified it as the camera belonging to the school.

Mitch didn't get it. Why steal a valuable camera, then throw it away? "Was there any film in the camera?" he asked Virgil.

Virgil said that there hadn't been. Mitch hung up as the truth came to him. The thief didn't steal the camera to sell it. He'd wanted the pictures Carrie Lou Dunning had taken of the booger dance. Therefore, the thief had to be the person who'd been wearing Vian Brasfield's costume that night. What he hadn't known was that Carrie Lou had already changed that roll of film for a new one.

But Mitch had seen the booger dance, and he hadn't recognized the person wearing Brasfield's costume. Would the pictures reveal something he hadn't seen at the dance? He'd go by the high school tomorrow and ask for copies.

He phoned Rhea, who was still at the clinic, and made a date for the weekend. Emily came in while he was on the phone and stacked her notebook and a couple of textbooks beside Mitch's case file folders on the kitchen table.

Mitch said good-bye to Rhea and cradled the phone. "Hi, sweetheart," he greeted Emily. "How was your day?"

She made a face. "The pits. All my teachers decided to pile on the homework at the same time. I'll be up half the night."

"Well, sit down and get started," Mitch told her. "I'll scare up something for dinner." He opened the refrigerator door and scanned the shelves. They were pretty bare. A head of lettuce, a single tomato, a chunk of cheddar cheese and a leftover chicken breast. He needed to schedule a trip to the grocery store. "Could you get by on a chef's salad and an apple? I think we've even got some of that carrot cake from the bakery left."

"Whatever," Emily murmured. She sat down at the table and opened her notebook with a heavy sigh.

Mitch got out the salad ingredients and began putting together two salads.

"Was that Rhea on the phone?" Emily asked.

"Yes. We were making plans for Saturday night." He got out the cutting board and chopped up the chicken breast. "I figured you'd have plans of your own."

She was watching him closely. "You like her a lot, don't you?"

"Yeah, I do. Is that a problem for you?"

She scooted her chair back and bent over to grab a pen that had rolled under the table. Then she stood to face him and said, "Not really. Only . . ." Her brown eyes clouded. "I guess I'm kind of jealous."

"No reason to be, honey."

"I know, and I got used to Lisa, so I guess I can get used to Rhea." Lisa had been Emily's English teacher and Mitch's lover before she moved to California last summer. "But Daddy, you won't forget Mama, will you?"

Mitch put down the knife and gathered her into his arms. She clung to him and pressed her face against his chest. "Never," he said. "Never, ever will I forget your mother."

They embraced in silence for a moment while Mitch tried to swallow the knot in his throat and suspected Emily was doing the same thing. When she spoke, her words were muffled against his shirt. "Did you know, when Mama died I was mad at God?"

Mitch stroked her hair. "Were you, honey?"

She pressed her cheek hard against his chest. "I talked to Reverend Whitaker about it. He helped me a lot."

Mitch hadn't known that she'd felt the need to talk to her minister, and felt as though he'd let her down somehow. "That's good."

She lifted her head and gave him a misty smile. "I know you get lonely, Daddy. And I like Rhea, really I do. I'm glad you can spend time with her."

It was a darned mature statement for a sixteen-year-old. Mitch studied his daughter's face and decided that, in spite of her misgivings, she really meant it—or wanted to. "Thank you, sweetheart."

All at once, they were both a little embarrassed by the exchange. Emily drew in a deep breath, sat down, and began leafing through her notebook. Mitch turned back to the counter and finished making the salads.

He carried them to the table, along with two glasses of milk. As he sat down, Emily pulled a folded paper from one of her textbooks. "Here's the school paper," she said, offering it to him. "Carrie Lou's story about the Cherokee dances is in it."

Mitch opened the paper and read the article as he ate. Carrie Lou was a good writer, with a knack for description. He could actually see the booger dance and the Eagle Dance as he read what she'd written about them. One picture accompanied the article, a shot of the booger dancers. The photograph was a little grainy; the high school's photography equipment wasn't up to the standards of a regular newspaper. But you could, at least, tell what you were looking at, if you looked closely. Which he did.

Frowning, he turned the paper so that the light fell on it better. Among the boogers, there was a frontal shot of the dancer wearing Vian Brasfield's costume.

"I was going to drop by the high school tomorrow and ask to see the pictures Carrie Lou took at the dance. Did she keep copies?"

Emily looked up. "I don't know. She could probably get them, though. I think the boy who develops the pictures keeps the negatives till the end of the school year."

Mitch pointed to the person in Brasfield's costume. "Ask her if she can crop this so the only dancer left is this guy in the middle, just from the waist up. Tell her I need an eight-by-ten."

"Sure. I'll call her."

But Carrie Lou wasn't at home. So Mitch called the journalism teacher and explained what he wanted. Blaylock said he'd try to find the kid who developed the pictures for the school newspaper. He'd get Mitch a blow-up of the photo accompanying Carrie Lou's article as soon as possible.

29

Blaylock dropped the enlarged photograph off at the house Saturday morning. The picture's clarity was better than Mitch had expected. The dancer was facing the camera, with his head turned slightly as he looked to his left in the direction of the bleachers. The mask completely hid his face and the quilt draped over his head and clutched beneath his chin with his left hand hid the rest of him. The only skin showing was that hand and a few inches of wrist, and that's where Mitch's attention was focused.

In the enlarged photograph, he could see clearly what he'd only suspected was there in the much smaller picture reproduced in the school paper. He took the picture up to his bedroom, where he looked at it some more and tried to fit what he saw into what he already knew. Finally, he tapped the photograph with one finger and sucked in his breath.

"Gotcha!" he muttered.

After the first rush of excitement, he realized it might not be enough. He had to lay some groundwork before tipping his hand, talk to a couple of people and show that plastic disk encasing Mary Kennedy's picture to a woman he had yet to meet.

On Monday morning he directed Shelly and Duck to bring the suspect in for questioning.

Hunter Kennedy strolled into Mitch's office, where Mitch had chosen to interrogate him rather than the interrogation room, thinking he'd feel less threatened there. Kennedy pulled up a chair to Mitch's desk and sat astride it with his arms across the chair back. He looked as if he were about to lecture some troublemaker who'd been sent to his office and had struck the pose to put himself on the same level. Just one of the guys.

"I need to get back to school pretty quick," he said. "I'm giving achievement tests today. This is about my father's suicide, I suppose."

"We don't think it was suicide," Mitch said.

"Of course it was. He left a note."

"Somebody left it."

He looked a little less relaxed now. "Somebody *else*, you mean? Oh, that's not possible. Who would do a thing like that?"

"We think we know who, Mr. Kennedy." Mitch opened his desk drawer and took the disk with Mary Kennedy's picture in it. He pushed it across the desk under Kennedy's nose. "Recognize this?"

"Why, that looks like . . ." Kennedy picked up the disk to study it. "That could be a picture of my mother taken many years ago." He put the disk down. "I can't say for sure."

"Yes, you can," Mitch said. "You carried that on your key ring for years."

Something flickered in his eyes. "That's absurd. I don't know where you got that information, but—"

"From your wife," Mitch interrupted. "I showed it to her this morning." The Kennedys had been out of town over the weekend, and Mitch hadn't been able to talk to her until an hour ago. "She said you'd had it on your key ring for as long as she'd known you. She didn't know you'd lost it. Wanted to know where it was found."

"She's mistaken." Kennedy seemed to be holding it together pretty well.

"I didn't tell her that it was found where you parked your car the morning you murdered Vian Brasfield and Arnett Walsh."

"Now, see here, I had nothing to do with that. Good God, I didn't even know Walsh. And why would I kill Vian? He gave me my first administrative job, even passed over Troy Reader and overlooked who my father was to give me a chance."

"The job was his way of trying to assuage his guilt. Of course, you didn't know that then. You learned it after you took the job. I think you began to suspect him when you and Brasfield attended that conference in Oklahoma City, when he got drunk. According to what you and Reader told me earlier, he cried with remorse over things he'd done in the past, begged for forgiveness. You told me Brasfield was asking Reader to forgive him for not giving him the vice-principal job. But Reader said Brasfield wasn't looking at him when he said it. If he wasn't looking at Reader, he must've been looking at you. It was *your* forgiveness he wanted. I don't know if you realized that then, or if you figured it out later, when you took him back to his hotel. At any rate, Brasfield put you on the track to finding out what had become of your mother."

Kennedy heaved a disgusted sigh. "Vian had no way of knowing anything about that."

"Oh, he knew all about it because he killed her. He found out she was leaving town with his wife and he went to the hotel where she was waiting for Nicole Brasfield and tried to talk your mother into moving on without Nicole. I don't think he went there intending to kill her, but when she refused to leave without her lover, he lost it. I don't pretend to know what was in Vian Brasfield's mind at that moment, whether he still loved his wife at that point, or whether he just couldn't stand the humiliation of Nicole leaving him for a woman. At any rate, Mary refused to leave without Nicole, and he killed her."

Mitch had told Nicole Brasfield the same thing that morning and asked her to recall again what her husband had said and how he acted when he returned from Tulsa after seeing Mary. In light of Mitch's suspicions, Nicole remembered that Vian had seemed agitated, even shaken. She also remembered that it was only *after* she had repeatedly asked him "What have you done?" that he insisted they would stay together for the children's sake. Upon reflection, Nicole agreed that Vian could have read more into her words than she'd meant. He could have thought she suspected he'd killed Mary and was determined to stay with her and keep repeating his story until she believed him. Nicole admitted that if he'd killed Mary and thought Nicole suspected, he would have wanted to have her around where he could keep an eye on her.

"You've got a big imagination, Chief," Kennedy said, his cool slipping a little. "But your story doesn't hold water. Vian Brasfield would never have lost control of himself like that. He was the most even-tempered man I ever knew."

"He wasn't always that way. Several people have told me that Vian had a hot temper when he was younger, that he had worked hard at controlling it. It makes perfect sense. Killing your mother in a rage of temper was a wake-up call. He got away with it that time, but he knew he could never let anything like it happen again."

Kennedy sat back in his chair, folded his arms over his chest, and gazed stonily at Mitch. "I don't have to sit here and listen to this."

Mitch leaned forward and planted his hands on the desk. "Yes, you do. There are a couple of officers outside who'll stop you if you try to leave without my say-so."

"I may end up suing you for harassment when this is over," he said. "But as long as I'm here, tell me more. You think you've given me a motive, as far-fetched as it is, for killing Vian Brasfield. Why did I kill a game warden I'd never even met?"

"That's easy. Arnett Walsh was in the wrong place at the wrong time. He came upon you in the woods as you were killing Brasfield, or afterward before you had a chance to move the body to your father's pond."

Kennedy rolled his shoulders to loosen the tenseness that had settled there. "This gets wilder all the time."

"Wild it may be. But that's what happened. You spelled it all out for us in that note you typed after you killed your father. You killed Brasfield, then Walsh, dragged Walsh's body into a nearby cave, and moved Brasfield's body to his pickup, then drove out to his place and left the pickup in those trees. You dragged Brasfield's body to the pond, pushed it in, and left his handkerchief on the bank for us to find. Then you ran a couple of miles back to the lake—no problem for a dedicated runner—and got your car. To muddy the waters even further, you went back out to Brasfield's that night, put on his booger costume, and made an appearance at the dance. Your wife and kids were visiting her family, so there was nobody to ask why you left so early that morning and where you went that night. But you couldn't let it rest, could you? You were afraid it would take too long for someone to find the body or for us to zero in on your father. That's the trouble with some killers, they get too clever. You couldn't stand the suspense, so you pointed us in the right direction. You went out to the farm, pretending to be concerned about your sister, who you talked into going for a walk so you could spot the pickup and report it."

A bitter laugh escaped him. "Are you saying I deliberately tried to frame my own father for two murders?"

"That's what I'm saying, Kennedy. You blamed him almost as much as Vian Brasfield for the loss of your mother. You reasoned that if your father hadn't been the way he was, your mother would never have left him. To get us used to thinking about your father, you started by making those anonymous phone calls to the Cherokee clinic. They were all made during your planning period at school. I got your schedule from Virginia Craig a few minutes ago. But throwing suspicion on your father for the phone calls wasn't enough. Framing him for the murders must have seemed more appropriate. But, after all of the evidence you'd so carefully planted, we didn't arrest him. And maybe he found out something that threatened you, I don't know. But you decided he had to confess. Your wife told me that you slept on the couch the night your father was killed so you could answer the door when the Bregmans came for their daughter. After everybody was asleep, you slipped out, went to the farm, killed your father. I think you rousted him from bed, and when he came to the door he had his handgun. You took the gun away from him, shot him, and left that note confessing to the murders. The Bregmans didn't get back to town until one A.M. Plenty of time for you to have done it and been back home when they arrived at your house."

"You can't prove any of this." Kennedy stood up and started toward the door.

Mitch came around the desk. "Listen to me, Kennedy. We found a couple of fingerprints on the table holding your father's typewriter that don't match his. I'm betting they're yours, that you got careless. It was awkward typing with gloves on, so you pulled them off. You thought you wiped off all your prints later, but you missed a couple. You are going to be convicted of three murders, Kennedy. You're facing the death penalty."

Kennedy threw open the door and had taken only two steps before Duck loomed in front of him. "Did you say he could go, Chief?"

"No," Mitch said. "Come back in here, Kennedy." From his desk drawer he pulled the eight-by-ten photograph that Carrie Lou had sent him and thrust it under Kennedy's nose. "This was taken the night after you'd killed Brasfield. Recognize the dancer?"

"How could I? He's wearing a mask."

"That's Brasfield's costume, but it's not Brasfield because he was already dead."

"So you say."

Mitch pointed at the elaborate watch on the dancer's wrist. The red line around the watch face was clearly visible in the enlarged photograph. "You forgot to take off your watch, Kennedy. I don't know anyone else in town who has one like it, do you?"

Kennedy stared at the photograph for a long moment and something essential seemed to drain out of him. Maybe it was the resentment over his mother's seeming abandonment and the rage he'd carried for his father all those years. Maybe it was just that he knew there was no longer a way out for him. He turned his back on Mitch and covered his face with his hands. For a few moments, the silence was so profound Mitch could hear himself breathing.

The man who finally lifted his head and looked at Mitch was not the man who'd coolly tried to brazen his way past Mitch's accusations. This man's eyes were bleak and hopeless. He was beaten. "Call my wife and tell her to get me a lawyer."

"Okay," Mitch said. He walked to his open office doorway. "Duck, read him his rights. Shelly, get the camera and the fingerprint kit."

"Come on, Kennedy," Duck said.

Kennedy gazed sorrowfully at his mother's picture once more before walking slowly away. At the office door, he turned back. "I didn't mean to kill Vian. I just wanted him to tell me what he'd done with my mother. He tried to deny everything, told me I had misunderstood what he said that night in Oklahoma City."

"What did you hit him with?"

He looked at the floor. "A tire iron."

"If you didn't intend to kill him, why did you have it with you?"

A muscle worked in his jaw, and he didn't answer for a moment. "I was upset. I wasn't thinking clearly. I didn't even realize I had it with me until I'd hit him with it."

"You may have a hard time convincing a jury of that, Kennedy, especially since you also used it on the game warden who came upon the scene while you were killing Brasfield."

"I panicked. He caught me dragging Brasfield's body to the pickup. He tried to run, to go for help. I had to stop him. What other choice did I have?"

"I can think of several, all of them better than three cold-blooded murders."

He shook his head. "My father . . . I just wanted to stop his stupid protests. That's why I made those calls to the Cherokee clinic. I thought if the police questioned him, he'd lay off the protests and letters to the editor. I wasn't planning to get him arrested for the murders. I knew he'd probably be suspected of killing Vian, but I didn't think you could prove it. I—I certainly never meant to kill him. But he saw me . . . that night."

"What night?"

"That Friday night at the dance ground. After I'd danced, I took Vian's costume back to his truck and—"

"You ran into Carrie Lou Dunning and grabbed the school's camera?"

He nodded dumbly. "I wanted to destroy those pictures. When I drove away, I took the film out of the camera, un-

rolled it, and threw it in one direction and the camera in another."

"Carrie Lou had already exchanged the film for a new roll."

"I figured that when I saw the picture in the school paper.
I had no idea Dad was outside that night, but he saw me getting into Vian's pickup."

Mitch remembered Dane Kennedy's hesitation that night,
when he'd asked the old man if he'd seen anyone. He'd lied to
protect the son who wanted nothing to do with him, the son
who repaid him by killing him and trying to pin two murders
on him.

"I didn't know he'd seen me," Kennedy was saying, "until I
tried to talk to him that day at the high school, when he was
picketing. He lost his temper and threatened me. He said I'd
better get the school to let him distribute his literature, or he'd
tell the cops I'd been driving Vian's pickup the Friday night it
disappeared. I knew I couldn't get the school's okay, but trying to reason with Dad was useless. I—I had to shut him up."

"I guess murder gets easier after you've done a couple,"
Mitch said coldly.

Kennedy flicked Mitch a sideways glance so full of devas-
tation it was almost painful to see. "My life is ruined, I know
that. But I want my mother to have a decent burial."

Mitch stared at him for a long moment. "You tell me
where the body is and I'll see to it."

"She's buried on Brasfield's acreage. In the southwest corner."

"He told you that?"

He gave an almost imperceptible nod in Mitch's direction.
"When I hit him the first time, he fell, but he was still con-
scious and he started begging me to spare him. I said I

wouldn't hit him again if he told me what he'd done with my mother."

"So he told you, and you hit him, anyway."

There was no remorse in his desolate eyes. "He had to pay for killing my mother."

"You made him pay, all right," Mitch said. "But the fallout is doing major damage to four families, including your sister's and your own. Was it worth it?"

Without responding or even meeting Mitch's gaze again, Kennedy followed Duck wordlessly to the booking desk.

30

Two weeks later, Mitch was enjoying a leisurely Saturday afternoon with Rhea at her house. Rhea had decided to put out a few Easter decorations and invite Mitch and Emily for Easter dinner. She was arranging a centerpiece of rabbits and eggs on the low table in the living room while Mitch lounged in a chair and watched.

"Where's Emily this afternoon?" Rhea asked as she moved a small stuffed rabbit a couple of inches to the left.

"Temple Roberts's mother took the girls to Tulsa to shop for Easter dresses."

She moved another rabbit. "Has she mentioned me—us, I mean?"

"Yes," Mitch said. "We have her permission to see each other."

She threw him a quick grin. "Sweet of her."

"I thought so."

"Seriously, Mitch, it must be hard for her to know you have a woman in your life who isn't her mother."

"I think she's worked through that."

"I do hope so." She walked around the coffee table, studying the centerpiece from all angles. "What do you think?"

"About Emily?"

"No, the centerpiece."

"Oh. I think it looks fine."

She turned to him, hands on her hips. "There's a safe reply if I ever heard one."

"What am I supposed to say?"

"How about charming or delightful?"

"The centerpiece is charming and delightful, Rhea."

She made a face and came over to sit on the arm of his chair. "I guess that'll have to do. Now, can we talk about the Kennedy case? I've been dying to ask if there are any new developments ever since you got here."

"The judge bound Hunter Kennedy over for trial."

"I already knew that. Is he out on bail?"

Mitch shook his head. "The judge didn't want him out, so he set bail at a million. His wife's family has money, but I hear they aren't going to bail him out. Kennedy's going to be with us till the trial, I'm afraid. That's set to start in a couple of weeks." He put his arm around her waist and pulled her into his lap. "There's something else too. I guess I can trust you not to talk about it."

She drew away in order to look into his face. "I'm not a gossiping woman, Mitch."

"I know, sugar. That's one of the many things I like about you."

"Later I'll want a list of all the others, but now tell me about this something else."

"We found Mary Kennedy's body."

"Oh, Mitch. Where?"

"Buried on Brasfield's acreage. Before he died, Brasfield told Hunter Kennedy where he'd buried it. We knew generally where to look, and we've been digging out there for days."

"I didn't know that."

"We tried to keep it quiet."

She laid her head on his shoulder. "Do you think Kennedy will be convicted?"

"You can never be absolutely sure about a jury, but we've got a good case. We tracked down a principal in Oklahoma City who attended that conference with Kennedy and Brasfield. He was actually with them in the bar the night Brasfield got pie-eyed and after Reader left, he remembers Brasfield saying that giving Kennedy a job was a penance for his past sins. The guy said Kennedy laughed and said, 'What did you do, murder somebody?' "

"My word. What did Brasfield say?"

"He broke down, sobbing, and grabbed hold of Kennedy and started begging for forgiveness. The guy didn't pay much attention, figured Brasfield was too drunk to know what he was saying. Then Kennedy got him on his feet and helped him out of there."

Rhea sighed. "I keep thinking about Hunter Kennedy's wife and children. Those boys are too young to know what's happening now, but they'll understand someday. Meantime, they'll grow up under a cloud."

"They're staying with Mrs. Kennedy's parents somewhere in Texas."

"It's all so sad."

"Let's don't talk about it anymore," Mitch said, and kissed her.

The telephone rang and Rhea grumbled "Darn" and ran to answer it in the kitchen. Rhea couldn't bring herself to just let a phone ring, in case it was one of her patients. She came back into the living room. "It's for you, Mitch."

"Who is it?"

She shook her head. "A man. He didn't give his name."

Grumbling, Mitch got out of his chair and went to take the call.

"Mitch, it's David Parling."

How had the district attorney known to call him at Rhea's? "Yeah, Dave, what's up."

"Sorry to bother you on your day off. I called the station and Virgil Rabbit gave me this number. I didn't think you'd want to wait till Monday to hear this. I just had a call from Hunter Kennedy's attorney."

"Oh, really? What's cooking?"

"Kennedy is willing to bargain."

"Bargain! He killed three people."

"I know how you feel, Mitch. But his lawyer says Kennedy will plead to three counts of murder one in front of a judge if we can guarantee he won't get the death penalty."

"Sounds like he's convinced a jury will convict him."

"Right. I think there's a ninety-five percent chance of a conviction too. But Kennedy's going to give them a sob story about growing up with no mother and a crazy, abusive father. And later, when he's finally gotten his life together, he finds out he's working for his mother's murderer."

"Give me a break. He was half grown when his mother left."

"It wouldn't surprise me if he claims to have no memory of the killings."

"He told me he killed Brasfield and Walsh."

"You know how it works, Mitch. He'll probably say he was coerced, that he said whatever you wanted him to say just so you'd leave him alone."

"Bull."

"I'm just giving you my thoughts on it, Mitch. Even if we get convictions, which I think we will, the jury is liable to think extenuating circumstances and recommend life instead of death. We could take the plea bargain and save everybody the hassle and expense of a trial."

It was obvious there was no point in arguing. The D.A. wanted the plea bargain. "Will the judge go for it?"

"I think so. I'm going to talk to him, but I wanted to let you know first."

Parling was probably right, Mitch admitted reluctantly. Even if they got a death sentence, the appeals could stretch on for years. This way, life on three counts—probably life without the possibility of parole—was a sure thing, and that would be the end of it. Kennedy's wife and kids and the other families could get on with putting their lives back together. "Okay, Dave," Mitch said.

He hung up and went back to the living room, where Rhea waited in the armchair they'd shared earlier. He told her what the D.A. had said.

"You don't look happy with the bargain," Rhea said.

"In my job, you don't expect happy. Sometimes a compromise is all you can hope for. Anyway, it's done."

She gave him a sympathetic look and got to her feet. She rubbed the back of her hand caressingly across his cheek. "There's nothing more you can do, then. Try to forget it."

"Excellent idea," he said, but he knew it would be a very long time before he forgot the young father who committed three brutal murders.